"None of this is yours!" Aelia exclaimed.

Her father had been dead merely a month, yet this usurper had moved in as if he had every right to do so. As if her father had never been lord here.

"You think not, my lady?" Mathieu Fitz Autier took hold of her arm and led her roughly to the window. "Observe. All that you see is mine. You are vanquished, Saxon."

Aelia turned to slap his arrogant face, but he caught her hand and pressed it against the cool metal hauberk covering his chest. 'Twas a place where no normal heart pulsed, but a cold and cruel one.

Yet he did not strike back. He lowered his head, his face, his lips coming but a breath away from hers.

And then he kissed her. He slid his hands around her waist as he lowered his mouth to her jaw, then her ear and her throat, sipping, tasting Aelia.

* * *

Saxon Lady
Harlequin® Historical #798—April 2006

Praise for Margo Maguire

The Virtuous Knight
"These are memorable characters whose story plays out against a well-researched backdrop."
—*Romantic Times BOOKclub*

His Lady Fair
"You'll love this Cinderella story."
—*Rendezvous*

Dryden's Bride
"Exquisitely detailed...an entrancing tale that will enchant and envelop you as love conquers all."
—*Rendezvous*

Celtic Bride
"Set against the backdrop of a turbulent era, Margo Maguire's heart-rending and colorful tale of star-crossed lovers is sure to win readers' hearts."
—*Romantic Times BOOKclub*

**DON'T MISS THESE OTHER
NOVELS AVAILABLE NOW:**

#795 THE DUKE'S GAMBLE
Miranda Jarrett

#796 THE VENETIAN'S MISTRESS
Ann Elizabeth Cree

#797 THE SCOUNDREL
Lisa Plumley

Margo Maguire

SAXON LADY

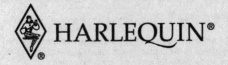

HARLEQUIN®

TORONTO • NEW YORK • LONDON
AMSTERDAM • PARIS • SYDNEY • HAMBURG
STOCKHOLM • ATHENS • TOKYO • MILAN • MADRID
PRAGUE • WARSAW • BUDAPEST • AUCKLAND

ISBN 0-373-29398-4

SAXON LADY

Copyright © by Margo Wider 2006

This edition published by arrangement with Harlequin Books S.A.

® and TM are trademarks of the publisher. Trademarks indicated with ® are registered in the United States Patent and Trademark Office, the Canadian Trade Marks Office and in other countries.

www.eHarlequin.com

Printed in U.S.A.

This book is dedicated to Kate Blessing, a reader, musician and scholar. May your last high school years be as full of grace and brilliance as your first.

Please address questions and book requests to:
Harlequin Reader Service
U.S.: 3010 Walden Ave., P.O. Box 1325, Buffalo, NY 14269
Canadian: P.O. Box 609, Fort Erie, Ont. L2A 5X3

Chapter One

Northern England
Early Autumn, 1068

It was all Lady Aelia could do to keep her men calm before the battle ensued. She walked the perimeter of the palisade and spoke to the archers, bolstering their courage, praising their prowess in battle.

"'Twas not for lack of skill that we've survived against the enemy these past months!" she called to them. "You are worthy warriors, you are Ingelwald's heroes! Fear not the Norman bastard, Fitz Autier, who invades our lands. He is no different from Gui de Reviers, or any of the others whom you killed in battle— he is powerless against our might!"

Aelia hoped it was true. The tales of Mathieu Fitz Autier's conquests were many and terrifying. He had become a legend in Northumberland with his ruthless ways, sent by King William to conquer where other warriors had failed. No Saxon man, woman or child was spared when Fitz Autier won the day.

Aelia would just have to make certain that he won naught at Ingelwald.

It was nearly dawn, and a hazy mist hovered below. She could sense more than see the activity on the ground beyond Ingelwald's stone walls. Fitz Autier, no doubt, was marshaling his men into position. But Aelia refused to be unnerved by the enemy she had not yet seen.

Many formidable thanes of Northumberland had come to Ingelwald when their own smaller holdings had fallen, swearing fealty to Wallis, Aelia's father. Now that Wallis and so many of those Saxon warriors were dead, it fell to Aelia to deliver her people from the Norman peril.

A sudden, hard yank on her arm nearly pulled her off her feet. She whirled 'round and faced the angry countenance of Selwyn, her betrothed. His bearded face lacked the comeliness of a younger man, someone closer to Aelia's age. And now he lacked even the lands that had swayed Wallis's decision to give the man his daughter.

Wallis had wanted to ally himself with his closest neighbor, who had a fine estate to the south. And to keep Aelia near him after she married. 'Twas the primary reason he'd given his promise to make her Selwyn's wife.

"Get down with the women and children," he rasped angrily, spraying spittle from his darkened lips.

With distaste, Aelia pulled her arm from his viselike grip. "No. These are my father's archers. They look to *me* for—"

"Ingelwald is my ward now, as are you and young Osric," Selwyn asserted, and not for the first time.

"My father made no such provision," Aelia retorted, her temper flaring, "as you well know." Wallis had promised her to Selwyn only for the purpose of allying Ingelwald with its powerful neighbor, Selwyn's holding—which had already fallen to the Normans.

That purpose was moot now, and Aelia would have an end to this distasteful betrothal as soon as her battle for Ingelwald was won.

'Twas unnaturally quiet on the grounds below, the women and children huddled within the walls of her father's hall, praying for deliverance. It was not Aelia's intention to join them.

"Wallis never meant for you to dress yourself as some fabled shield-maiden in breeches and tunic," said Selwyn, "yet you stand here among the men with your quiver on your back, your bow at the ready. What think you, woman? That you are some fatal match for the bastard Fitz Autier?"

Naught would please Aelia more than to be the one whose arrow took the life of that Norman warrior. Yet she would be satisfied if any one of her father's men accomplished the feat.

"Aelia!"

She and Selwyn turned to see the young red-haired boy who ran toward them. Her brother was merely ten years old, but had the reckless daring and unyielding fortitude of a man twice his age. 'Twas all Aelia could do to keep the lad out of trouble even as she was careful not to crush his formidable spirit.

"'Tis dangerous up here, Osric," she said.

"Get away with you, boy!" Selwyn demanded.

Wary of unsettling the warriors who manned the battlements, Aelia drew Osric to a quiet corner and spoke softly to him. "Did I not give you a task—an important one?"

"Aye," he said.

"But you are here with the archers. Were you not instructed to assist the swordsmen with their armor?"

"Aelia, I cannot," the boy protested, his exuberance nearly palpable. "I am master of Ingelwald and I must—"

"Bah!" Selwyn's guttural retort sounded behind her, but she ignored him.

"You must return to the horsemen of Father's fyrd, Osric. They will need every hand to prepare for battle."

"They are mounted and ready for the dawn," her brother said. "My place is here with you. I have my bow."

And he could easily be shot. Aelia searched her mind for a new task to set him upon, something that would not seem trifling to him.

"Christ's bones, woman!" Selwyn growled. He pushed Aelia aside, grabbed Osric by the scruff of his tunic and shoved him toward the ladder. "Get you gone, boy! This is no place for a brat."

"Selwyn, cease! He is not your—"

Sunlight broke over the distant horizon and the first onslaught of enemy arrows came with it. Ingelwald's archers met the attack, arrow for arrow, as the armored horsemen in the courtyard prepared to exit the gates.

Aelia forgot about Osric for the moment as she took her place among the archers and looked down at the Normans who would seize her father's hall, his lands, her home. Taking aim, she found a target once, twice, then a third time before she noted a tall knight on a massive destrier rallying his men, keeping them in position.

Aelia could not see his face, for he was clad in armor from helm to spur. Even his horse was protected from stray blows by a coat of steel. When she realized that this knight must be Fitz Autier, Aelia raised her bow and took aim.

But he had no vulnerable spot. She closed one eye

and targeted him, ever ready should he raise an arm or bend his body in such a way that a vital part was left exposed.

'Twas to no avail. He was a seasoned warrior who knew better than to leave himself open to attack. His movements were powerful and controlled, his horsemanship without flaw. Still, Aelia kept watch on him as he battled the mighty Northumberland thanes.

When his helmet became momentarily dislodged, she saw that the Norman bastard was a comely demon. Even from a distance, Aelia could appreciate the masculine angles of his countenance, the strong lines of his jaw. His dark hair was long for a Norman—it lay in wet strands upon his brow, which was furrowed in anger— or frustration. So handsome was he that Aelia had no doubt many a Norman maid would mourn his passing.

She raised her bow, but her aim was disturbed by a sudden tremor that racked her narrow shoulders, and a strange light-headedness. She had all but forgotten her mother's portentous words years ago, but when the sight of the Norman warrior caused a burning heat to singe her from blood to bone, she remembered her saying: *"The earth will move and your body will quiver with awareness when you first see your one true mate."*

Aelia had always believed her prediction. It had happened to her mother and grandmother, and all the other women in her line, yet… It could not be a Norman—a *bastard* Norman.

Fitz Autier *could not possibly* be the man.

Aelia let the arrow fly and an eternity passed as she waited for it to meet its mark. Her breath caught in her throat and her hands clenched tight with anticipation when a sudden rush of blood burst upon the Norman's face. Aelia's heart jumped with jubilation, for she had accomplished what every thane in Britain had striven for: death and destruction of the Norman leaders who had come to take their lands.

But no…Fitz Autier was not slain, merely nicked. Blood gushed from the wound in his cheek, though Aelia's arrow did not protrude from the spot. With disappointment, she realized she must have only grazed him.

While she watched, he turned his gaze up to the battlement where she stood. Their eyes met and held, and in that moment, Aelia realized that Fitz Autier knew it was *she* who had wounded him.

And she wondered if he felt the same racking tremor that she experienced once again when he looked at her.

The battle raged all morning and far into the afternoon, and Aelia managed to shrug aside the uneasy notion that what she'd felt when she looked upon Fitz Autier was exactly what her mother had predicted.

Her mother, dead after Osric's difficult birth, could never have known that Aelia would one day find herself face-to-face with this fierce Norman enemy. And *that* was the only explanation for the odd sensation she felt when she looked at him.

Aelia had no further opportunity to dispatch the Norman bastard. Though Ingelwald warriors managed to hold the gate, too many archers had fallen. Her Northumberland swordsmen outside the walls managed to carry the day. As dusk set in, the Normans retreated to their camp beyond the southern wood to prepare, no doubt, for battle upon the morrow.

Within the stone walls of Ingelwald, torches illuminated the courtyards and the interiors of every building. Half the village was here, within the safety of the walls, but Ingelwald had expanded over the past few generations, and much of it lay outside. Those villagers whose homes were outside the walls had abandoned their cottages and now sheltered inside.

Aelia toiled in her father's great hall, tending the wounded, bolstering the men of Ingelwald's fyrd, and the thanes who had come to Wallis when their own lands had been usurped by the French invaders. "Victory is yours!" she called out amid the groans and misery. "Your wounds were well earned, and Ingelwald takes pride in your valor, your sacrifice!"

Those whose injuries were not mortal rallied at Aelia's words. They stood or pushed themselves up to hear their lady, taking heart in her praise. She stayed among them until all their wounds were bound, and food was distributed, then left the hall to make her rounds in the enclosure, visiting the families who had come from the village for shelter and protection.

Food stores were low, but there was fresh water from the well behind the great hall. If tomorrow's battle went as Aelia planned, the Normans would be routed, and life at Ingelwald would return to normal.

Aelia made her way to the well, where she drew water and washed the grime of battle from her hands and face.

She had not seen Selwyn among the thanes in the hall, nor was he on the battlements. Though Aelia had no desire to wed the man, she wanted to pay him her compliments, for he had fought well for Ingelwald, leading the battle outside the stone walls of her father's holding.

She took a long draught of clean, clear water and heard her name called by one of Osric's young chums. A moment later, the lad reached her side. "Osric is gone!"

She wiped the water from her face. "What were his orders?"

"Modig told us to climb to the top of the storehouse and call the alarm if we saw any Normans trying to breach the wall."

"And Osric left his post?"

"Aye, but—"

"When you find him, tell him he'll answer to me," Aelia said, though she knew that Osric had no fear of her. He was a headstrong lad, overindulged by their father in his grief these last two years, since the death of their elder brother, Godwin. Still, Osric was aware that these were unusual times, and that his actions would be severely scrutinized.

"No! He's gone, my lady! Outside the wall!"

Aelia's heart dropped to her toes. "Outside? What do you mean, Grendel? Where?"

"He went through the tunnel under the east wall…said he would kill the bastard, Fitz Autier, himself!"

Aelia steadied herself against the trunk of the sapling oak in whose branches Osric and his friends had spent so many carefree hours. There had been so much death of late. She'd lost Godwin, and less than two months ago, her father. She could not lose Osric, too.

"What did he tell you?" She tamped down her panic and moved away from the well and the peaceful, familiar surroundings. "What plan did he have?"

"None beyond wanting to kill Fitz Autier as he slept. Osric said Selwyn treated him like a helpless bairn, but he would show that old man."

Aelia should have known Osric would react thus. He took much of what was said as a personal challenge. And even if Selwyn had given Osric a worthy task, her brother must have felt insulted to be excluded from the battle.

She had to raise the alarm and assemble a company of men to go to Osric's rescue. 'Twould mean going to battle in the dark, in territory that was unfamiliar to many of the Saxon warriors who had come from distant lands. Such a conflict could very well prove disastrous.

Mayhap there was a better way.

Sending Grendel to the armory to sup with the men, Aelia made her way to the east wall, where a narrow tunnel had been dug a generation before. There was no point in sending a battalion of men into the Norman camp when one small warrior could accomplish the task, at far less risk.

Aelia knew the territory well. She'd been raised in these lands, had ridden her steed there and hunted with her father and Godwin.

She would try to catch Osric before he had a chance to get into the Norman camp. If he somehow managed to elude her, Aelia would decide upon another likely course.

The ferocity of Ingelwald's defense came as no surprise to Mathieu Fitz Autier. That they would send a child assassin was either ridiculously stupid or colossally brilliant. The boy claimed to be Wallis's heir, and if it were true, he would make a fine hostage.

But the matter could wait until the morrow. His men were battle-weary and the boy was safely gagged and tied for the night. If Wallis wanted him back, he could surrender at daybreak when all parties were rested. Then Mathieu would take the Saxon lord prisoner, along with his sons and the daughter, Lady Aelia.

King William's orders had been clear. Mathieu was to personally escort his Saxon prisoners to London, where they would be publicly displayed and executed.

All was quiet in the encampment. Mathieu did not believe Wallis would attempt an attack in the dark, but he had posted guards to give early warning in such an event. Carrying a torch, he walked among the small canvas shelters that housed many of his soldiers, and headed toward his own tent. It was a large dwelling, serving not only as his sleeping quarters, but as the place where he and his commanders met to strategize, planning their movements and battles.

He ducked under the flap and pulled it closed after him, then walked to the center of the tent. Tugging his tunic over his head, he poured water into a basin and tended his own wounds. For the first time, he allowed his thoughts to touch upon the archer whose arrow had sliced so close to his cheekbone.

It had been a maiden.

Even from a distance, with golden hair tinged red in the sunlight, she was a delicate beauty who'd stood out among the rough soldiers on the battlements. An odd prescience had come over him when he'd first seen her, taking hold of him like an iron fist squeezing his ribs and the bones of his spine. The ground had seemed to shiver under his feet. The sensation had disoriented him sufficiently to put him at risk, and he'd only come to his senses when his helm had been torn from his head.

A moment later, when the arrow grazed him, he'd looked up and caught her gaze. It was as if…

No, he was no young swain easily infatuated by a comely face. Besides, this was a Saxon woman, one who would kill him if given the opportunity. She had nearly succeeded this morn.

Mathieu washed the wound in his cheek. It likely needed sewing, but he would not disturb Sir Auvrai now to tend him. Mathieu stretched his shoulders and back and took note of several new bruises. 'Twas the price of war: no more, no less. But this time, when William's enemy was routed, he would be master of the spoils.

Victory here assured Mathieu of the land he'd craved for years, and marriage to the most beautiful woman in all of Normandy—Lady Clarise, daughter of Lord Simon de Vilot.

Mathieu had served William for years. As the bastard son of a noble father, he had fewer rights than his legitimate half brothers, and no possessions beyond his horse and his armor. Yet he'd earned the respect and affection of his liege lord, who was now king of England. Soon, Mathieu would collect his reward. As overlord of Ingelwald and all its neighboring lands, and as son-in-law of Simon de Vilot, Mathieu would be no less than his brothers' equal.

No, he would surpass them.

Aelia derided these ignorant Normans for making camp right beside the river. Did they not know that the rushing water masked whatever sounds an intruder might make as she slipped unseen into their midst? There was clutter here, too, making it easy for her to hide as she watched the men bed down for the night.

Silently, Aelia slipped under a discarded tarpaulin, keeping one corner lifted in order to see out from beneath it. She closed her eyes and took a deep breath. With deliberate effort, she slowed her breathing and calmed her nerves as she settled in to wait. She had not seen Osric in the flickering torchlight, but all was quiet

in the camp. If her brother had killed Fitz Autier,
'twould not be so, unless the Norman's dead carcass remained undiscovered.

Where would he be?

A moment later, Fitz Autier walked into sight and
that odd, shivery feeling came over Aelia once again.
This time she was sure it must be fear for Osric that
caused the strange sensations. The bastard strode
through his camp, passing right in front of her. This
Norman whose reputation had preceded him to Ingelwald was just a man, not some warrior god with pow-
ers beyond those of any mortal.

Yet his physical stature was greater than any Saxon
she'd ever known. Without his armor, his chest was a
wall of granite and his arms thick with muscle. His
hands worked at the buckles and laces of his tunic and
chausses as he walked, and Aelia wished he would de-
sist. Surely he would not disrobe before reaching his
shelter, not when the night was so chilly. She had no interest in seeing his flesh bared.

He finally ducked into his tent, and Aelia would have
made a run toward it, but two sentries came close, taking away her moment of opportunity. Was Osric waiting for Fitz Autier inside that tent? Would he be able to
kill the Norman without help?

Osric thought much of himself, and though he knew
how to handle a knife, he was no match for a full-grown
man—especially not one like Fitz Autier, who was as
likely to spit a young Saxon lad on his sword as he was
to take him hostage.

Aelia had to move. She had to get Osric out of there
before he found himself on the wrong side of the blade.

Though anxious to leave her hiding place, she had
no choice but to wait for the sentries to pass out of

sight. She forced herself to remain still and watch for activity within the camp, half expecting Osric to emerge stealthily from the Norman's tent with his bloodied knife in his hand.

Waiting for the best possible moment to move, worrying all the while, she observed the guards on the perimeter of the camp, wondering whether or not Osric was inside Fitz Autier's tent.

If he was not, then Aelia herself would accomplish what her brother had set out to do. Osric's idea had been a good one, though 'twas not suitable for a young boy to carry out.

When the guards and their torches were out of sight, Aelia slid quietly from the tarp and crawled to the Norman's tent. She lay perfectly still, listening intently for sounds within. But all was silent. She heard naught.

Was Osric inside, awaiting the perfect moment?

The flap was loose and Aelia slipped under it, disturbing the canvas as little as possible.

Once inside, she held still for another moment to allow her eyes to adjust to the gloom. Campfires burned outside, casting a small amount of light through the fabric walls. Aelia's eyes were drawn to the figure who lay upon a fur pelt.

He was unmoving, but not dead. And Osric was not here. Aelia heard the Norman's breathing, deep and even in sleep. She drew her knife from its sheath at her waist and crept toward him, past the center pole, past the suit of armor that lay in an orderly arrangement near the far wall.

When she was close enough to see the stubble of dark whiskers that grew upon his jaw, she raised her arm and struck.

Chapter Two

Mathieu moved with a speed that belied his size, grabbed the woman's wrist and pinned her beneath him. 'Twas ironic that the very wound she'd inflicted upon him earlier in the day had throbbed sufficiently to keep him from sleep, making him aware of her the moment she crawled into his tent.

"Lady Aelia, I presume."

"Get off me, you...you Norman swine!"

"I see your aim is better than your manners. Fortunately, your skill is unmatched by your size, or I might have had something to worry about."

She pushed and squirmed under him, but Mathieu did not yield. "Do you Saxons plan to assault me one by one until I've beaten every last one of you?"

"One by one?" she gasped. "My brother...he is here?"

'Twas some time since he'd had a woman under him, but though he was aroused by her soft feminine flesh, Mathieu was no rapist. He was disgusted by his own father's preferred technique. Instead, he favored an enthusiastic partner rather than a combative or submissive one. "Do you mean the red-haired maggot who tried to stick me with his puny sword?" Mathieu quipped. "If Wallis is reduced to sending children to vanquish his enemy, then I've lost all respect for the man."

"My f-father is dead."

Her words surprised him. Who, then, had led Ingelwald's defense? Wallis's elder son? "Then 'tis Godwin who rules Ingelwald?"

Lady Aelia did not answer, but renewed her efforts to free herself. She jabbed her knee forward, hitting Mathieu ruthlessly between the legs. He groaned and rolled to the side, still holding her wrists in his fists.

"You have already done sufficient damage to me, *demoiselle*," he said through gritted teeth as she continued to kick and flail against him. "Cease. You are going nowhere." He lay across her, pinning her legs as well as her hands, and wondered how she'd managed to slip past the sentries who patrolled the boundaries of the camp. He had to concede that her small size had served her well in this instance.

"Where is my brother?"

"Stowed safely away," he said roughly. His face was so close to hers that he could see a few light freckles dancing over her smooth, flawless skin. Her bared teeth were white and evenly spaced, her lips full and pink and slightly parted. He could almost taste them.

As appealing as that would be, he resisted the urge. "Should my men be watching for Godwin, too?"

"Release me!"

That was something Mathieu had no intention of doing. At least, not until she was properly restrained. He made another quick move and turned the wench facedown on the pelt that made up his bed. Placing his knee in the center of her back, he shoved her long blond plait aside and held her hands tightly behind her with one fist. With his free hand, he reached for a length of rope to bind her, then turned her again, to tie her hands in front.

He was not a cruel man. His ruthless reputation had been exaggerated, but it had served his purpose as he battled for the king. If only Wallis had heeded what he'd heard of Fitz Autier, the Saxon lord would still be in possession of his holding. Instead, he had rebelled against William's authority, refusing to accept him as king. William had had no choice but to send an army to quell the rebellion.

When the woman was securely tied, Mathieu allowed her to sit up and face him. "Will Godwin negotiate for your release?"

She pressed her lips tightly together and looked away, refusing to answer. But Mathieu saw her throat move convulsively, and noted a slight tremor in her mouth. She was not merely being obstinate. If he was not mistaken, 'twas raw grief that made her tremble.

Her brother was dead.

He ignored the twinge of sympathy that arose from some place deep within him. 'Twas the way of war. Soldiers as well as innocents lost their lives, especially when those innocents did not surrender peacefully to the conquering armies. Mathieu had made warfare his business, and he was not in it to save anyone—particularly not this Saxon wench who stood between him and his deepest wishes.

Mathieu rose to his feet and placed the woman's knife on top of his hauberk as he considered what to do with her. At first he thought of taking her to the supply wagon and leaving her there with her brother, but decided against it. Better to keep them separated.

"Who is in charge at Ingelwald?" he asked.

She raised her chin and refused to meet his eye.

"It does not matter." He tossed a fur pelt down to the floor beside the one where the Saxon woman sat. "Tomorrow morn, when you arrive at Ingelwald gate, trussed up and draped over my horse's rump, someone there will deal with me."

"Where is my brother?" she snapped.

Mathieu laughed. "You are in no position to demand answers, *demoiselle.*"

"He is just a child—send him home."

Mathieu reached for the knife. "You do not yet understand, Lady Aelia. The boy no longer has a home. Nor do you."

She let out a huff of breath as if he'd struck her. If there had been any compassion in him, he might have spared some of it for this proud woman who'd braved the dark forest paths, then a legion of enemy soldiers, to rescue her young brother. If Mathieu were of a baser nature, he would allow her beauty and her womanly curves to entice him.

But he had one purpose here. He was to win Ingelwald for William, who in turn would grant it back to him as the king's trusted vassal. 'Twas a rich holding, and a far greater reward than either of his brothers had achieved. He had already been named baron of Ingelwald by King William.

He reached for a length of rope and wrapped it twice 'round the Saxon woman's waist, tying it behind her. Then he took the loose ends, tied them to one of his own wrists and lay down upon the extra pelt.

Aelia twisted her body to take hold of the rope that bound her to him, and tried to pull free. "If you think I'm going to lie here—"

"I am weary, wench," he growled as she continued to struggle. She kicked him and tried to beat him with her fists, but Mathieu shoved her to the floor once again and took hold of her hair at the nape of her neck, where the long plait of gold-red began. He leaned down and spoke softly in her ear. "I can call to my men, and if you prefer their company to mine, you can pass the night with them."

"You would do such a thing, Norman!" she cried, wriggling to get away. "Set an innocent woman—"

"Innocent?" He turned her and pulled her face close to his. "This bloody gash in my cheek had naught to do with innocence. The arrows that rained down upon my soldiers were not meant as goodwill tokens, *demoiselle*. Be grateful that I am more civilized than you, and be still. Sleep or not, but rest assured that your continued good health and that of your bratling brother will depend upon your conduct tonight!"

Aelia could see no way out. Fitz Autier had turned away from her and settled down to sleep, but she could not rest.

Nor could she escape.

One tug on the rope that bound her would rouse him from slumber, and he was even more formidable at close quarters. 'Twas appalling to her to admit it, but she was afraid to cross him.

She'd thought him comely from a distance, but now that she could see his features *and* his massive chest and arms, bared for sleep, she knew that there was much more to Fitz Autier than a handsome face. His nose bore a slight bump at its bridge, indicating that it had once been broken. A narrow scar marred his forehead, cutting through his thick dark brow. And from this day forward, he would always bear a reminder of her arrow upon his cheek.

Would that it had been a true shot! Then she would not be in this predicament.

She tried to loosen the bindings on her wrists, but could not. The knots he'd tied at her back were unreachable, and she was unable to twist them to the front, where she could see them and work on them.

The walls of the tent were staked firmly to the ground, so Aelia could not slip underneath, even if she were to manage to free herself. She glanced 'round the shadowy interior of the tent, looking for anything she might be able to use as a weapon, or to cut herself free. Of course, Fitz Autier had placed her knife upon his far side, and she could not reach it without climbing over him.

An unlit lamp hung from the center pole, and a small wooden trunk stood fast against the far canvas wall, a wooden carving of a wolf lying on top. Besides the Norman's armor and his discarded tunic, hauberk and boots, there was nothing else. No way to kill him, and no way to escape.

Even if she could somehow slip past him to get out, she did not know Osric's location. If she left, she would have to search every inch of the camp for him, and if she failed to find him and take him back to Ingelwald, Aelia had no doubt the Norman would make good his threat.

Osric would be killed.

Aelia sighed in frustration and lay down uneasily behind Fitz Autier, watching him breathe deeply and regularly in sleep. He was remarkably relaxed for a man who lay beside a captive bent upon destroying him.

He was uncovered, yet his body radiated heat. The

thick muscles of his shoulders rippled with every breath, and Aelia swallowed uneasily as she took note of his size and remembered the strength of his grip on her wrists.

He could crush Osric—or even *her*—between his big hands.

Aelia could not relax. She had never slept beside a man before, and was not about to start with a Norman, particularly this bastard. She pushed herself as far as possible from him, inadvertently tugging the rope and waking him.

She cursed his quick reflexes as one of his hands shot out and grabbed her. He pulled her inexorably toward him and quickly enveloped her in his arms.

"By all that's holy, wench, 'tis the last time I'll tell you to settle yourself, else I'll send you to the guards. Lie down!"

Aelia knew she would be worse than a fool if she tried to fight him. 'Twas not just her own life at risk, but Osric's, too.

She lay back on the fur pelt beside him, but he allowed her no space. He stayed facing her, and she was caught between his broad chest and the taut canvas wall.

As his breathing quieted, Aelia turned her thoughts from the brawny Norman and considered the coming morn. She had to think what to do when she was offered in exchange for Ingelwald.

Selwyn would not care as much about her safe return as he would about keeping Ingelwald for himself. Aelia had had to remind him far too many times since her father's death that the holding was Osric's birthright. King Harold had promised that Wallis and his heirs would continue as earls of eastern Northumberland.

With her brother, Godwin, gone these past two years, the honor fell to Osric. Certainly not to Selwyn, whose stature was insignificant in the English hierarchy.

Aelia eased herself down beside Fitz Autier and shivered, whether with cold or nerves, she did not know. But seeming of its own accord, her body inched closer to his warmth, and he threw one arm over her waist. The quiet sound of his breathing relaxed her, and she found her eyelids drooping. Her thoughts became disjointed.

Ingelwald's warriors would battle the Normans to the death. Selwyn would not yield until the walls were breached and every man, woman and child was killed.

But what if Selwyn could be eliminated first? 'Twas possible her father's huscurls would trade her and Osric for peaceful entry.

How many lives would be spared if Ingelwald accepted the Norman's terms?

Ingelwald's warriors were vastly outnumbered by these Normans, whose stores of armor and weapons—and food—seemed unending. The supplies at home were growing scarce. There were only so many arrows left, and even fewer bags of grain until the fields were harvested. Aelia did not know how long her people could hold out before starvation, if not slaughter, vanquished them.

Aelia saw the face of her brother's young friend, Grendel, before her eyes, and those of his sisters and his parents. There were countless others whose lives were precious to her. There was Beorn the Carpenter, who built lyres and harps, and all manner of other musical instruments. And Erlina, daft as she was, who made potions and poultices for any who had need of them. If Ingelwald surrendered, would the Normans allow her people to live in peace, working their land as they'd done for generations?

'Twas a disturbing question.

Fitz Autier tightened his grip on her, as though he had heard her painful thoughts and wanted to give comfort. He pulled her close, sliding one thick knee between her soft thighs. Afraid of waking him, she did not pull away, but held her breath while his hand caressed her back, sliding down across her buttocks.

Aelia's eyes drifted closed and she did not resist when he increased their intimate contact. She did not have the energy to fight him, and the warmth of his body drew her to him, as did the sense of being gathered into a cocoon of security. It had been so long since Aelia had felt safe. She'd lost her brother, then her father, in skirmishes against the bastard king's armies. Now she had to contend with Selwyn, who wanted to take Ingelwald from Osric. It sometimes felt as though the strife would never end.

Fitz Autier made a soft sound in his sleep and changed position slightly. Though he might be indifferent to what he was doing, Aelia could feel her pulse pounding in every sensitive part of her body. And when his leg slid even higher, she could not breathe.

She was as fatigued as she'd ever been in her life, yet the pressure of his thigh made it impossible to sleep. Her sense of security and repose was soon replaced by a strange tension and a pleasure so acute she had to press her mouth closed to keep from sighing aloud. Inadvertently, she clasped her legs tightly 'round his and shifted slightly, finding the most responsive part of her body and moving against him.

She was afraid of waking him, yet she could not make herself stop. Every nerve within her seemed centered in that one extraordinary place, and when the urgent sensations flooded together and peaked, Aelia thought her heart would burst from her chest. She closed her eyes and let the strange euphoria wash over her, feeling exquisitely sensitive to everything around her.

She felt Fitz Autier's breath in her hair, heard his heartbeat, felt the dark crisp curls of his chest against her cheek. He smelled like a freshly washed male, his skin warm and taut against hers, and once again Aelia felt the shuddering awareness she'd experienced when she'd first seen him on the ground beneath Ingelwald's battlements.

But he was her enemy!

These odd sensations had naught to do with the predictions her mother had made so many years ago, when Edward was king and William merely a troublesome Frenchman. Her mother had never known of the disasters to come, of the terrible toll the Normans would take from Ingelwald. She had never meant that a Norman would be Aelia's one true mate, her body recognizing him even as she did her best to kill him.

'Twas ridiculous.

Chapter Three

Mathieu never dreamed at night, but decided he might enjoy the practice if all his dreams were as arousing as the one he'd just had. No doubt his proximity to the Saxon woman through the night had been responsible for it. He'd awakened in a tangle of soft arms and legs, and the scent of feminine arousal.

Whatever he'd dreamed had been merely a trick his mind played upon him. If she'd been aroused at all, 'twas with thoughts of murder, nothing more.

The Saxon wench still slept, looking surprisingly innocent. But Mathieu would take no chances with her. There was no doubt she would kill him as soon as look at him.

Without waking her, he reached for her knife and sliced through the rope that bound her to him. Her lashes fluttered, but she did not awaken as he left the pallet they'd shared.

Events could not have worked out better. For Lady Aelia to have fallen so conveniently into his hands was a gift from God. 'Twas obvious the Saxons could not go to battle when their lady's life was at stake. Ingelwald would belong to King William before the morning sun cleared the trees east of the castle walls.

In good spirits, Mathieu tore off the braies in which he'd slept. Reaching into his trunk for fresh garments, he considered how best to approach Ingelwald. A full-blown battle was likely to ensue if he rode there with his army behind him. No one would notice that he carried Lady Aelia. Ingelwald's archers were certain to be ready, just as they had been yestermorn.

Perhaps 'twould be best to ride in with merely a herald and a small battalion at his flanks.

Or he could tie the wench to a horse and send her first into the clearing so that—

A sharp intake of breath behind him made him turn to the bed.

"How dare you!" she sputtered.

He stood unabashedly naked before her, but her presumption angered him. 'Twas *his* tent, and *she* was the interloper. "You forget, *demoiselle,* that you were not invited here."

"Common decency—"

"Would have prevented you from entering my tent with homicidal purpose."

With color flashing in her cheeks, she turned abruptly away, presenting him with her back. Her movements were awkward, hampered by the ropes that still bound her. 'Twas difficult to believe this was the same soft woman who'd cuddled close to him for warmth during the night. This morn, she was all hard angles and planes, her obstinacy demonstrated by her rigid posture.

Mathieu stepped into his braies and belted the garment at his waist. Then he sat on his trunk and pulled on his chausses, keeping one eye on the Saxon.

"I would see my brother, Norman."

Mathieu had no intention of uniting her with the boy, not until it suited his own purpose. He continued dressing, sliding his arms into the sleeves of a clean tunic, then pulling it over his head. When he picked up his hauberk, the woman turned to him once again.

In the early morning light he could see that her eyes were green, and they flashed with anger. Or desperation. Mathieu rubbed the back of his neck to dispel the odd feeling that arose when he looked at her, and watched her push herself to her knees.

"Set me free and I will go to Selwyn."

"You insult my intelligence, *demoiselle*." Mathieu shoved her knife through his belt and picked up his sword. He turned to the tent flap and pushed it open.

"I can persuade him to surrender to you."

"Who is Selwyn?"

"He is my betrothed…. He will have taken command of Ingelwald in my absence."

"And why would you want to surrender Ingelwald to me now?"

She dropped her gaze to the floor. "My people… I would see no more of them killed for my sake," she said as he left the tent.

Norman soldiers greeted their lord as he passed, and it sounded as if Fitz Autier gave them their orders in return. Aelia was grateful to Father Ambrosius for teaching her the Normans' language, though she did not hear anything useful now.

She stood up and followed their leader outside, only to be stopped by a wall of chain mail. She lost her balance, but the burly knight on guard outside Fitz Autier's tent grabbed her arm and kept her from falling. His face was hard and unmoving, his action not one of kindness, but of expedience.

He was taller than Fitz Autier, and broader, too, though his hair was so blond it was nearly white. His was a craggy face, one that might have been frightening with its scars and one empty eye socket, but Aelia refused to be intimidated by him.

He released her and stepped aside, allowing a smaller warrior to push past her, balancing several items in his arms. He set everything down in Fitz Autier's tent, then gathered up his leader's armor and started to leave.

"Food and drink," he said.

"I am neither hungry nor thirsty," she replied defiantly, wishing she could cross her arms over her chest to punctuate her words. But alas, her wrists were still tied. "I have need of…" She glanced toward the perimeter of the camp and the woods beyond it. "…of a moment's privacy."

The big, blond knight pushed her back into the tent as the young man left. "You're not leaving. Baron Fitz Autier sent all you will need."

The man lowered the tent flap behind her, and Aelia saw that a large metal pot had been left for her, along with a bowl of water, a thick slice of bread and a cup of ale. Awkwardly, she picked up the pot in her bound hands, and with a cry of frustration, heaved it against the wall of the tent, resulting in a loud clang and a burst of male laughter outside.

The heat of humiliation burned her cheeks, along with the awareness that her situation would likely become worse as the morning progressed.

Her hands were still tied and Aelia would damn her own soul before asking any of these Normans to cut her loose. She pulled against the ropes, twisting her hands every possible way to free them. Then she tried her teeth.

"You scorn our meager rations, *demoiselle?*"

Aelia's head jerked up at Fitz Autier's voice and she met his eyes, the same cool blue of the cloudless sky.

He'd looked formidable without clothes. Just the thought of his densely muscled body, and the impressive manhood he'd so flagrantly displayed, made her mouth go dry. But in his armor, he was an overwhelming adversary.

Aelia decided she could be just as daunting. She was an earl's daughter, after all. In her father's house, she had entertained all manner of royalty, including kings and queens. One Norman knight was barely worth her notice.

She lifted her tied hands, holding them out in front of her. "'Tis full light. Surely you do not fear my escape now, not with all your men on guard 'round this tent."

He pulled her own knife from his belt and slid the blade between her hands.

Aelia felt his gaze upon her face, but she did not look up. She kept her eyes trained on the ropes that bound her. In one quick slice she was free, but guarded as she was, she could do naught with her freedom.

Fitz Autier stepped away from her and toyed with her knife before putting it back through his belt. He was taunting her, demonstrating which of them had the power here.

"Will I see my brother this morning?"

He pushed the flap open behind him, and Osric fell into the tent. Her brother lay gagged, with his hands bound behind him. A length of rope was looped around his neck like the lead on a goat.

Aelia ran to the boy, dropping to her knees beside him. She started to slip the rope from his neck, but Fitz Autier's boot came down upon the loose end before she could free Osric.

"You are a barbarian!" she cried, looking up at him. "He is just a child!"

Fitz Autier's face hardened. "This *child* nearly severed one of my men's fingers with his teeth! He kicked Raoul de Moreton in the ballocks so hard the man will be worthless if we battle today! Furthermore—"

"He merely defended himself!" she protested. When she pulled off his gag, Osric let loose a stream of Saxon curses. "Let me untie him!"

Fitz Autier drew his sword. "Do so at your own peril, *demoiselle*."

The Norman was deadly serious. Aelia smoothed Osric's bright, coppery hair away from his dirty face and shushed him. 'Twas important to remain calm, never allowing the Norman to see how he'd rattled them.

"Aelia," Osric said in their own tongue. "When I say the word, you feint to the side and I'll grab—"

"Do not be an idiot," she replied. "First of all, he could very well understand our language. Secondly, you are tied! We have no chance against them. They are armed, we are not. There are so many of them, and we are only two. We'll have to let them trade us for peace at Ingelwald."

Osric rolled to his side and pushed himself up. "Never! Ingelwald belongs to us! We—"

"*Hush* before you get us killed," she said, blocking her little brother from any action the Norman might take.

She had known Osric would never yield to his captors. He was not an easy child, even in the best of circumstances. Their father and older brother had indulged him unrelentingly, spoiling him, making him feel as privileged as a king. He was a bright lad, but young.

And headstrong. She could just imagine the havoc he'd wreaked upon the Norman camp during the night.

"Make ready to ride, wench," Fitz Autier said. "The boy will wait outside."

Mathieu took the Saxon boy by the scruff of his neck and hauled him away from his sister. "You will ride with Sir Auvrai d'Evreux," he said, aware that the boy spoke French.

The little fiend turned suddenly and kicked Mathieu's shin, then fled. Since Mathieu's leg was shielded, no damage was done, but he did not follow. He allowed Osric to run all the way to the bordering woods, where two sentries caught him and carried him back into camp. They dropped him unceremoniously at Mathieu's feet, where the child spat out the only Saxon words Mathieu had learned, and they were not fit for a child's tongue.

"Are all Saxons as badly behaved as you, boy?" he asked, without expecting an answer.

He just wanted to get this business over—bargaining for the woman's and her brother's lives for the peaceful surrender of Ingelwald. He turned to Auvrai, the tall, blond warrior who was his second-in-command. "I'll carry Lady Aelia. You take the boy. I want ten men on each of our flanks and the rest of…"

All activity and every conversation going on around Mathieu and Auvrai suddenly ceased. Mathieu looked in the direction of his men's gazes and saw that Aelia had moved outside.

She might have been wearing a gown of the finest silk, with a circlet of gold upon her brow, yet her garments were merely a common tunic and breeches. She'd straightened those poor clothes and done something to her hair. 'Twas now a glorious mass of golden curls, cascading across her shoulders and down her back. She'd washed her face, and Mathieu could appreciate every feminine feature, from her delicately arched brows to the hint of a cleft in her chin.

Yet he refused to be moved by her beauty. She was his hostage, and her life would be forfeit if Selwyn refused to negotiate. He had no sympathy for her position.

With utter poise, Lady Aelia approached him, stopping at the place where Osric lay curled on his side. "I am ready, Norman," she said, reaching down to help her brother to his feet. She spoke softly to the lad in their Saxon tongue, then looked unflinchingly at Mathieu, with eyes the clear green of England's fertile fields.

Mathieu clenched his jaw and turned away, barely noticing the squire who led his horse into camp. He would not be duped by her quiescent manner, or swayed by her comely form. There were far more beautiful women in Normandy, one of whom would become his bride as soon as he returned to London.

Mathieu mounted his horse and Auvrai lifted Lady Aelia up to the saddle in front of him. She felt small and insignificant for all her apparent composure, and he felt her tremble slightly against his armor.

She had good reason to be nervous. Unless Selwyn was strongly motivated to save Aelia's life, the man would have no reason to negotiate at the cost of losing Ingelwald for himself. As the warrior chosen to wed Wallis's daughter, Selwyn had become Ingelwald's legitimate leader. Would the Saxon care more about losing Aelia and her intractable brother, or giving up Wallis's rich holding in what was certain to be another bloody battle?

Without a doubt, Aelia was a desirable woman. Having spent the night dreaming of her sensual awakening, then observing the noble manner in which she'd approached him just now, Mathieu could not imagine a man in all of England who would not want her.

But Mathieu did not know Selwyn, nor did he know how matters stood between him and the lady.

He pulled down his visor and waited for Auvrai to mount his horse and situate Osric in front of him. A moment later, the rest of the company was ready, and Mathieu led the throng away from camp.

He considered what to do if Selwyn refused to negotiate. There were several trees just outside Ingelwald's walls. Mathieu had noticed one in particular, with a thick, horizontal branch suitable for hanging. If Selwyn did not surrender, Mathieu would set these two Saxons upon one horse, tie ropes 'round their necks and send the horse a-galloping. The two prisoners would strain and choke as they hung by their necks, and their legs would jerk and quiver as all of Ingelwald witnessed their deaths.

Mathieu took a deep breath and inhaled Aelia's scent. He felt her softness against him and hardened his thoughts against any unwelcome mercy.

She was his prisoner, nothing more. And there was no excuse for his thoughts to keep returning to his arousing dream, or to wonder if he could make those sighs of pleasure that he'd imagined real. Better to think of Lady Aelia with a stout rope around her pretty neck.

Or not think of her at all.

Mathieu and Auvrai took the main path, while the men who flanked them rode through the sparse woods. Mathieu had decided to approach Ingelwald with only a few men visible. The rest would remain beyond the line of trees near the Saxon holding, awaiting the results

of the parley that would take place with Selwyn. He had
already instructed the herald, Gilbert de Bosc, on what
was to be said, and that he wanted the Saxon's words
translated.

"Will you allow me to speak to Selwyn?" his captive asked.

"I am no fool, Lady Aelia. Either he agrees or he does
not. I am prepared for either decision."

She took a shuddering breath. "If he agrees, then we
will become your slaves. If he refuses, then you must
execute me. And Osric."

Chapter Four

'Twas still early when they reached the walls of Aelia's home. The morning was cold and clear, all the better for Selwyn and the others to observe her sitting astride the Norman's massive steed. To bear witness to her defeat.

Aelia swallowed reflexively. A light breeze ruffled her hair and her muscles tightened in spite of her resolve to appear serene. Her body was so tense with her hatred for this Norman scoundrel, she felt her bones might break if she moved even slightly.

The Norman herald rode forth and blew his horn. Then he called out to those who waited beyond the walls. "Hear ye, men of Ingelwald!"

Aelia clasped her hands into fists in her lap and gazed up at the high battlements. Without a weapon, and with no hope of escape, she could do naught but wait upon Selwyn's pleasure. Would he trade Ingelwald for her life?

Aelia felt Fitz Autier's breath in her hair, his powerful arms like steel bands around her. His armored thighs bracketed her hips, making her feel inadequate and small. Fitz Autier was ready for battle, but what about her? She and Osric were unprotected. If Selwyn commanded the archers to fire upon them, Aelia and her brother could easily be wounded or killed.

She glanced over at Osric, who was struggling against the Norman knight who held him fast, and felt an unrelenting urge to grab him and run.

'Twas impossible. They were doomed, unless some practical plan suddenly came into her head.

But she'd been over it a hundred times. Selwyn would never give up Ingelwald for her. If he could win this battle against the Normans, her father's rich holding would belong to him. The Normans would kill her and Osric, and Selwyn would have no rival for possession of the estate.

Aelia could not see any way for her to win.

"Selwyn will not barter for me."

Fitz Autier said naught, but Aelia felt his breath leave him. Whether 'twas in anger or frustration, she did not know. He must have hoped he could engage in a peaceful exchange—her life for Ingelwald. Now he would have to win it in battle.

And execute her on principle.

"After my father died, I told Selwyn I would not wed him. He has no claim to Ingelwald unless I am dead."

The Norman tightened his grip on the reins and turned his horse, signaling Sir Auvrai to follow. "You might have mentioned this before now, *demoiselle*." His tone was gruff, ill-tempered.

She took a deep, quavering breath and held on to the horse's mane. "I thought—"

Aelia heard the first arrow hit Fitz Autier's armor, but he seemed to suffer no damage. He retreated so fast she had difficulty seeing whether the other knight followed him to the safety of the trees. They were under attack, and Aelia felt the Norman lean over her to protect her from the volley of arrows that rained down from her father's high walls.

She did not understand. Why didn't he just throw her into the line of fire and be done with her?

Fitz Autier's mounted regiments advanced, but the soldiers made way for their leader as he rode through their ranks, retreating well behind the line of battle.

He beckoned two of his foot soldiers. "Take this woman and her vexing brother back to camp!" She felt his hands encircle her arms and he swung her to the ground. "Tie them securely, and don't take your eyes off them." He lowered his visor and turned toward Ingelwald as Sir Auvrai dropped Osric unceremoniously beside her.

Aelia watched the two Normans turn to the battle. Neither one looked back.

The sounds of battle horns and clashing swords raged in Aelia's ears. She barely noticed her hands being bound by the Norman guards, nor did she heed Osric's torrent of curses and complaints when they were tied together with a sturdy rope. She heard men's angry voices in the distance, and the clash of steel upon steel. The unmistakable tones of taut bowstrings and loosed arrows filled her ears.

One of the guards gave her a shove and they started on the path toward the Norman camp. There was a better route, but Aelia would not show it to them. There might come a time when she and Osric would need to use it, and 'twould not do to have the Normans too familiar with the terrain.

Ingelwald would fall to Fitz Autier. The absolute certainty of it shook Aelia, and she stumbled blindly as they trod across the uneven ground in the woods. Her life as she'd known it was over, but perhaps her people would go on as before. They were no threat to these French bastards. This war was between Saxon landholders and the Norman encroachers, Frenchmen who would take all that the Saxon lords had built, and steal it for their own.

The people of Ingelwald would go back to their cottages and fields, but Aelia dreaded to think what would happen to her and to Osric. Were they to be sold as slaves to the Scots who raided Ingelwald lands when they had need of cattle and laborers? Mayhap Fitz Autier would send them back to Normandy, to face a future of servitude there.

She shuddered at the thought that they might yet be killed as an example to her vanquished people.

The fighting was now confined to the third level of Wallis's hall. Mathieu fought hand to hand, with Auvrai at his side, until they reached the last pocket of resistance. Five men defended the uppermost chamber, a circular tower with arrow nooks opening in each direction. Mathieu was certain the man giving the orders was Selwyn, Lady Aelia's spurned betrothed.

He was no suitable husband for as beautiful a maid as Aelia. Selwyn was middle-aged, with grizzled features and a decided lack of respect for the woman whose family had given him refuge. Mathieu knew that the man's lands had already been confiscated by King William, and that Selwyn had sought refuge at Ingelwald.

"This is the worm who would not negotiate for his lady's life," Mathieu called to Auvrai. He crossed swords with the man, letting his anger dictate every parry, every thrust of his blade. "He would prefer to steal her family's holding from her than keep her from harm."

Auvrai did not reply, nor did Mathieu expect an answer as they fought the cohorts of this Saxon lord. The battle was fierce, and when one of the whoresons swung his ax toward Auvrai's blind side, Mathieu skewered the man.

He used both hands to wield his broadsword, slashing and hacking until one of the men swung his mace and nearly caught him in the throat, where his helm offered little protection. Mathieu ducked the blow and shoved the Saxon out the door, causing the man to pitch down the stairs. Selwyn bellowed at him in his Saxon tongue, clearly castigating him, but Mathieu had had enough. Too many of his men had been killed or wounded. Fires burned in the castle courtyard, and there was panic among the women and children. 'Twas ungodly hot in his armor, and Mathieu was out of patience.

"Yield!" he shouted.

Selwyn responded, but clearly did not yield.

"Your last warning, Saxon! Give in now, and I will consider sparing your life!"

Selwyn lunged, but Mathieu speared him with one last fatal thrust. Only a breath away from death, the Saxon tried to wield his sword again, muttering incoherently. He took one step toward Mathieu, but collapsed before he could raise his arm.

There were still two Saxons standing. When they saw Selwyn's fate, they gave up their weapons.

"Pick him up," Mathieu ordered, gesturing toward Selwyn with the tip of his broadsword.

The men did not understand his words, but Auvrai showed them what was required. The largest of the men hoisted Selwyn's body to his shoulder and carried him to the stairs, then down to the main hall, where Norman knights continued to fight furiously for domination over their Saxon opponents.

One by one, the battles ceased as Ingelwald men caught sight of Selwyn's bloody carcass. They pointed and exclaimed, and soon all were subdued by Mathieu's men, who seized their weapons and herded them outside. The elation of victory was upon the Norman soldiers, and Mathieu knew there would be hell to pay if he did not take steps to protect that which had not yet been destroyed.

"Auvrai, Gilbert! Restrain them!" he shouted. "Osbern, find the ale…get some food. Divert these men from their bloodlust. I want the village and all who dwell within left intact!" Mathieu ordered. He would not begin his tenure here as a hated overlord.

'Twas several hours before Ingelwald was fully secured and his own warriors well occupied. Women and children were spared, as were any Saxon men who willingly laid down their weapons. Mathieu made his rounds, surveying the damage done, taking note of all that could be salvaged. He walked through Wallis's hall—Aelia's home—and gave instructions regarding the former lord's possessions.

He entered a bedchamber that overlooked a courtyard, and realized he was in Lady Aelia's private quarters. There could be no other occupant whose size fit the suit of *cuir-bouilli,* the hardened leather armor that lay on the narrow feather bed. When he picked up one of the gauntlets, his own hand dwarfed it, and he was appalled to think he might have met her in battle had she not ventured into his camp the previous night and become his prisoner. He would have assumed he was fighting an adolescent lad, not a woman.

'Twas not to say he had decided what to do with her. Should he hang her and the red-haired brat to demonstrate his power to the villagers? Or take her to William, where she would suffer a public humiliation before her execution?

Both options were difficult to swallow, though he knew not why he should care. Lady Aelia and her brother were no more than two obstacles to that which Mathieu desired with all his heart—this land, and the prestige of being one of William's conquering champions…and the pride of bringing a beautiful, wellborn bride here, to his own rich holding.

A stringed instrument stood propped against one of the chamber walls, and a beautifully carved fruitwood recorder lay upon a trunk at the end of the bed. As one who had spent many a leisurely hour making his own carvings, Mathieu appreciated the fine craftsmanship of the piece, even as he imagined Aelia's lips upon the instrument, and the music she would make. He opened the trunk and removed several articles of clothing—delicate chainsil and sturdy woolens. Placing the recorder across the center of the pile of clothes, he rolled it all into a neat package and carried it from the chamber.

"Find something to put this in," he said, handing the bundle to one of his men. "And put it with the packs that will return to London with me."

Hours passed, with no news of what was happening to Aelia's home, to her people. When the acrid smell of smoke permeated the air around her, chafing her nose and burning her throat, she blinked back tears and vowed revenge. "The village!" she whispered to Osric. "They've torched our village!"

So many cottages, the shops, the livestock. All would be destroyed by the Norman bastard, who would take her father's land and enslave her people.

Osric jumped to his feet, pulling the rope that bound him to Aelia. "I will kill him," he said. But one of the Norman guards shoved him to the ground once again. "And you, too!"

"Take care, little brother," Aelia said, blinking back her tears. *She* would be the one to exact their revenge upon Fitz Autier. She did not know how she would manage it, but somehow, she would kill the bastard and take Ingelwald back for their people.

As dusk grew near, riders approached and dismounted. "We're to break camp," one of them said. "And get these two back to the hall."

Hall? Aelia almost laughed at the absurdity. *What hall?* She fired her questions at the Normans, but they did not give her the courtesy of a reply, merely ordering her and Osric to start walking.

Osric denounced the Norman guards in English, in French and in Latin as he trudged back through the forest toward Ingelwald. Aelia was too angry to say a word, and worried, too.

Would Fitz Autier kill her and Osric now? Had he waited until his victory was assured before executing them?

As they came closer to Ingelwald, the smoke became thicker, hovering low amid the branches in the woods. Aelia's eyes teared so badly that her vision was impaired when they reached the edge of the wood and entered the village that lay outside the walls.

"'Tis still here!" Osric exclaimed.

Aelia wiped her eyes, though her sight still was not clear. "Hardly, Osric." She knew about the Normans' tactics—the devastation they wrought that took years to repair.

Yet Aelia gradually saw that the cottages remained intact, for the most part. The tannery, the weaver's shop, the tavern…none had been destroyed. Fowl and swine ran loose between the buildings, and people called to her from their doorsteps.

Aelia's throat felt too raw to answer. She stumbled blindly through the village until they reached Ingelwald's timber gate, which lay shattered on the ground beneath her feet. Inside the walls, she heard the sounds of weeping. Here was proof of the Normans' brutality.

The smallest of the buildings within the walls had been burned to the ground. Her father's house remained, only because much of it was constructed of rock and stone, but Aelia had no doubt that the Norman bastard would raze it, too, when it suited him.

Osric pointed toward the area beside the armory, where a long row of bodies lay upon the ground, and a number of women stood holding each other, weeping.

Aelia's heart lodged in her throat. Heedless of the knight who shouted at her, she walked toward the grieving women. Dead Normans and Saxons lay beside one another, as though they'd not spent their last days trying to butcher each other.

"My lady!" cried one mourning widow. She grabbed Aelia's sleeve and knelt, pressing her forehead to Aelia's knee. Her tears soaked through the soft wool of Aelia's braies. "My Sigebert! 'Tis my Sigebert lying at your feet! What am I to do? Our children…"

"Hilda, come," said another of the women.

"No! These Norman bastards killed him…my Sigebert…."

The woman took the widow away as others knelt and kissed Aelia's hands.

Aelia swallowed. Her hatred had become a palpable thing. Everything in her field of vision became clouded by a red haze of rage, and her hands itched to do violence. She would vent her anger, but not just any Norman would do. When she loosed her wrath, 'twould be upon the leader of these vermin.

The guard tried to lead her back toward the great hall, but Aelia shrugged him off, pushing Osric ahead of her. "A weapon," she said to her brother. "We must find something to use against these foreigners."

"On the bodies," Osric replied. "One of them must have a knife or… Look, Aelia," he said. "'Tis Selwyn."

True enough, the man who'd been chosen to be her husband lay among the dead. Aelia mourned him, not because of any particular fondness for the man, but because he was Saxon. He did not deserve this ignominious fate. Aelia vowed that he and all the other Saxon warriors would be decently buried.

Aelia reined in her temper and walked down the line of bodies, hesitating at each one to say a short prayer, while she searched for an overlooked weapon. When she came to the body of a woman laid out among the warriors, she gasped. 'Twas Erlina One-Ear, the pitiful crone who lived in a tiny cottage at the farthest end of the village. In recent years, Erlina had started muttering incoherently to herself as she walked through the village, and though her behavior seemed to become more bizarre with every passing month, she was harmless.

"'Twas murder," Aelia said to Osric.

"There is no wound upon her."

Aelia whirled 'round to face Fitz Autier, who stood

watching her with his hands casually perched upon his narrow hips. He closed the distance between them. "Don't try to convince me that you weren't thinking the worst of me and my men. We didn't kill the old woman."

"Then how did she die?"

"Mayhap you should examine the body and tell me."

"I am no leech, Norman. But neither was she a soldier."

He wore a long, split hauberk, but his head remained uncovered. His hair was not barbered in the usual manner of Normans, but neglected and left to grow as it would. With one day's growth of beard and the terrible slash across his cheek, he looked imposing and dangerous. Still Aelia found herself alarmingly drawn to him.

He slid her knife from his belt and sliced through the rope that bound her to Osric. "Take him to the prisoners' quarters."

"No!" Aelia cried, reaching for him. "He's just a child!"

"I'm no child, Aelia!" Osric countered angrily. "I will stay with our men until it is time."

"Time for what?" Fitz Autier asked, his voice an ominous growl of pique and displeasure. "Time for what, boy?"

Osric stared defiantly at the Norman leader, then spoke through his teeth. "For my execution, bastard."

"Osric, no!" Aelia's breath caught in her throat and she resisted closing her eyes against the surety of what was about to happen.

But rather than gutting the boy with the knife in his hand, Fitz Autier motioned to the guard to take him away.

"What will you do with him?"

Fitz Autier took hold of the rope that bound Aelia's

hands and pulled her beside him. "Better for you to consider what I will do with you, *demoiselle.*"

Aelia swallowed hard and stumbled alongside the Norman as he strode into the great hall of her father's house. A fire burned in the massive hearth, providing the only light in the cavernous hall. A number of Frenchmen with bloody wounds lay upon pallets here, sleeping or moaning in pain.

Fitz Autier continued walking until he reached the stairs, then pushed her in front and made her climb. "Where are you taking me?"

"Keep moving," he replied.

"I—I'm hungry." She had not eaten all day.

"Gilbert!" He did not stop moving, but shouted to someone below. "Send food."

"You…you can't…I…"

"Say your piece, *demoiselle,*" Fitz Autier said. "You've had no trouble speaking your mind before now."

They climbed to the topmost floor and stepped into the circular tower that was her father's bedchamber. Fitz Autier freed her hands.

Aelia felt the blood rush from her head as she gazed into the once-familiar room. Wallis's belongings were gone. The feather bed had been stripped of its hangings, and Wallis's trunks were missing. One thin blanket lay at the foot of the bed, and a massive suit of armor had been placed in the farthest corner beside a three-legged stool.

Her father had been dead merely a month, yet this usurper had moved in as if he had every right to do so. As if her father had never been lord here.

"None of this is yours!"

"You think not, my lady?" He took hold of her arm

and led her roughly to the window. "Observe. All that you see is mine. You are vanquished, Saxon."

Aelia turned to slap his arrogant face, but he caught her hand and pressed it against the cool metal hauberk covering his chest. 'Twas the place where no normal heart pulsed, but a cold and cruel one.

Yet he did not strike back. He lowered his head, until his lips were but a breath away from hers.

And then he kissed her.

Chapter Five

'Twas meant to punish her for her impertinence, her utter disregard for his authority. Lady Aelia needed to understand who was in control at Ingelwald—and it was not she.

Lust played no part in his actions. He was merely demonstrating his mastery over her when he urged her mouth to open under his, when his tongue touched hers, when he tipped his head for better access to her lips.

Yet he damned the chain hauberk that kept him from feeling her soft breasts pressing against his chest, and the fluttering of her heart. Her shoulders were small and yielding under his war-hardened hands. Her back was narrow, her stature surprisingly delicate, considering her fiery nature.

And Mathieu wanted to consume her. He slid his hands around her waist, touching the crests of her hips as he lowered his mouth to her jaw, then her ear and her throat, sipping, tasting Aelia. She was a powerful elixir, drugging him, dissolving his common sense.

And when he realized that, he pulled away.

Mathieu released Aelia so suddenly she stumbled

back a step before regaining her balance. Her face was flushed and he saw confusion in her green eyes, but Gilbert de Bosc pushed open the door to the chamber and strode in before either of them managed to say a word.

"Your supper, Sir Mathieu," he said, looking for a place to set the platter of food.

"Put it on the bed," Mathieu said as two more of his men entered. They carried a large trunk and a washstand, and set them on the floor in the far corners of the room.

Mathieu sat down on the bed and made a deliberate show of turning his attention to the food. The kiss meant naught. 'Twas only to demonstrate his complete dominance over her.

"There are Saxons below who are ready to swear fealty to you, Sir Mathieu."

"No!"

Shock and outrage rang clear in Aelia's tone, but Mathieu studiously avoided looking at her. He poured ale into a cup and took a healthy swallow. "Give them a meal and have them wait for me."

"You bribe them for their loyalty!" Aelia cried. "'Tis a thin mark of fidelity that you win here, Norman."

Mathieu stood abruptly. "What makes you so sure, Lady Aelia? What has changed for these people, besides the name of their liege lord?"

"They—"

"Naught," he said as he walked to the door. "They will go on as before, but in the future, they will have an overlord who will protect them."

"Who will grow rich through their labors."

"As your father did not?"

"Our people respected and revered Wallis! He was a fair and generous man—"

"Who overindulged his offspring. Cease your chatter now, and partake of this meal before it's taken away!"

He walked out and let the heavy door slam behind him. "She is not to leave this room," he said to the guards who awaited him.

"Yes, baron."

He could not get down the stairs fast enough to suit him. The woman was impossible. Tedious. And he had more important things to do than dally with her in the chamber he planned to use for the duration of his stay at Ingelwald. He did not care whom it had belonged to before his victory here.

There was no weapon in the room. He wouldn't leave her armed, but Aelia could not help but hope she would find a forgotten dagger among his things.

She pulled the door open, but came face-to-face with two Norman guards who would not let her pass. "Am I a prisoner here?" she demanded.

"Yes, my lady," one of the men replied.

Aelia huffed indignantly and returned to her father's chamber, slamming the door behind her. She hoped it fell off its hinges.

But when it did not, she was reduced to pacing the length of the room while she cursed her Norman captor. Repeatedly.

If she'd been hungry before, that kiss had taken away her appetite. What had she been thinking, allowing him such intimacy? The man had butchered her people and taken away their homes. He'd bound and imprisoned her brother, a mere child. And now he'd usurped her father's own chamber.

The truth was, she had *not* been thinking. His kiss

had been pure sensation—a tingling heat that had frozen her mind but warmed her body. She hadn't realized that a simple kiss could do such a thing, and wondered if Fitz Autier had felt the same.

No, most likely not. Or he would not have broken away from her just as she'd begun to feel the same ravishing sensations she'd experienced the night before. Aelia took a deep breath and turned her thoughts to a more productive line. 'Twas pointless to give any further consideration to that kiss, or anything she'd felt while imprisoned in his tent.

She had to figure a way to defeat the Norman knight. Mayhap his army was stronger than hers, but if Aelia could kill Fitz Autier, his men would have no choice but to surrender and return Ingelwald to its rightful masters.

How was she to kill him? Without a weapon, there was little hope of that.

Aelia sat down on the edge of the bed and eyed the platter. She had not eaten since the night before, yet food no longer interested her. There was a gnawing pain at her center that had naught to do with hunger. Her belly roiled at her defeat, her imprisonment, her humiliation.

Her life should have been forfeit when Selwyn refused to surrender. Yet she still lived and breathed, while he lay dead in the courtyard.

The line of bodies had not been as long as Aelia had anticipated. Only twenty Ingelwald men lay dead, alongside another twenty Normans. Even so, none of those brave Saxons had had to die. If the greedy William had not sent his knights to every corner of England, there would have been no reason for the death and destruction wrought over these last two years.

Her father would still be alive.

Never had her need for his counsel been so great, nor her desire for his fatherly embrace. Aelia felt like a lost child again, frail and vulnerable, and in need of protection. Wallis had always provided that.

She pressed one hand against her chest as if she could hold in her anguish, and dropped to her knees beside the bed. Her father was gone and she'd had little time to shed her tears when, weeks ago, they'd put him in the ground. Tears pooled in Aelia's eyes now as she lowered her head to the bed and wept for her father and Godwin, and all that had been lost.

Mathieu was weary of war. After two years of death and destruction, he wanted nothing more than to settle here at Ingelwald in peace. He was no fool, though. The Saxons of Wallis's fyrd who'd just sworn fealty were no more loyal to him than they were to King William. They'd merely done the most expedient thing in order to get on with their lives.

Auvrai d'Evreux would remain at Ingelwald to deal with them and to keep order when Mathieu left for London. Auvrai would be the one to oversee the reinforcement of the protective walls, and the improvements to the hall. When Mathieu wed Lady Clarise, she would have an impressive home here at Ingelwald.

He picked up a lamp and started up the stairs toward the master's chamber. Sleep would be a welcome amenity just now, but Mathieu did not know if he would be able to rest with Lady Aelia in the room. 'Twould be best if he found himself a bed elsewhere, but—

The rasp of unsheathed steel made Mathieu swing 'round abruptly and reach for his sword. The figure on the landing was swathed in shadow, but his blade gleamed bright in the lamplight, and it was poised to strike between the loosened buckles of Mathieu's hauberk. Mathieu raised his sword arm in a gesture of resignation.

When the assailant moved slightly into the light, Mathieu saw that he was merely an adolescent boy with the downy fur of his first beard. However, the boy's age would not keep him from moving in for the kill, Mathieu knew.

"The lady…" the lad said. "You have no right."

His French was passable, though his accent was thick. His sword hand trembled.

"You would protect Lady Aelia from me?"

"She is lady of Ingelwald," the boy said. "All men here protect…*honor*…her."

All Mathieu had to do was toss the lamp to one side and pull away from the point of the sword. But throwing a candle, even though 'twas enclosed in the lamp, would be a perilous choice. The manor house was made mostly of wood, and the rushes on the floors were extremely combustible.

"Your devotion is admirable." 'Twould be an easy task to disarm and kill this boy. But his death, when they'd just won peace here, would cause far more trouble than Mathieu wanted. Still, he would not be cowed by a youth with a weapon. "I intend no harm to the lady."

"Release her!" the boy demanded.

Mathieu felt the sword pierce his flesh, and he gritted his teeth against the pain and eased away. "That will not be possible."

He made a sudden feint to the right, pulling away from the boy's blade. Raising his own weapon, he found 'twas an easy feat to knock the boy's sword from his hand and back him up against the wall.

At the sound of the scuffle, guards from the hall

below and the upper floor took to the stairs. When they arrived upon the landing in between, Mathieu already had the situation under control.

"Your loyalty does you credit," he said, pulling the boy's arms behind him. "And because of it, your life is spared."

The Saxon, gone pale either with fury or fear, did not speak.

"What is your name?"

"Halig."

Mathieu turned him over to the guards. "Lock him up with the others."

"Lady Aelia is good woman, Norman," the boy said. "You take her—"

"No harm will come to the woman as long as she behaves."

Mathieu could not fault Halig for attempting to protect Aelia. 'Twas what he would have done had Queen Mathilda or any other innocent woman been in peril. But Aelia was no innocent. She'd donned armor and raised her bow against his men. Mathieu himself bore a gash upon his face as a result of her arrow.

Yet she had the loyalty and love of her people. Mathieu had taken note of the homage they'd paid her when she'd walked across Ingelwald's grounds. Old and young alike revered her. 'Twas Aelia's defeat—more than Selwyn's—that had won Ingelwald for Mathieu.

He continued up the staircase, more watchful now as he approached the master's chamber. One of the two guards he'd posted at the door was still on duty. Mathieu passed him and entered the room, half expecting an attack upon his life, even though he'd been careful to leave Lady Aelia no weapon.

Lamplight flickered in the periphery of the room, casting her sleeping form in shadows.

Her head lay upon her crossed arms on the mattress, but her body was curled on the floor at the bedside. Her eyes were closed, her breathing slow and regular. 'Twas as if she'd sat down beside the bed to await his return, but had fallen asleep instead.

The food on the plate was untouched, and Mathieu wondered when she'd last eaten. Earlier, she'd complained of hunger.

'Twas not his concern. If she refused to eat, he could do naught but watch her starve herself.

But he would put her to bed, then go and deal with his newest wound. Mathieu crouched down to pick her up, and she made a small sound, much like a sigh, yet more. 'Twas the sound of despair.

And there was moisture upon her cheeks.

Mathieu gathered her into his arms and lifted her to the bed, grimacing when her body touched the gash in his side. He didn't think the boy had done much more than scratch him. Mayhap the wound was worse than that.

He lay Aelia upon the bed, then set the plate of food on the trunk, and covered her with his blanket. When she stirred restlessly, he moved away from her, quietly removing the battle horn that was still strapped over his shoulder. He lowered the heavy hauberk to the floor and walked toward the lamplight, unlacing his thin undertunic. The lower right side was covered with blood.

With a muttered curse, Mathieu pulled the sherte over his head and looked at the wound. 'Twas deep enough to need stitching, though not bad enough to cause him serious worry. He'd had worse, but he was going to need help tending it.

He opened the door and spoke to the guard, sending him to find Sir Auvrai, a man who knew more about healing than any surgeon Mathieu had ever known. Then he closed the door and went to the washstand, where a basin of water and several clean cloths awaited him.

Stitches were likely to chafe and bother him on the journey to London, but there was naught to do about it. He had no intention of putting off his return to William's court, thereby delaying his betrothal. The sooner he wed Clarise and returned to Ingelwald, the better.

"What happened?"

Mathieu turned and watched Aelia swing her legs over the edge of the bed and stand. Even from across the room, he could see that her eyes were red-rimmed and wary.

"You're bleeding. Did the mighty Norman knight suffer a mishap with his sword?"

"'Twas a lucky jab from your overzealous swain." He turned away from her, but heard the floor creak under her feet as she approached. "Why are you not sleeping?"

"I never meant to sleep."

Mathieu sucked in a breath when she touched the laceration.

"This needs sewing."

"And what would you know of it?"

"More than I like. Give me that." She took the cloth from his hand and swabbed the wound carefully.

"You didn't eat."

"Having a Norman in my father's bedchamber turned my stomach." Mathieu held his breath as she pressed the edges of the cut. Her touch was gentle, yet knowledgeable.

"You have some skill here, *demoiselle*."

"Not by my choice, Norman," she replied. "My father said 'twas a lady's duty to tend the sick and injured of her estate. I learned all I know from Erlina—the old woman who lay dead in my father's courtyard. She was a fine healer before her mind turned." Aelia took a clean cloth and dropped it in the basin of water. "Whoever speared you missed anything important."

"'Twas one of your admirers, defending your honor."

Aelia's hand stilled and she gazed up at Mathieu with contempt. "Did you kill him?"

"He was just a boy. Of course I did not kill him, even though—" A sharp knock at the door interrupted him. "Enter!"

'Twas the herald, Gilbert de Bosc, carrying the leather satchel in which Sir Auvrai kept his medicines. Gilbert was no warrior, but a man fluent in the Saxon tongue. Mathieu had never seen him wield a sword in battle and did not know if he would be able to defend himself if necessary. Still, he had his uses, besides functioning as an interpreter. His administrative skills were immense, and he was free to tend the sick and wounded. "Sir Auvrai will be here presently."

"Tell him not to bother. Lady Aelia will attend me." Mathieu took the satchel and handed it to her.

"Baron, are you certain—"

"Auvrai has more pressing duties, and the lady has convinced me she is competent."

It seemed overwarm in the chamber. Aelia pushed open the shutters to let in the evening air before turning once again to face the Norman's naked chest and rippling muscles. 'Twould not be possible to overpower him. Still, his sword lay nearby, and he'd placed her dagger upon the washstand. If she could—

"If you're thinking of using the moment to do me some damage, *demoiselle,*" he warned, taking her blade in hand and stabbing the sharp tip into the wood of the stand, "I urge you to reconsider."

Aelia bit her lip and pushed up her sleeves. "This will be easier if you lie on the bed."

He pushed the wooden stool closer to the lamplight and sat down, letting his knees drift apart. "This will do."

"You expect me to kneel before you?"

"Do what you will, *demoiselle,*" he said. "But get the sewing done."

He raised his right arm and rested it upon the washstand, giving Aelia better access to the laceration in his side, as well as a better view of his brawny chest and shoulder. Aelia had no doubt that the visual display was meant to intimidate her.

She glanced at the wound, then at the needle in her hand. The gash needed five stitches to hold it closed.

She knew how to make it ten. There was more than one way to kill a Norman and she would discover it before the evening was out.

Chapter Six

Mathieu made a fist with his left hand and pressed his other against his thigh when Aelia pushed the needle through his skin. He concentrated on her mouth while she worked, on those soft, pink lips that had responded so intensely to his kiss.

He'd managed to avoid thinking about it until now, and he knew it would be in his best interests to concentrate on something else.

But she was so close he could see the faint freckles on the bridge of her nose, and the fine line of a tiny scar that fanned out from the corner of her eye. He could feel her warm breath and see the pebbling of her breasts against the soft wool of her tunic.

He sucked in a breath.

"Brace yourself, Norman," she said, unaware that he'd barely noticed her needlework. She leaned closer, and several loose tendrils of her hair brushed against his chest. "I'm not yet finished."

Mathieu gritted his teeth. 'Twould be so easy to kiss her again, to draw her to her feet and lead her to the bed, where he would lay her on her back and make her forget he was her enemy.

But he knew 'twas better to concentrate on the needle passing through his skin. Bedding Lady Aelia would be the worst possible course he could take. The situation was already far too complicated.

"Enough, woman!"

He pushed Aelia aside and stood. "I am no altar cloth on which to ply your needle."

Shouts outside the window caught Mathieu's attention and he crossed the room to see what the commotion was about. "God's breath! The grain storehouse is on fire!" 'Twas where the prisoners were held. He threw the tunic over his head, then grabbed his sword. Taking Aelia by the hand, he ran from the room.

"To the storehouse!" he called to the guard as he passed.

"Osric!" Aelia cried as they flew down the steps. "My brother is in that building!"

"And you will be staying here, in the hall, with Sir Gilbert and the wounded men while I get him out." Mathieu knew she would resist him, but he had no intention of allowing her to join the chaos outside. All his men would be needed to put out the fire and collect the prisoners. There would be no time to deal with whatever trouble Lady Aelia could accomplish.

As he fastened his sword belt, he backed her up to a chair against the wall and watched her fall into it. Her cheeks were flushed with color and each breath seethed with outrage.

"I'm going out there," she cried. She tried to get up from the chair, but he stood before her, his knees to hers. She tried to push her way free, but Mathieu trapped her in place, leaning over her and placing a hand on each arm of the chair.

He leaned close. "*Demoiselle,* you will stay here, and give Gilbert no trouble. I will find your brother and assure his safety."

"No! You can't leave me here!"

Mathieu straightened and Aelia tried again to slip out of the chair. "Aye, I can." He pushed her back where he wanted her. "Gilbert! Tie Lady Aelia in place and see that she does not leave the hall."

A moment later, he clipped down the steps and raced toward the storehouse.

Ingelwald's hall had never looked like this, Aelia thought as she entered the room.

The huge oaken table that had dominated the large chamber was gone, as were most of the chairs. In their place, ten or twelve injured men lay upon pallets on the floor, moaning or sleeping, as was their wont. Aelia did not take time to notice anything more, but bolted for the door, having easily eluded Sir Gilbert. The hapless Norman came after her, but became distracted when one of the injured men started to retch. She took advantage of the diversion and beat the herald to the door.

Thick smoke filled the yard and choked Aelia the moment she went outside. Undeterred, she headed toward the source of the smoke, the storehouse where Osric and the men of the fyrd were being held. There was already a line of men, women and children passing water-filled buckets toward the stable, which stood beside the grain storehouse, and carrying the emptied ones back to the well. Normans as well as Saxons worked to prevent the fire from spreading, but it seemed to be gaining in strength rather than waning. The heat from the flames was stifling.

'Twas a terrifying sight.

The fire had taken hold of the stable roof, and men

were leading horses out to safety. They'd already given up on the storehouse beside it, the place where Osric had been held.

Aelia ran to the front of the water line, where a number of Saxon men lay covered with dirt and ash, coughing and trying to catch their breath. A Norman warrior caught an empty bucket from the roof and handed it back down the line.

"Did everyone get out of the storehouse?"

"Who's to know?" he replied. "At least some of them got out, but we don't know if there are any more in there."

"What about a young boy—a small, red-haired boy?"

The Norman took the next bucket and handed it up to a man on the stable roof. Aelia grabbed his arm. "The boy! Did you see a small boy come out of the storehouse?"

"No. Move aside or help, lady. There is no room here for bystanders."

Aelia's heart lodged in her throat. If Osric was still inside the storehouse, he would burn to death.

She heard Fitz Autier shouting orders, and looked up toward the sound of his voice. He had shed his tunic and stood on the stable roof, pouring water from the buckets that were handed up to him.

Aelia ducked away before he could take notice of her, and picked up a discarded rag from the ground. Covering her head and mouth with it, she whispered a silent prayer and ran into the burning storehouse.

She didn't think she'd ever felt anything hotter than the flames outside. But within the storehouse, 'twas worse. Her throat burned and her eyes watered as she searched the smoke-filled spaces for anyone who might still be inside, but she could see no one. Nor were there any bodies.

"Osric!"

Since 'twas summer's end, the storehouse was nearly empty, but piles of burning debris obstructed Aelia's progress through the building. She pressed the rag against her mouth and nose, but soon began to have difficulty catching her breath. A fiery beam cracked and fell in her path, and she tripped.

"Osric!" Her voice was a mere rasp now, and she did not know if he would hear her. She had to move on. If he was still inside the building, he could very well be unconscious.

She heard a groan nearby, and pushed herself up. "Where are you?" she called out.

"Here!" 'Twas not Osric, but an older man called Leof, who had once been a warrior in her father's fyrd.

Aelia crawled to the man and helped him to a sitting position. "Have you seen Osric?"

"No, my lady."

Aelia swallowed her frustration and spoke quickly. "You must get out of here!"

"I cannot walk. My leg—it's broken!"

The fire roared around them. Finding Osric was hopeless now, and Aelia knew she would be lucky to get herself and Leof out of the storehouse.

"I'll help you up. Lean on me!"

Another beam crashed to the floor nearby, and Aelia knew the roof was likely to fall in at any moment. Somehow, she managed to get Leof to his feet. She pulled his arm 'round her shoulders and held on to him, supporting his weight as he limped back in the direction of the door.

But Aelia could barely see where she was leading him.

"I cannot breathe," Leof rasped.

"Keep moving!"

Aelia heard a man's voice call her name, and wondered if it was her imagination. Another crash behind them spurred her on. "Come, Leof—not much farther!"

"Aelia!"

Fitz Autier's face came into view. He wasted no time, but knelt before Leof and pulled the man into an awkward embrace. When the Norman stood again, Leof lay draped over his shoulder and he was moving away from her. "Let's go!"

She blinked smoke from her eyes and followed in his wake, grateful for his assistance and trusting that he knew the way out. Yet she despaired Osric's loss. The building was about to collapse and Aelia knew she could not go back. The heat was unbearable as it was.

And Osric was likely already dead.

Aelia choked on a sob and blindly followed Fitz Autier out of the storehouse. She was torn, desperate for air and cooler temperatures, but horrified by her inability to save her brother. She felt light-headed and ill, struggling for every breath.

"Move, Aelia! I cannot carry both of you!"

Aelia bristled. Fitz Autier would *never* have to carry her. She hurried alongside him, ducking the falling embers and skirting the debris on the ground.

A wall of flame roared up behind them and Fitz Autier grabbed her hand and pulled her along with him, until they were outside and clear of the building. Aelia fell to the earth, coughing.

She was still trying to catch her breath when the entire storehouse collapsed. Aelia heard shouts and screams of panic all 'round her, but paid them no heed as she coughed and wheezed.

Fitz Autier lowered Leof to the ground and knelt beside Aelia, fighting to catch his own breath. His bare arms gleamed with sweat and his face was covered with soot.

"Of all the witless… What were you thinking, going in there?" he demanded angrily between bursts of coughing.

"Osric! He's…" The full impact of Aelia's loss hit her, and she began to weep. She had failed in her duty to Ingelwald, and had been unable to rescue Osric. What happened to her now was of little consequence. If Fitz Autier chose to execute her here and now, 'twould be no less than she deserved.

Mayhap the black ash in her lungs would kill her first.

She pushed herself up off the ground, but her movement was impeded by Fitz Autier's iron grip on her upper arm. Aelia shook off his hand and rose unsteadily to her feet, turning to gaze upon the site of her brother's death. Emotion welled in her chest and she whirled away from the charred storehouse amid the shouts of the people all 'round her. Tears blurred her vision, but she managed to see Fitz Autier's big, blond companion push his way through the crowd, dragging a kicking, screaming boy with one massive hand.

Osric!

"Tell the bastard to turn me loose!" he bellowed as though he were lord and master here. As if he had not just barely escaped with his life.

The blood rushed from Aelia's head and she remained standing only because someone slipped his arm 'round her waist and supported her from behind. "Osric!" she wheezed.

An expressionless Auvrai d'Evreux held on to Osric as he pulled the boy toward Aelia and dropped him unceremoniously at her feet. "This is the one who torched the storehouse."

"You lie, Norman. My brother would never—"

Osric jumped to his feet and dashed away from Sir Auvrai's reach. "I knew they would have to set us free if the building was on fire!" His tone was defiant.

The blood suddenly drained from Aelia's head. "Osric, no! You could have killed so many…" She tried to swallow, but her throat was too dry. There had to be some additional explanation for Osric's actions. Surely he had understood the danger of a fire in the center of the village. And now he risked immediate retaliation by their Norman conquerors. "Leof almost died in there."

"As did your sister, boy," said Fitz Autier. He kept one hand at her waist as he confronted Osric. "Lock him in again with the other prisoners, Auvrai. The boy's a menace. He needs to be watched all night."

"Please let me stay with him!" Aelia cried, relieved once more that Fitz Autier had not seen fit to kill them both.

"And wreak more havoc on this holding? No. He will remain under guard until I order otherwise."

With little effort Auvrai lifted Osric and tossed him over his shoulder. The knight was impervious to the boy's kicks and blows as he carried him away from Aelia, who felt suddenly weightless. She would have fallen to the ground had Fitz Autier not held her up.

"But I can see to it that he does no more damage."

"No, *demoiselle*. He is no longer your responsibility."

"He is my brother. I—"

"Enough! Look around you!"

Her people were quiet now, all watching scornfully as Sir Auvrai carried Osric away. They'd heard Osric admit that he'd set fire to the storehouse, putting so many Saxons in danger. He may have intended to get them all free, but had endangered all the buildings in the village. As it was, the storehouse was gone, and the stable had nearly been destroyed.

The Saxons must view Osric as the enemy now—not Fitz Autier, who had risked all to stand on the stable roof, toiling at his own personal risk to douse the flames.

'Twas a horrible end to a dreadful day.

Mathieu was furious. He did not know what made him angrier—knowing that the little Saxon brat had set the fire intentionally, or seeing Aelia run into the burning building.

She might have been killed.

He forced himself to release her. Whatever he'd felt when he'd seen her dash into the storehouse was just a momentary distraction from his purpose here. He needed his prisoners alive and well enough to travel to London. King William expected it.

"Where will your knight take Osric?"

Her face and clothes were filthy. One sleeve of her tunic hung by threads from her shoulder, where a large abrasion glowed red in the light of the fires that smoldered nearby. Several of Mathieu's own stitches had torn free, but he seemed to have more than enough to hold the edges of the wound together. He would suffer no more sewing, at her hand or anyone else's. "I hope Auvrai finds a cage to put him in."

Aelia's eyes darted around her. "Our people…they're looking at Osric as if he were a fiend."

"What would *you* call someone who tried to burn fifty men alive?"

"He did not intend to hurt anyone," she countered.

"Tell that to the old man." Mathieu gestured toward

the Saxon he'd carried out of the storehouse. "I'm sure he will be gratified to know it."

Mathieu was shaken by the disaster. Every man in the storehouse might have been burned to death. All the other timber buildings within Ingelwald could have been destroyed—an inauspicious beginning to Mathieu's sovereignty over the region. As it was, several valuable animals had died in the stable fire.

He should have carried out his threat to execute both the boy and his sister. None of this would ever have happened—from Halig's ill-advised attack on the stairs, resulting in the troublesome wound in his side, to Mathieu's intractable urge to drag Aelia up to his chamber and bury himself inside her until he did not know where she ended and he began.

"He is still very young," Aelia said. "He did not understand the—"

"The boy lacks discipline, not to mention good sense." Mathieu could see no evidence of training or restraint in him. "He is reckless."

"What will you do to him?"

"He is no longer your concern, *demoiselle*." Mathieu nudged Aelia forward, toward the hall. Auvrai would find a suitable place to confine the boy, and see that he was well guarded through the night. 'Twas up to Mathieu to do the same with Aelia.

"He *is* my concern." Aelia stopped in front of him, turning to place her hands upon his forearms. Given her torn and soiled clothes, her voice heavy with fierce loyalty to her brother, he should have felt no surge of lust at her touch.

But he'd tasted her once already, and his body hungered for more.

"Hugh! Durand!" He called to two of the knights

who'd come to Ingelwald earlier with Gui de Reviers, and ignored the proud but pleading look in Aelia's eyes as he turned her over to them. "Find a secure chamber in the hall and lock her in. Do not leave her unguarded."

Each man grasped one of her arms, and they led her away from him, taking no particular care of her injured shoulder. These two would not let her escape as Gilbert had done.

Mathieu strode away and returned to the stable. He climbed to the roof and went about helping to quell the smoldering embers before he could change his mind about what was to be done with Aelia.

Chapter Seven

It stank in Aelia's little prison room, of disuse and of her sooty clothes and body. The candle she'd been given had burned down to its last hour. Though there were no windows in the little pantry, Aelia was certain 'twas past dawn from the distant sound of chirping birds.

They had to let her out.

The only furnishings in the pantry were the four empty burlap sacks Aelia had used as a bed once exhaustion had prevailed over her sorrow and worry. Now that she was awake again, she could not help but fret over Osric's situation. She went to the door and pounded, ignoring the heavy ache in her shoulder. "Open the door!"

There was no answer, so Aelia began to pace as she'd done the night before, after she'd been locked in this tiny, dark room.

She had not been able to read the expression in Fitz Autier's eyes as he'd sent her away with his men. But she worried that he had already decided to condemn her brother to death.

What else could the Norman do? Osric had done the

unthinkable. In his desire to release the Saxon prisoners and gain his own freedom, he'd endangered everyone in Ingelwald, not just the Norman soldiers.

He was a foolish child, and she had to convince Fitz Autier to take that into consideration…if he had not already had the boy executed.

She blinked away the tears that welled in her eyes, and pounded on the door again. "Take me to Fitz Autier! I must see him!"

If there was any Norman who would kill a child, 'twould be Fitz Autier. The man's reputation for ruthlessness had preceded him. For months they had heard rumors of his exploits, of the terrible toll exacted upon the Saxon lords at his hands. Aelia wondered if there was anything that could sway him from putting Osric to death.

She had naught to offer but the riches of Ingelwald, and he'd already claimed them, from the lowliest cottage outside the walls to her father's own hall. What more could she give him?

The candle sputtered and died just as the heavy wooden bar rasped against the door. Aelia took two steps toward it and pulled the door's handle, anxious to get out, whether or not that was what her guards intended. The door suddenly gave way and she staggered back into the pantry.

Durand grabbed her arm and pulled her from the room. In the moment it took for her eyes to adjust to the light in the anteroom, he shoved her forward.

The man was as dark as Fitz Autier, and there was a scar upon his cheek that mirrored the one Aelia had given his master, along with a cruel glint in his steely gray eyes that was unlike any expression she'd ever seen in Fitz Autier's. The man was as brawny as the

Norman who'd killed her father in battle against Gui de Reviers, but that knight had worn an armor helm, so Aelia would never know who had struck the fatal blow.

She recoiled at Durand's touch and pulled her arm away as the other guard spoke. "Fitz Autier wants to see you."

"Where's my brother? What has he done with him?"

Durand struck her, knocking her to the floor. Aelia was stunned by the man's brutality, though she should not have expected anything less. These men were her enemies and she would do well to remember it.

"On your feet, wench!"

In silence, Aelia did as she was ordered, and the men flanked her as they made their way to the great hall, where Gilbert the Herald still tended the wounded. Aelia bit her lip to keep her chin from trembling as they walked outside.

'Twas a dank and rainy morn, but Aelia was glad to be free of her confinement, no matter what the weather. Fitz Autier stood in front of the village bake house, looking freshly washed, wearing a black mantle over his hauberk, and clean, dark chausses on his legs. He seemed impervious to the rain as he spoke to the one-eyed knight who'd carried Osric away from her the night before. Fitz Autier turned slightly and caught Aelia's gaze, and his conversation seemed to stop.

A moment later, Aelia realized she must have been mistaken, for he resumed his discussion with Sir Auvrai as if he had not noted her presence. She stumbled and nearly fell, but her escorts were relentless, pushing her in the direction of the stable, where a saddled mare stood.

"Mount up."

Aelia took a shuddering breath. She could not leave

Ingelwald without asking after Osric again, nor could she ride away without knowing her destination. But she was afraid.

She damned her weakness and tried to form the words to question her guards, but her throat would not work. There was no doubt that any questions would raise the brutal guard's ire, and Aelia was not inclined to suffer another blow.

"Damn useless Saxon. Don't suppose you can ride."

She bit back a retort that would only cause her more pain. Of course she could ride. And if mounting this horse would get her away from these two oafs, Aelia was all for it. She would go to Fitz Autier and ask him her questions directly.

She put her foot in the stirrup and mounted as Sir Hugh took hold of the bridle; it seemed she would not be allowed to escape her guards, after all. When the men led her to the bake house where Fitz Autier stood, Aelia allowed herself to hope she could get some answers from him, though she now knew 'twas too much to hope she could convince him to release Osric.

The Norman baron did not spare her a glance, but mounted his own saddled gelding. A contingent of Norman warriors rode toward the gate and stood waiting for him—and her. Aelia fought back tears and tried to compose herself enough to ask about Osric…and her destination.

"Durand! Hugh!"

Mathieu beckoned the two guards toward him.

"Did my orders include abuse of my prisoner?" His voice sounded low and menacing to his own ears, but that could not be helped. He maintained strict discipline among his ranks, and though these two had been bound to Gui de Reviers, who had fallen before Mathieu's arrival at Ingelwald, they had clearly overstepped their orders.

At Mathieu's question, Hugh looked abashed, but Durand's expression darkened. Mathieu had not taken particular note of the man before, but he had an attitude of defiance and superiority that would not be tolerated.

"No, seignior," Hugh replied, but Durand remained silent.

"Turn yourselves over to Sir Auvrai. 'Twill be your task to deal with the stables. From the manure on the ground to the thatched roof."

Mathieu felt Lady Aelia's eyes on him as he gave his order, then turned and rode through Ingelwald's gate to the land beyond.

"S-seignior…" she stammered.

The welt upon her cheek did not concern him. She was no longer a noblewoman, but merely his prisoner in this battle for her homeland. She was his slave, and if King William did not execute her in London, Mathieu had no doubt he would ship her to Normandy, where she would be compelled to serve on one of his many estates.

She caught up to him. "My brother…?"

"Will remain in custody at my pleasure, *demoiselle*." He looked away from the worry in her eyes. Her troubles could be of no consequence to him. "And your cooperation buys the boy's continued good health."

Once Mathieu turned her over to the king's men in London, 'twould be an end to whatever connection was between them. He intended to be well occupied celebrating his betrothal and his victory at Ingelwald, and there would be little time to think of Lady Aelia. Or her fate.

"'Tis time for you to show me Ingelwald."

"But I—"

"*Demoiselle,* you are most qualified to do so, and with you, language does not pose a problem. I wish to assess the holding before I leave for London."

She hesitated. "Ingelwald is too vast," she finally said, no doubt keeping in mind Osric's tenuous position. "Its southern border is two days' ride from my father's hall."

"Fine. We'll ride north."

"As you wish, seignior." Her words were clipped, her posture stiff as she rode beside him. The morning's rain had turned into an annoying drizzle, and Aelia's torn and ragged clothes were soon soaked through. Though the weather was mild, Mathieu knew she would become chilled.

"Take this," he said, pulling his mantle from his shoulders. "Put it on."

She took it and draped it 'round her like a shawl, covering her head. "Thank you," she muttered. "The path joins the river beyond those trees."

"It flows south?"

"In parts. It has a circuitous route, but mostly flows east."

"By way of the mill—and Ingelwald's northern wall."

"Aye."

"And away west? What lies past those fields?"

"The hills in the distance are Ingelwald's. We graze our sheep up there. Beyond that is Grantham, held by Fugol the Bold."

Not any longer. Fugol had been taken to London when Baron Richard Louvet had conquered the Saxon lord's holding. Mathieu had seen the man hanged in London a year ago. He cleared his throat. "How many sheep?"

"Hundreds."

'Twas no wonder Wallis had fought so hard for this land. There was wealth here beyond anything Mathieu had expected. 'Twas likely a richer holding than his father's estate in Normandy. Autier de Burbage would not be pleased when he learned that one of his many bastards fared better than he. "What of raiding Scots?" Mathieu asked, unwilling to expend any energy thinking of his father. "Do they harry your borders?"

Aelia shook her head. "No. My father maintains— *maintained* patrols that deterred them."

"And without these patrols?"

"While you Normans besieged us, 'tis likely the Scots came down from the hills and helped themselves to whatever livestock were out grazing. 'Tis likely you are now lord of ten sheep and five cattle."

Mathieu ignored her gloating tone and looked out toward the hills. The clouds had cleared and 'twas turning into a fine, warm day, but he could barely see the dots of white there, the Ingelwald sheep. They would need to be guarded, beginning today.

'Twas problematic. He'd planned to return to London with a large contingent of men. Now those men would be required to stay at Ingelwald and guard the holding from Scottish raids.

If only he did not have to return to London.

Mayhap 'twould be better to travel with a smaller contingent, anyway. They would be able to move faster and attract less unwanted attention that way, but he would have to be very cautious. Saxon outlaws hid in the forests, poised to attack careless travelers, and there were displaced Danes who had no love for the Normans.

Mathieu's party traveled north beside the river until

it widened and became a rapidly flowing torrent, crashing and foaming over large boulders in its bed.

"Where is the waterfall?"

Aelia turned to look at him with a crease in her brow and astonishment in her eyes.

"'Tis never good to underestimate your enemy, *demoiselle*. Of course there must be a waterfall nearby—with the broadened river and these rapids. And the terrain rises sharply ahead. How far is it?"

Aelia kicked her heels into her mare's sides and galloped on. Her move was unexpected and rash, and Mathieu was unsure whether 'twas an attempt to escape him or perhaps lead him into some sort of trap.

Did she know if there were Scots waiting 'round the next bend? Or mayhap Saxon outlaws camped nearby?

Neither was likely. 'Twould not have been possible to organize an attack here, when his own plans had not been settled until a few moments before they'd ridden from Ingelwald.

"Raoul, stay on the path," he ordered. "I will rejoin you shortly."

He raced after Aelia, following the trail she'd left in the muddy earth, until the sounds of a waterfall roared loud in his ears. The trail climbed and swerved away from the river for a time, but Mathieu never lost sight of her tracks. The fool woman wasn't very far ahead.

Craggy cliffs became visible beyond the tops of the trees and he could see the crest of the waterfall, a wide cascade crashing down to the riverbed below. Aelia's tracks veered east, in the direction of the waterfall, but she no longer climbed. She'd left the path and ridden directly toward the water.

Mathieu dismounted and led his horse through the underbrush. The waterfall and rushing river blocked out all other sounds, including any that Aelia might make in her flight from him. However, there were signs of recent passage. He was certain he hadn't lost her.

Aelia knew it had been foolish to ride off the way she'd done. But these few moments of freedom—out of that cursed pantry, and away from Ingelwald—had gone to her head.

So had the desire to keep Fitz Autier off balance.

He hadn't expected her to bolt, and she had taken full advantage. She just hoped he didn't find her too quickly. There was no clear path to the cavern where she and Godwin had come as children with their mother, to the deep, placid pool behind the waterfall, to swim. 'Twould be at least an hour before he found his way here.

Sitting on a rock behind the waterfall, she dropped the Norman's dark wool mantle and untied the laces of her shoes. She needed to clear her head and heart of the terrible events of the last few weeks, of her fear for Osric…and for herself. The cool water might not save her, but it would certainly refresh her. Besides, she could not stand her filthy, fetid skin any longer. She jumped into the water fully clothed.

It felt wonderful. Somehow, she managed to rub away the grime of two days—had it only been two days? It seemed like weeks since Fitz Autier's men had overrun Ingelwald. Months since Selwyn had died.

Years since she'd lost her father.

Aelia could not imagine what would happen next. Fitz Autier had threatened to execute her and Osric if Selwyn would not negotiate for them. The battle had come and gone, yet she and Osric were still alive.

The Norman planned to take her and Osric to London. Was Fitz Autier coldhearted enough to turn them over to the king for execution there?

Aelia swam to the bottom of the pool and put such thoughts out of her mind. They served no purpose, nor did they change the course of action she had chosen.

Since 'twas proving impossible to kill Fitz Autier, Aelia was going to find Osric and free him, then the two of them would flee Ingelwald. Many of the neighboring estates had been overrun by Normans, but Cælin of Thrydburgh still held his hall and his land. 'Twas a three-day journey to his holding on horseback, but Aelia had no qualms about making the trip on foot. Wallis had had his differences with Cælin, but whatever their disagreements may have been, 'twas Saxon against Norman now. Surely the man would give them shelter.

The cool water soothed the ache in Aelia's bruised shoulder and washed away the blood and despair of the last few days. She felt refreshed and renewed as she pushed off the pool's rocky floor. She was a strong swimmer, but she took her time rising to the surface of the pool, enjoying the peaceful solitude of the water surrounding her.

When Aelia broke the surface, she took a quick glance all around. Fortunately, there was no movement anywhere about the waterfall, which meant Fitz Autier had not yet caught up to her. Aelia lay back and floated, letting her mind drift as she gazed absently up at the water as it cascaded down the rocky hillside. 'Twould be so easy to believe that all was well, that she and—

A creeping tentacle slid 'round her ankle and pulled her down. 'Twas strong and unrelenting, and Aelia was certain her last moment had come. She could stay submerged another minute, but would surely drown if she could not get free of this…

What had hold of her? There was no muck at the bottom of the pool to support vines or any other plant that could possibly ensnare her. She fought the current to bend down and try to free herself from whatever was pulling her.

And suddenly, she was loose.

She shot upward like an arrow, and filled her lungs with air while she paddled frantically to the edge of the pool. Until she knew what had pulled her down, she could not remain in the water. With tremendous effort, Aelia climbed out of the pool and dropped to the rocks beside it—onto a pile of woolen clothes and a cold, metal hauberk that lay beside her shoes.

Indignation, annoyance, embarrassment—all these emotions vied for dominion in Aelia's heart.

Fitz Autier! The blackguard had nearly drowned her! He had sneaked up and pulled her down, keeping her under just long enough to make her panic.

Aelia grabbed her shoes and started to stalk away, but when she heard the damnable Norman's laughter, she became infuriated. There had to be something she could throw at him—a rock large enough to do damage to his thick skull and end all her problems. She dropped her shoes and picked up a small boulder. She would show him that she was not one to be toyed with.

But when she turned, he was climbing out of the pool, his body naked.

Aelia gaped at him as he walked toward her with water sluicing off his brawny frame. Muscles flexed and bulged as he moved with the sure ease of a powerful animal certain of his strength. Aelia swallowed and took a step back, but could not take her eyes off him. He was beautiful. 'Twas not an apt description for a man, but she could think of no better word.

She should have felt chilled after leaving the pool, but a vaguely familiar heat kindled deep within her, and she had to remind herself to breathe. Hot color bloomed in her face, but she could not look away. This man had kissed her. He'd taken her into his arms and made her forget her own name.

And by all the saints, she wanted him to do the same now.

Horrified by her thoughts and worried that he'd seen some foolhardy longing in her eyes, she dropped the rock from her hand. Aelia whirled away from him. "You have no shame, seignior!"

"And you are wearing too many clothes, *demoiselle,*" he said, closing in on her. "They're wet. You'll catch a chill."

Aelia felt his breath on her neck as water dripped and puddled at her feet. She did not know what she would do if he touched her. In his sleep two nights before, he had pulled her close, unconsciously caressed her, and produced in her an amazing experience unlike anything she'd ever known.

Aelia's knees went weak and her heart pounded at the thought of what might have happened that night. Had he been awake, and aware of what he was doing to her, would her pleasure have been enhanced? Here he stood in all his naked glory—big and threatening, yet so inviting.

She stepped closer to the cavern wall, crossing her arms over her breasts to keep from turning to him. She was not really tempted by him. 'Twas only the novelty of the intimacy between them that confused her.

Perhaps now would be a good time to put some distance between them, while she learned of his plans for her and Osric. "What are you going to do?"

"Do?" He had followed her and stood much too close.

Aelia started when he touched her shoulder. Gently, he turned her to face him, but she pressed herself back against the cool cavern wall as he lowered his head.

"What would you have me do, *demoiselle?*"

Their mouths were inches apart, and the space between them was quickly diminishing. She could feel his breath upon her lips and the heat of his naked body against her. Panic seized her. If he kissed her again, she would be lost.

She pushed away from him and jumped back into the pool, letting its waters cool her heated blood.

Chapter Eight

Mathieu could not explain what happened to his rational mind when Aelia was near. He responded to her with his body—a hard, feral reaction that coursed through his blood and demanded satisfaction. And she was not indifferent to him.

'Twas an incendiary combination.

He jumped into the pool to extinguish the fire.

Aelia had already mounted her horse and started to ride off, but she encountered Raoul and the rest of their escort before she could get away from the waterfall. Signaling to Raoul de Moreton to ride on without him, Mathieu let her go.

He needed to put some space between himself and Aelia.

Even bedraggled as she was, she could make him lose all sense of purpose. He'd had one idea when they'd ridden out from Ingelwald: to assess his new holding. Aelia was the most knowledgeable person to show him the land, having lived here all her life. But she had managed to distract him once again.

Mathieu took a breath of air and dunked his head,

diving deep into the cooling water. Would he ever be able to visit this place without seeing Aelia's face, without recalling that he had been merely seconds from laying her upon the damp stone and satisfying his lust?

'Twas only a matter of time before he purged her from his mind. There were much more weighty matters vying for his attention, not the least of which were the questions of how to secure Ingelwald before leaving for London, and how many knights would need to stay and defend the holding as well as the livestock.

He'd planned on returning with at least half the men who'd come to Ingelwald with him. Now it seemed his traveling party would have to be reduced to a mere escort. Could he go with so few men?

Mayhap a smaller company would be safer. A smaller group would be much more suited to maneuvering off the beaten trail, and they would be able to carry fewer supplies, attracting less attention, though remaining more vulnerable.

His plan had been to leave Auvrai d'Evreux in charge of Ingelwald. Auvrai was an old friend, and as competent a knight as any Mathieu had ever known. However, it might be better to have another strong warrior in their party, rather than leaving Auvrai at Ingelwald.

Taking leisurely strokes that propelled him across the pool, Mathieu considered all the possibilities. By nightfall, he would have to make a decision as to who would go and who would stay, for he planned to leave early in the morn. There was no time for this imprudent pastime, and 'twas even possible his swim had done some damage to the wound in his side.

He swam to the edge and climbed out. Quickly appraising the damage to the gash, he decided no serious harm had been done. If anything, the wound looked better now than when he'd started out this morn.

Pulling on his clothes, Mathieu looked 'round the cavern. He would never have noticed this niche behind the waterfall had he not caught sight of Aelia in the pool. 'Twas a perfect location for a tryst, and when he returned from London with Clarise, he would bring her here for just that purpose.

There would be no better way to expel Lady Aelia from his mind.

Her shoes lay at the edge of the pool, and Mathieu pictured her bare feet, so small and delicate for such a fierce warrior. She had bared no other part of her body, yet his imagination wandered over the soft curves that lay hidden beneath her tattered clothes.

He shook his head to rid it of such provocative images; they served no purpose beyond raising his frustration to a maddening level. Mayhap 'twas time to find a willing maid in the village and slake his lust before he was blinded by it. Naught was special about Lady Aelia; any woman would do.

His men were far ahead of him when Mathieu finally took to the trail. He followed it as it wound around the hillside, and had an excellent vantage point from the high ground at the brink of the waterfall. He took a moment to survey all the land before him.

His land.

'Twas no mean conquest for the bastard son of a scullery maid. The king had been confident of Mathieu's victory here, where others before him had failed. The winning of Ingelwald would not only please William and gain more honors for Mathieu, it would secure his betrothal to Simon de Vilot's daughter. Now there was no question that Lady Clarise would be his wife.

The betrothal would take place as soon as Mathieu arrived in London, and the marriage would soon follow. When he returned to Ingelwald, his bride would travel with him.

Mathieu had yet to meet Lady Clarise. He'd seen her once in Rouen, and only from a distance. At the time, he'd been merely a bastard warrior in William's army, certainly no likely suitor for the well-born daughter of Simon de Vilot. But now that Mathieu had been promised this rich holding, the dark-eyed, raven-haired Lady Clarise would be his wife. He was honored to have been chosen by her father and the king to be her husband, when any number of Norman noblemen might have made a more prestigious match. This marriage was a great deal more than a bastard son could ever have expected. The king had raised Mathieu's stature even higher than that of his half brothers, who each had nobly born wives and fair estates in Normandy.

Mathieu had a clear view of his men riding in double file with Aelia in their midst, her blond head uncovered in contrast to the soldiers' helm-covered pates glinting brightly in the sunshine. She rode well, with a regal posture that belied her status as his prisoner.

He was anxious to be rid of her. Once they reached London, he would turn her over to the king's guards, and have no more to do with her. 'Twould be a relief.

Wooded hills surrounded his men as they traversed a deep, barren vale. Mathieu caught sight of movement in the trees east of his troops, and narrowed his eyes to see if he could discern whether it was anything more than the sunlight reflecting off the river.

Mathieu could not tell from such a distance what caused it, but when the light flashed again, far from the riverbed, he knew it was trouble.

Someone, mayhap Scots marauders, lay hidden among the trees. If they attacked by surprise, his men would be at a distinct disadvantage.

Mathieu had to take action. But shouting to them, even if his voice could be heard at this distance, would alert the warriors in hiding. Riding after them would do the same. 'Twould precipitate a battle, and Aelia would be in the midst of it.

Mathieu could not think of her now. He took another moment to observe the area in question and became even more certain that outlaws of one kind or another lurked there. Whether 'twas Scots, displaced Saxons or marauding Danes made no difference. He had to act.

He dug in his heels and spurred the gelding down the hill, leaning forward and keeping his body low. Stealth and diversion were his best strategy.

Veering east into the wooded area where the rogue warriors were hidden, Mathieu was distracted by thoughts of what would happen to Aelia if he did not warn his men of the danger beside them. He'd never before given much thought to the bystanders of war, and how their lives were changed by it. He'd always known there were victims all 'round.

But Aelia was different. Mathieu had never known or even heard of such valor in a woman. Yet she rode without armor or weapon now. If they were attacked, she could do naught to protect herself.

Mathieu continued riding northeast, deep into the cool, damp woods. His pace was slower, for there was no established track, and the underbrush was thick in places. He rode carefully, listening for sounds that would orient him to the location of the hidden army, certain they'd seen his men's approach and were preparing to attack.

When Mathieu heard the jangle of metal hitting metal, he knew he was closing in on them. He dismounted and tied his horse, then continued on foot, following the sounds of stealthy preparation. He stayed out of sight, crouching low and keeping to the trees, but managed to advance far enough to see who was cloaked within the forest, and how serious a threat they posed.

They were Saxons. Dressed in skins and ragged wool, some wore *cuir-bouilli,* some had helmets. They strapped on their daggers and tested the edges of their axes in preparation for battle.

There were many of them, at least two to every one of his men. If these Saxons planned an ambush, they would be able to encircle the Normans and crush them.

Mathieu slipped back to the place where he'd left his horse, and mounted again. He climbed a small hillock that bordered the Saxons' east side. There were fewer trees, which meant less cover, but he did not doubt that the Saxons were entirely focused upon the Norman soldiers who rode in the vale, not on the hilly terrain behind them.

When he was well hidden and a good distance away, Mathieu rolled several small boulders down the hill, then put his horn to his lips and blew. The reaction was exactly what he had hoped for. There was immediate confusion in the Saxon ranks. 'Twould take some time before they understood they were not under attack from behind, and in those few moments, Raoul de Moreton would be well warned and prepared for battle.

Aelia sat stiffly in the saddle. She did not know where Fitz Autier was, nor would she turn to see whether he'd joined them.

She hoped he had put his clothes back on. The man

was unnerving enough while fully dressed, but when she saw the physical power that lay beneath his warrior's garb, she nearly lost her sense of proper restraint. Why had her father not wed her to a warrior of such prowess as Fitz Autier? Mayhap if Aelia had such a husband, she would not be quite so susceptible to the physical power the Norman displayed with such arrogance. He seemed to think naught of flaunting his naked body before her repeatedly—as if she were some simpleton slave, and anxious for his favors.

The Normans rode silently north, through a deep valley surrounded by thick woods and tall cliffs. Aelia had never been permitted to venture so far beyond the waterfall. According to her father and Godwin, the path through the vale was too vulnerable, with Scottish lands a mere day's ride from here. Wallis had always been loath to invite trouble.

The hair on the back of Aelia's neck prickled and she knew something was amiss. "Sir Raoul…"

She did not wish to appear the frightened maiden among these Normans, yet something was not right. Whether 'twas her father's misgivings about this place or the possibility that there was truly danger here, Aelia did not know. She looked to the east, then west, trying to see into the dense woods. Naught was visible, but the undeniable sense of peril raised gooseflesh upon her arms.

"I think we should turn back."

To his credit, Raoul did not ignore her. "What is it, *demoiselle?*" He cast his eyes about him, as if evaluating the risk of continuing on. "My orders are to—"

The full, resonant cry of a battle horn sounded in the distance. All the horses reacted, and Aelia's mare reared, throwing her and galloping up the path. The

Normans paid no attention to her plight as they drew their swords. Battle cries burst from the trees east of them. Bruised and barefoot, Aelia ran behind the line of warriors as they arranged themselves to face the attack.

She reached for her knife and remembered that Fitz Autier had it. She had no bow, no weapon to use when they were attacked by whatever enemy dwelled within the woods.

But something strange happened. The voices in the forest scattered, some moving north and others to the south, accompanied by the unmistakable sounds of horses, swords and clanging armor. The horn sounded again, but it seemed even farther away.

"'Tis the baron!" Raoul called to the men. "He's leading them away!"

The Normans left Aelia behind as they charged into the woods. She tensed, but her only fear was for Fitz Autier. What kind of fool would attempt to draw off an army alone?

And why did she care?

In truth, she did not care. Her concern was for her own safety, how she would escape from whatever danger lurked in the woods and get herself back to Ingelwald—to Osric. Fitz Autier's fate did not concern her beyond his ability to escort her home.

Yet she found herself searching for some sign of him.

The clash of swords rang in Aelia's ears. She wondered if she should turn and flee, retrace her path through the vale and beyond the waterfall. She knew the eastern road well, and could get herself back to Ingelwald without her Norman escort. But if she turned west, she could go to Thrydburgh…to safety. Surely Cælin would allow her to stay.

Her horse had run off and Aelia could see no sign of it. She could not walk the distance to Thrydburgh without shoes, and if she left the Normans here, 'twas doubtful she would ever see Osric again. Fitz Autier held him hostage against her cooperation.

Would he kill her brother if she disappeared? Fitz Autier was a ruthless warrior, but Aelia had never seen him hurt any women or children. After last night, however, Aelia doubted anyone would consider Osric an innocent child.

She had no choice but to stay and wait out the battle.

Her position was much too exposed, so she walked cautiously forward, using the trees and low shrub as cover. She felt naked without her dagger, and knew her best protection was to get into a position where she could watch the skirmish. She advanced, staying under cover and keeping some distance from the battle. The fighting was disorganized, but the Normans were clearly outnumbered by a ragged band of Saxon warriors.

An unbearable sadness filled Aelia's heart. As numerous as they were, the Saxons stood no chance against these Normans. Her vision blurred with tears when Fitz Autier suddenly came into sight, riding into the thick of battle, wielding his sword like a coldhearted executioner.

She could not tear her eyes from his powerful form. He moved like a proud stag of the forest, swift and dangerous, yet light and agile. Aelia experienced the same wrenching heat she felt whenever she watched him from afar. 'Twas difficult to catch her breath when she saw him like this, in full mastery over his enemy—her own people.

Fitz Autier shouted orders to his men, and they started to hem the Saxons in a wide circle, with no room to maneuver. Aelia could not bear to watch.

She backed away, shaking her head to clear it. Her mother had to have been mistaken about the odd feelings engendered by the sight of him. Fitz Autier could not possibly be her one true mate—not even if his touch made her heart flutter and her bones turn to ash.

With overwhelming sadness, Aelia turned away. She started to run, but someone came at her from behind and shoved her down. She landed hard, and before she could make a sound, her Saxon attacker drew his ax and swung.

Aelia screamed and rolled to the side to escape the blow, then quickly pushed herself up to her feet and ran. 'Twas not her fate to be hewn this way—by a man who was likely once an ally of her father.

"Now you die, Norman whore!"

The words cut her to the bone and she stumbled, with the Saxon right behind her. This was not the time for tears. She had to keep her wits about her or she surely *would* die. In a desperate attempt to keep her balance, Aelia scrambled up and ran ahead, but the Saxon fell upon her and shoved her to the ground. Dropping his ax, he grabbed her hair, yanked her head back, placed the cold steel of a knife blade against her throat.

Aelia held her breath and stayed perfectly still, even when he muttered another insulting remark about her. Telling him that she was also Saxon would do no good. The man would only see her as a traitor.

She felt the burn of the sharp edge and the trickle of blood down her neck. But before she could react, the Saxon let go, dropping her to the ground.

"Aelia!"

On hands and knees, she scurried away, but Fitz
Autier's enraged voice, and the clash of swords, caused
her to turn. Too shaken to do more than press one hand
against the cut on her neck, she drew her legs up to her
chest and wrapped one arm 'round them. She took a
shuddering breath when the Norman baron finished off
the man who would have killed her.

Fitz Autier gave her no time to recover, but took her
hand and pulled her to her feet. With one finger under
her chin, he tipped her head back and looked at the
wound. "'Tis not deep."

Aelia could not speak, and it galled her to stand
trembling before the Norman.

"Hold still," he said, gripping her torn sleeve and rip-
ping it the rest of the way off her tunic. He slid it down
her arm and folded the cloth, then pressed it against the
wound in her neck.

Aelia wished he would not be so kind. She wanted
her hatred for him to be a clear, pure thing, uncompli-
cated by any demonstration of compassion or benevolence.

At the same time, she wished he would hold her
until the trembling stopped.

"Let's go." A moment later, she found herself being
lifted and tossed upon his horse, with Fitz Autier mounting behind her.

"I can ride," she said, though her voice sounded thick
and unsteady to her own ears.

"Not this time."

"I have seen battle, seignior. I have never…"

"I know, *demoiselle*. I will forever bear the scar of
your arrow upon my face." He shifted in the saddle, then
draped something warm about her shoulders. 'Twas the
mantle she'd worn earlier, and she was grateful for its heat.

"You…saved my life," she said. She would have to thank him for that, at least.

"Think naught of it. 'Twas no more than what I'd have done for anyone under my protection."

"You drew the Saxons away from your men," she said. "You warned them with your horn."

"'Tis a useful weapon."

"Your horn? 'Tis not a weapon at all."

He pulled her close. Aelia did not understand his reason for making such a comforting gesture, but since his hauberk was surprisingly warm, and Aelia felt chilled to the bone, she did not complain. "You do not believe the horn was an effective weapon? It drew the Saxons away from my men, did it not?"

"But swords are weapons. Axes, knives… Aye. Your horn diverted the Saxons from their prey. I concede."

The voices of Normans and Saxons fell behind them as Fitz Autier guided the gelding out of the forest and onto the valley path. "You're leaving the battle?" she asked.

"I've seen enough of killing. Raoul will prevail and take prisoner any Saxon who yields."

Aelia felt her throat thicken. More of her people would be enslaved, and she could do naught to help them. "What will you do with them?"

"There is room at Ingelwald, is there not?"

"For more Saxons who hate you?" Aelia could have bitten her tongue for those cutting words to the man who had just saved her life, but they were out, and their truth could not be denied.

But Fitz Autier just gave a laugh that sounded more bitter than mirthful, and rode on.

The woman needed some clothes. What she wore was torn and stained, and misshapen after her swim behind the waterfall. Not that Mathieu did not appreciate that she'd kept her clothes on. In hindsight, 'twas best that one obstacle had remained between them.

Men and women were at work inside Ingelwald's walls when he and Aelia arrived. The rubble of the burned storehouse was gone, and the stable roof had been repaired. Normans and Saxons collected debris and swept it away from the paths while the scarred knight spoke with a Saxon shopkeeper. When he saw Mathieu, he turned and approached.

"Speaking the Saxon tongue now, Auvrai?"

The knight shrugged. "What happened to you?"

Mathieu told him about the attack as he dismounted and assisted Aelia from his saddle. He should send her away with one of the guards to the enclosure where the rest of the Saxon prisoners were held.

But he was not ready to part with her.

"The lady could use some of your salve, Auvrai." He reached for her shoes and his mantle, and took them from the saddle.

"And what of you? I've yet to see that wound in your side."

"It looked clean this afternoon."

Auvrai shrugged again. "You'll find the salve in my pack, with Gilbert in the hall." He'd never been one for questions beyond the essential, but he was as loyal as any man could be, and had matters well in hand here.

Aelia did not wait for Mathieu, but walked toward the hall, as though she were still daughter of the lord, even though she was dressed like the most pitiful pauper in the realm.

Mathieu followed her. She did not look back but went to the stairs and climbed. He picked up the leather bag that held Auvrai's salves and bandages, and went up after her. He climbed all the way to the master's chamber, but Aelia was not there.

Mathieu should have known she would not retreat to the room he'd taken as his own. The place she would seek refuge would be her own chamber—the one that had belonged to her before he'd had it stripped. The room was barren of all her belongings, of all comforts other than a plain, straw mattress. Yet she'd gone to the place where she'd likely spent many a carefree hour, he discovered when he went there.

She stood at the window, looking out. Her arms rested at her sides, one of them bare, the other covered by a puckered woolen sleeve. Her hair had come loose from the thick plait that bound it, yet Mathieu could easily imagine how she would look dressed in her Saxon finery, with her hair shining and flowing loose to her hips.

Was she remembering the better times when she was the lady of Ingelwald?

"I want to see my brother," she said without turning.

Mathieu dropped her shoes to the floor. "No."

She turned then. Though she tried to keep her expression neutral, she could not hide the fury in her eyes. "My cooperation ensures Osric's well-being, does it not?"

He ran one hand across his face. "To some extent, *demoiselle*. But his own behavior also helps to determine how he is treated."

She came to him in two steps, placing her hand upon his arm. "He is just a child! He cannot be held responsible—"

"He is without discipline."

"But he's a good lad."

Mathieu found Auvrai's salve in a small pouch

within the satchel. He untied the string that held a thin hide over its top, and uncovered it. Taking Aelia's chin between his thumb and finger, he raised it to gain access to the cut in her neck.

She would not look at him, but kept her eyes downcast. Mathieu could not help but notice the thick crescent of russet lashes that shadowed her cheeks. The pulse in her throat raced, and he could imagine how it would feel against his lips.

He cleared his throat and ignored the delicate curve of her neck. He would not think of how close she'd come to losing her life. "Turn toward the light."

She did, and he smeared the musty-smelling ointment on the wound. When he stopped, she backed away.

He caught her hand. "I'm not finished."

She took an unsteady breath and waited for him to wrap a length of white linen 'round her throat, then remained still as he examined the scrape on her shoulder.

"The salve will do some good, but it will rub off on your clothes."

"That does not seem to be a problem, seignior," she said with a pointed glance at the tear in her tunic that left her shoulder and arm bare.

"I'll have someone find you some clothes."

"Do not trouble yourself," she said, and this time, walked away from him. She bent down to pick up her shoes. "What would a slave need with decent clothing?"

"You are not a slave."

"A prisoner, then. Tell me, Fitz Autier, what will you do with us—with Osric and me?"

If she'd intended to neutralize the intimate moment between them, she succeeded.

"I have orders to take you to the king in London."

Chapter Nine

Aelia would not go to London. The thought of facing that murderous Norman, William, was more than she could stomach. She was not afraid of the man, but she could not deny that Fitz Autier's orders unnerved her. What could the bastard king possibly want with her?

Ingelwald was her place. She was needed here in the aftermath of so many battles and such devastation. The people had always looked to her father and his men for direction, and there were many who owed work or rents. Now that Wallis was gone, 'twas up to Aelia to take charge of the holding. There were hundreds of acres under cultivation, and huge numbers of livestock, with pounds of grain and weights of meat owed to her bondsmen, food that would sustain them throughout the year. 'Twould soon be time for harvest, and Aelia had yet to miss one.

She lay back upon the lumpy straw mattress in her room and tried to find a comfortable position. How could she refuse to go with Fitz Autier? She had no power, no say in what happened to her. In that, she was no better than the lowest slave.

At least she'd been given one day's reprieve. Fitz Autier had not been able to leave Ingelwald as soon as he wanted. Too many of his men had been injured in the skirmish with the renegade Saxons, and now there were even more prisoners to deal with.

She spent a restless night locked in her own chamber, and was awakened from an uneasy slumber by a knock at her door. 'Twas Rowena, one of the housemaids. She was much younger than Aelia, a very pretty girl who'd garnered much attention from Ingelwald's young swains. She carried a bundle of cloth in her arms and spoke perfunctorily, her voice expressionless. "The Norman sent me with this."

Aelia took the parcel, taking note of the girl's pallor and the dark circles under her eyes. "Are you unwell, Rowena?"

The girl bit down on her lip and shook her head, cowering before the Norman guard who stood beside the door, watching their every move.

"Then what is it? What are you—"

"'Tis naught, my lady. I'll not speak of it."

Aelia frowned, taking note of a red scrape upon her neck—no, 'twas a bite mark! "You were assaulted. One of these bastards…did he rape you?"

Rowena trembled and tears streamed down her face. Aelia tried to draw her inside the room, but the Norman guard interfered.

"Move, you Norman oaf! I will speak to her here. In private!" Aelia shoved herself between Rowena and the guard, eased the girl into the chamber, then shut the door.

"I am so sorry, Rowena," Aelia said as an unholy rage flared within her. Why couldn't the man have chosen an older maid, one more experienced, and more willing? Nelda, perhaps, who was known to give herself freely. "Is there aught to be done for you?"

Aelia remembered the day her father had brought Rowena to work in the hall. The girl's father had drowned and there'd been no other family to care for her.

"I may be with ch-child, my lady…." Her voice was tremulous.

"I'll see the swine punished. Who is he?"

Rowena shook her head and wept. "You can do naught! 'Tis done now—"

"If there is a child, I'll see that the bastard takes care of you both."

"No! I wish never to lay eyes upon him again!"

"Tell me who it was."

"A Norman! You know him…s-so big. Dark." She pressed a hand to her cheek. "Scarred."

Aelia's anger grew to a seething, pulsing rage. She yanked open her chamber door and pushed past the guard as Rowena whimpered behind her. It took but a moment to climb the stairs to her father's chamber, slip away from the guard once again and throw open the door.

"Fitz Autier!"

He was fastening his belt over a dark blue tunic.

"How dare you!"

He looked up at her. A crease formed between his brows and he spoke, but Aelia barely heard the guard's apology to his baron, or Fitz Autier's dismissal of him.

"How dare I what?"

"Rowena is still a child, barely thirteen years old!"

The crease grew deeper. "Rowena?"

"You know very well, seignior." His dagger lay untended upon the end of the bed, beside his gauntlets.

Aelia's hand darted out and grabbed it. She held it up in a threatening manner and hoped he would come after her for it. Godwin had taught her how to deal with a man of Fitz Autier's size. Once he came toward her, she would quickly feint to the side, then slide her foot 'round his ankle to trip him.

When he fell, she would drop on top of him and mete out the punishment he deserved.

"Am I to understand that someone called Rowena has been wronged?" He did not move, other than to cross his arms over his chest. Fury made her heart pound and her breath come in short spurts. She tightened her grip on the knife and widened her stance. "You did not even know her name, did you?"

"How could I, *demoiselle?*"

"'Tis just like a Norman to take from another…to steal what is precious, without regard to—"

"Are we speaking of a woman?"

"A girl! An innocent child!"

Aelia lunged.

Fitz Autier moved so fast she missed him, and before she could strike at him, he took hold of her wrist and shook the knife free. It fell to the floor and he pulled her arm up behind her, shoving her facedown on the bed.

He dropped beside her, holding her in place. "Explain what this is about."

"Get off me!"

"Talk!"

"'Tis pointless! You Normans would never admit to raping a young girl, unless 'twas to boast of it to your despicable companions." She tried to push up, but could not oust him from his position.

"Rape?"

"Aye. I'm sure you've heard of it." She spat out the

words, laden with sarcasm. "'Tis when a man without honor takes a woman against her will, holding her down and—"

He released her abruptly and stood back.

Aelia pushed herself off the bed and would have gone for the door if he'd not stood in her path.

"She accused me? This Rowena?"

"Who else is so tall and dark...and bears a scar on his cheek?"

His jaw clenched dangerously. "A number of us, *demoiselle*. We have seen many battles. Who among us is not scarred?"

"Do you deny it, then?" There was more bluster than threat in her tone, and they both knew it. His eyes, icy blue, pierced her, but she felt little fear of him. Could Rowena have been mistaken about her attacker—or had Aelia come to the wrong conclusion?

"There is only one woman at Ingelwald who is of interest to me," Fitz Autier said, his voice low and ominous. "And the only reason her virtue remains intact is that I have no desire to force myself upon an unwilling woman."

His meaning became clear, and Aelia found herself unable to speak. She watched his eyes peruse her body as if he were a starving man looking to break his fast. Her throat tightened and she stood still for an interminable interval, then fled the room.

Aelia escaped to her own chamber and stood with her back against the stout wooden door, listening to the pounding of her heart in her ears. The only reason she felt so agitated was because of Rowena. And now that she knew Fitz Autier was not the one who'd raped the girl, Aelia would make it her business to discover and punish the man who'd done it.

Fresh water had been left for her, as well as a comb and a short leather strip to bind her hair. She made quick use of both, then dressed in the soft linen under-kirtle and green bliaut that Rowena had brought. The linen bandage Fitz Autier had bound around her neck chafed her, but she left it in place in her haste to leave the chamber and find the maid.

There were pointed questions to ask about her attacker.

Expecting an argument from the guard at her door, Aelia was surprised when he allowed her to descend to the great hall. Sir Gilbert still tended the wounded, along with the tall, blond, one-eyed knight, but she noted with relief that Fitz Autier was not in sight.

Ingelwald hall boasted two kitchens, and Aelia hoped to find Rowena in one of them. The first was empty, so she went outside to the separate building where most of the baking was done, especially in summer. There in the bake house, she found Grendel and his mother. "I'm looking for Rowena."

"She is not with you, my lady?" asked Elga. "I sent her to your chamber with the clothes given me by the Norman baron."

Aelia shook her head. "No. I saw her a while ago, but…" But she'd run up the stairs to take Fitz Autier's head off for something he had not done.

Still, he was responsible for the actions of his men. And if one of them had defiled Rowena, Aelia was going to see that he paid dearly for it.

"I'd hoped she would be safe with you after what—"

A piercing scream launched Aelia through the bake house door. 'Twas not the carefree shriek of a child at play, but that of a desperate woman.

Men and women came to the doors of their shops and cottages and looked out.

An old woman pointed to the chandler's shop, and when another scream came from that direction, Aelia did not stop to think, but went straight for it.

Mathieu looked out the window and saw Aelia. Though she was speaking to her own people, her posture was that of a warrior poised for battle. She wore women's clothes now, and her hair had been tamed into a soft cascade that teased her hips. But Mathieu knew her clothes would do naught to tame her temper.

She turned suddenly and ran, and Mathieu had no choice but to do the same.

Clearly, something was amiss, and the lady of Ingelwald intended to right it. He tore down the stairs and through the great hall, shoving his way out the main door. He heard Auvrai's shout behind him, but kept moving toward the place where he'd seen Aelia.

When he reached the courtyard, he heard it, too—terrified screams mixed with the shouts of a furious woman. A loud crash drove Mathieu forward, toward the chandler's shop.

'Twas deserted and there was little light inside, but Mathieu could smell the wax and discern shelves against two walls, filled with candles. Beyond three worktables, in the farthest corner of the room, he saw Aelia's green-clad figure.

Mathieu closed in on her as she wielded a stout wooden joist. "You are a demon!" she cried, swinging the beam, resulting in a fierce grunt when the blow met its target—a man crouched upon the floor in the corner.

When the unlucky fellow sprawled to the ground, a

child scrambled out from beneath him, crying, barely able to catch her breath. Without taking her eyes from her prey, Aelia shouted English words at the girl, who stumbled toward the door, stopping short when she saw Mathieu. She was a comely maid, but little more than a child. Her split and bleeding lip and the terror in her eyes sickened him, bringing an unwelcome reminder of his own mother's state after his *noble* father's visits.

"Move, Norman, and I'll spill your brains on the floor over the chandler's wax," Aelia said, taking Mathieu's attention from the girl, who regained her wits and ran, terrified, from the shop.

"You will regret this, Saxon wench." The man's voice was low and gravelly. Mathieu knew it belonged to Durand the Black, the man who'd struck Aelia when he'd been assigned to guard her.

Mathieu stepped forward. "Aelia."

"This animal raped Rowena," she said. Her face was covered with tears, but Mathieu did not think she even realized it. "Is this the way of the Normans?"

Durand rose to his feet, moving to wrest the beam from Aelia. She swung it again, the timber coming down hard, but missing Durand's arm.

Mathieu pushed past Aelia. Taking hold of Durand's tunic, he plowed his fist into the man's face, sending him to the floor in a slump. "Get yourself to the gates and help the carpenters there. And be ready to travel in the morning. You're coming to London with me."

The man got to his feet and skulked out of the shop, muttering under his breath.

Mathieu turned to Aelia and saw that her face was devoid of color except for the purple bruise on her cheekbone. And she was shaking. When her legs started to give out, he caught her in his arms. "Take a deep breath," he said.

She felt light and fragile when he lifted her, cradling her carefully as though she might break. Her face was still damp with tears.

Mathieu carried her to the chandler's living quarters at the back of the shop. Taking a seat on a wooden chair near the hearth, he pressed Aelia against his chest and waited for the trembling to subside. He touched her hair, slid his hand down her shoulder and arm...wanted to kiss away her tears.

He swallowed. "The girl is safe. I'll see that Durand goes nowhere near her again."

She nodded, moving her head against his chest. "I accused you. W-wrongly."

"Aye." He tucked her head under his chin, holding her until the shuddering stopped and her heartbeat slowed to normal.

"If he goes near Rowena again, I will kill him," she said in a whisper.

"I'll see that he doesn't." Mathieu was going to leave Ingelwald at first light, with Durand among the men who accompanied him. Until that time, the errant knight would be kept hard at work or confined under guard. There would be no more trouble from him at Ingelwald.

But the journey to London would be another matter. Mathieu had already decided who was to accompany him, and the number of men was small. Aelia and Durand would be in close quarters for several days. Somehow Mathieu would have to keep them separate.

He had spent a difficult night dealing with the new Saxon prisoners and conferring with Auvrai, who would remain at Ingelwald to oversee the repair of all the damage done by months of warfare, as well as improvements on Wallis's great hall. When Mathieu had finally gone to his bed, he'd had trouble sleeping as he considered every possible ploy to avoid taking Aelia to King William. But 'twas clear she could not remain behind. Besides his own ravening attraction to her, she was clearly well loved by her people. They would never accept Norman dominion as long as their Saxon lady maintained residence here.

But awareness of what William would do to her and her young brother curdled in Mathieu's belly. To parade them before jeering crowds, humiliating them before their own people, as well as their Norman conquerors, would be beyond cruel.

Her execution was something he could not even contemplate.

A sudden sharp pain in his jaw made him realize he was clenching his teeth. He had no choice but to take Aelia and her brother to London, but he was resolved to convince King William to deal compassionately with them. Mathieu was, after all, not without influence with the king. William had already shown him great favor by naming him baron and sending him here to relieve de Reviers, promising him this rich holding when he suppressed Wallis's resistance.

"You have been very…obliging…" Aelia quietly remarked. "I did not think you would care what happened to a Saxon woman."

"She is hardly more than a child, Aelia, as you well know." If his voice sounded harsh, 'twas only because of the dismal direction of his thoughts.

"And why should a Saxon child's welfare concern you?"

'Twas much more complicated than he liked. He had never spoken of how he felt to be the result of a brutal rape, and was not about to do so now. "All who dwell at Ingelwald are under my authority. Lawlessness and chaos serve no one."

"What compensation will you give Rowena for her lost maidenhead? For the child she might bear?"

"Durand will pay whatever her family demands."

"She has no family." Aelia pushed away from Mathieu and stood. She still did not appear altogether steady, but it seemed best to allow some space between them. He would see that they kept it.

"He will pay her the customary *wergeld,* then."

"Through me," Aelia demanded. Her appearance was regal though she wore but a simple gown, and her hair was only partially confined at her back. The color had come back into her face, giving a rosy hue to her cheeks and a blush to her lips. "And that brute is not to speak to Rowena. Ever."

"Agreed." Mathieu stood and turned his back to her. Distance was what was needed here. Miles if he could manage it.

Chapter Ten

A elia could not have been more surprised when Sir Auvrai took her to see Osric later that evening. Her brother was being held in a large building that served as servants' quarters, with members of her father's fyrd—men who refused to swear fealty to their Norman conqueror.

"You look well for a *prisoner*," the boy said derisively.

Aelia recoiled as if she'd been slapped.

"Osric…I know it has been difficult for you."

"What does the Norman plan to do with us? Will we hang?"

"No." She shook her head. "We will leave for London soon."

Osric turned away and folded his arms across his small chest. His red hair was filthy with the grime of the storehouse fire and his hours of confinement here. Aelia's heart splintered with the pain of seeing him brought so low. "Why? Why does he take us there?" he asked.

Aelia walked 'round to face him. "Fitz Autier will not say."

"Then it does not bode well for us, does it?"

Aelia feared he was right. But what could she do? Run away? She did not think the mighty Sir Auvrai would just turn his back and allow her to take Osric and leave Ingelwald. If they happened to get away, Fitz Autier would hunt them down.

"I don't know what it means for us," she said. "But there does not seem to be any choice in the matter. Fitz Autier has ordered it, and so we go."

"I refuse."

"Then he'll tie you to a horse and take you anyway."

"Father would disown you, Aelia."

"You are a child, Osric. Someday you will understand our situation. But for now, you should be glad to be alive, and do what is necessary to remain so."

She addressed the men who sat on the floor, listening to their conversation. "We are defeated. Fitz Autier has said he will be lenient with any Saxon who swears fealty to him. Wallis is gone. The day of Saxon mastery is past. Do what you must," she said, "but think of your families...of your women and children who do not want to lose you."

"You speak like a coward," Osric cried.

"I speak as one who has seen too much death."

She had resolved naught. Turning to leave, she tapped upon the door, but before Auvrai opened it, two of the prisoners called out to her.

"My lady...I will swear to Fitz Autier."

"You are right. 'Tis no use to resist any longer, my lady. We are defeated."

"We've got wives and children to see to."

"Crops to harvest."

A few others added their voices, and soon only Osric and four or five others remained silent.

Aelia's emotions were on edge as a group of Norman knights walked with her and the surrendering Saxons to the hall. Osric remained with the other prisoners who refused to accept Fitz Autier. She left them and walked across the courtyard to the wall, where she climbed the steps, reaching the palisade just as the sun made its final descent to the distant horizon.

Aelia could feel autumn in the cool evening air, and it chilled her. 'Twas likely they would depart for London on the morrow, and so this would be her last day here. She knew very well she would never see Ingelwald again.

Only one Norman guard paced the length of the high parapet, and he paid little attention to Aelia. Fitz Autier must consider her no threat at all if he'd given her leave to visit Osric and the other Saxon prisoners. And now she was allowed to walk freely within the walls.

Mayhap Osric was right. Mayhap she *was* a coward, going meekly to London where she had no notion of what would happen to her.

Aelia turned and looked out at the village and the land beyond the walls, at the rich, rolling fields of gold and green. 'Twas her father's domain, and Aelia was relinquishing it to their enemy. She had fought sedulously against the Normans these past months, holding out against the previous Norman leader who had pitted his skill against her. But when Fitz Autier arrived, all her defenses had come to naught.

Grief, raw and devastating, pierced her heart. Her father's death had been sudden and violent. Aelia would never forget the moment she'd seen him fall—his armor no protection against the brutal slash of a Norman broadsword. None of her arrows had pierced his killer's armor, nor had any of the men nearby been able to avenge Wallis.

Aelia had not even been able to reach her father until hours later…when his body had long been cold.

She needed him very badly now, as her world fell apart. Naught was as it should be. Her people had surrendered. They worked stolidly to rebuild that which had been damaged. Osric was irascible. And Aelia…too much was amiss within her own heart.

Fitz Autier was Ingelwald's conqueror. She had no business thinking of him as Rowena's valiant champion. Holding her after the nerve-shattering confrontation with Durand was naught but what any Christian knight would have done when met with a maiden in distress.

Except that his embrace, his caress, had caused a burning fullness in her chest and a quickening in her loins, much like what she'd felt the night she'd slept in his tent.

And to Aelia's dismay, she'd wanted more.

Her father would be disgusted if he knew what she felt.

Rowena stepped away from the well far below, and Aelia watched her carry a bucket of water toward the hall. The girl's life was irrevocably changed, as were all their lives, but Rowena had always been such a merry child, full of the potential of her womanhood. Aelia doubted the girl would ever again look at a young man with the same blush of innocence, without fear of being hurt and defiled.

A young Norman groom interrupted his own labors and approached the maid. From such a distance, Aelia could not hear what he said, and 'twas unlikely Rowena would be able to understand him. Yet she smiled and handed him the heavy water bucket, then walked beside him as he carried it to her destination.

Aelia's sigh was a painful one, constricting her chest

and choking her throat. It seemed that life would go on at Ingelwald without her, Saxons and Normans together.

"Much of what is here will remain the same, *demoiselle*."

Aelia whirled to face Fitz Autier, who had approached so quietly she'd not heard him. Or mayhap he'd stomped noisily across the palisade but she'd been so immersed in her doleful thoughts she had not noticed.

His words did not reassure her.

"Why must I go to London?"

Fitz Autier did not answer right away. He went to the parapet and looked down, resting his forearms on the wall, as though relaxed. But Aelia saw a muscle in his jaw tighten, and realized that her question had not been a simple one.

"Why not execute me here?"

Fitz Autier shoved away from the parapet and grabbed Aelia's arms. His sudden move surprised her and knocked her off balance, but he held her steady. "By God's holy cross, woman! What purpose would your death serve?"

She raised her chin and looked into his eyes. "I did not know a Saxon's death needed to serve some purpose."

He pulled her 'round to face the grounds below, where torches had been lit and people worked quickly to finish their tasks before retiring for the night. "This is what matters. Ingelwald."

"With you as its master. A bastard Frenchman."

He released her. "Aye."

Aelia felt cold. She hugged herself, rubbing her arms while Fitz Autier watched her with a closed expression. "The old woman who was killed—Erlina—she had a cottage outside the walls some distance from here. Osric and I could…we could stay there, and William would never know—"

The Norman turned and started to walk away, but Aelia followed, circling 'round to impede his path. "Please, seignior," she entreated. "Do not let your king enslave us. I promise—"

"And I gave my oath, *demoiselle*. I am bound by it to take you to King William."

She looked for some measure of kindness in the man, some hint of the benevolence he'd shown earlier. But there was naught. He was a hardened warrior, a man who would follow his orders no matter what the cost.

Mathieu walked toward the gate where the men were putting away their tools. The work would be finished upon the morrow, and the gate would be intact again. He could feel secure about leaving the holding well protected.

"Where is Durand?" he asked the men.

Most of them shrugged or replied that they did not know. One of the knights did not respond.

"Sir Hugh. Where is your cohort?"

"I have not seen him lately, baron."

His answer did not ring true. The two were usually together, and ever since Mathieu's arrival at Ingelwald, he'd noticed Durand's habit of using Hugh Picot whenever he needed a fool to cover for him. Mathieu did not know why Hugh permitted himself to be used in such a way, nor did he care. He just wanted to find Durand.

"I assigned him to work here. When did he leave?"

Even in the flickering light of a torch, Mathieu saw Hugh's eyes shift away. Something was amiss.

"An answer, Hugh. Now."

The man cleared his throat. "He was angry all day and spoke of leaving Ingelwald, baron. I did not see him go."

Mathieu would have taken a contingent of men and ridden after Durand, but the hour was late and there was much to do to prepare for his departure. "What was his destination?"

"I do not know. Likely to the west, where there is some chance that he...er..."

"Baron Richard Louvet's lands are west of Ingelwald," Mathieu said. "Will Durand go there?"

Hugh nodded. "Mayhap. Durand wants land, baron. Or a post. After he killed Ingelwald's lord, he thought Gui de Reviers would reward him generously. When you arrived to take Lord Gui's place..."

"He knew that I did not favor him, so he decided to seek opportunity elsewhere?"

"Aye. Especially after the incident today with the Saxon wench," Hugh replied.

Mathieu concluded his discussion with Hugh and went to the knights' quarters, where he found Auvrai, along with the men who would accompany him to London. He told Auvrai of Durand's desertion. "Hugh thinks he has gone west to Richard Louvet's holding, but he might lurk nearby."

"We'll keep watch," Auvrai said. "He will not disrupt Ingelwald."

But Mathieu did not like the possibility of Durand remaining in the vicinity, waiting for him to leave. "No, he will not. I'll go after him at first light."

"You will change your plans for this?"

Mathieu nodded. "I prefer to deal with the blackguard myself."

Mathieu did not like what he'd seen of Durand so far.

He did not feel comfortable leaving Ingelwald, suspecting the unscrupulous knight skulked nearby. Auvrai was more than capable, but Mathieu would not have it known that he'd left his estate when there was trouble afoot. He would deal with it himself.

He left Auvrai to his task, glancing up at the parapet where he'd left Aelia. If she was still there, he could not see her, which was for the best. It seemed that all he had to do was look at her and his nerves hummed. He'd managed to avoid her most of the day, and their confrontation on the parapet had not been pleasant.

But the tenor of their meeting had changed naught. He still wanted her in his bed.

Mathieu jabbed his fingers through his hair. He had no choice but to take her to William. He would never lie to the king about what had transpired here, and his orders had been quite certain. He was to bring Wallis and his family to London if they survived the battle for Ingelwald.

Had Wallis still lived, King William would have put him on display with the other Saxon prisoners, to humiliate them before the masses. And then he would likely execute them, unless he needed Wallis as a hostage against further rebellion.

Mathieu did not believe William would put Aelia and her young brother to death. He *could not* believe it, or he would be compelled to violate the king's orders. He would not take Aelia to London to be killed. Since Ingelwald seemed resigned to its Norman sovereignty, she would not be needed as a hostage. 'Twas more likely that William would marry her to a Norman soldier as a reward for service.

Mathieu clenched his jaws tightly. Mayhap the old woman's cottage was a viable alternative. King William had been primarily interested in Wallis, but the Saxon lord was dead. No purpose would be served by taking Aelia and the boy south, and their presence would only complicate the journey. Mathieu would not be able to travel as fast as he would like. And someone would have to guard them at all times.

The way Mathieu and Auvrai had figured it, Mathieu could take but a small escort with him to London. Merely eight men could be spared, in order to leave enough warriors here to secure and protect the holding. Mathieu and his party would have to travel swiftly and quietly, and try to avoid attracting the unwanted attention of marauders who roamed the countryside—like those who'd attacked them yesterday.

Mathieu walked outside Ingelwald's gate and into the village lane. He passed the church and inn, the tanner's and several other tradesmen's shops. There were numerous cottages with well-tended yards, and a mill at the opposite end of the village, near the river. No one was about at this hour, the villagers either finding their rest within the safety of Ingelwald's walls, or busy with their evening meals.

He reached the edge of the village, but continued on a narrow track, following it through a patch of tall grass until he came to an isolated cottage. It had to be the house where the old woman had lived, the place where Aelia had asked to stay.

The door was ajar and Mathieu walked inside. In the last light of dusk, he found a candle. Lighting it, he took a look around.

The room appeared not to have been inhabited for some days, and Mathieu grimaced at the stench of sour milk and spoiled food. Dust was thick on every surface, and he could hear the scampering of rodents that had taken up residence in the walls. A pallet of straw lay on the dirt floor at the end of the room near the hearth, and there was one broken stool lying beside a small table crusted with refuse.

'Twas not a fit home for anyone, much less his Saxon lady.

Frustration ate at him. Aelia could not remain at Ingelwald. A bride had been chosen for him and he would begin his marriage here with no distracting thoughts of Aelia living in this pitiful cottage. He wanted her as far away as possible.

Though Clarise might be the most desirable wife in the kingdom, Mathieu did not know how long he could resist his attraction to Aelia. Yet it made no sense. Unlike the beauties at Court, Aelia took no pains to make herself presentable. She wore no finery, nor was her hair arranged in any intricate fashion. She spoke her mind and showed her temper.

But it was all Mathieu could do to keep from pulling her close and fusing his lips to hers. He wanted to taste her, to feel her fiery spirit as he possessed her. His hands itched to feel the fullness of her breasts as he looked into her eyes, and his body ached to pierce through the barrier of her innocence, taking her for his own.

With a shaky breath, Mathieu extinguished the candle. He was trapped. He'd never experienced such unrelenting lust for a woman, not even Clarise. If only he could send Auvrai to London with Aelia and the boy…. But Mathieu was compelled to present himself in person for his formal betrothal to Clarise. And if he left Aelia here at Ingelwald, he had no assurance that this intense craving for her would abate by the time he returned.

His only option was to take her to London and leave

her there. And he would do everything in his power to avoid her as they traveled together.

A soft rain had begun to fall by the time Mathieu left the old woman's cottage and entered the gates to the hall. The grounds were deserted due to the rain, except for two people—women—walking together ahead of him. One of them was Aelia. Curious about her purpose, Mathieu followed the pair to one of the workshops.

The shop belonged to the master carpenter. Mathieu had visited every building earlier in the day, and talked to all the craftsmen, with Sir Gilbert as interpreter. But the carpenter had been ill and unable to speak with Mathieu. The man's wife and daughters seemed to believe he would not last out the day.

Mathieu wondered why Aelia had been summoned here. He stepped inside.

The workshop contained all manner of items crafted from wood—chairs and tables, stools and cupboards, as well as several beautifully carved musical instruments. But what interested Mathieu most were the pieces displayed on the shelves in the workroom.

The carpenter was a master carver. Mathieu picked up a crucifix the man had crafted with intricate detail. He ran his fingers over the smoothly planed and polished wood and took note of the careful strokes and cuts that made the piece remarkable. The next statue was the face of a young girl. 'Twas carved in such a way that it seemed to be emerging from a gnarled and weathered piece of wood unlike anything Mathieu had ever seen. He wanted to spend more time studying each piece, but the voices in the private quarters drew him.

Firelight cast a flickering glow on the room, but Mathieu could see that it was comfortably furnished. The priest was in attendance, and stood at the carpenter's bedside, anointing him and uttering the Latin prayers for the dying. The man's wife knelt in tearful prayer, as did two adolescent girls, presumably the man's daughters, while Aelia sat on a low stool, holding the craftsman's hand.

When the formal prayers ended, the carpenter spoke to Aelia. His speech was labored, and interrupted often by his efforts to catch his breath. Aelia listened patiently, then spoke to him. Mathieu could not understand her words, but her tone was gentle and kind, while her face bore the stricken expression she wore all too often.

When Aelia got up, she urged the carpenter's wife to take the seat beside her dying husband. Then she knelt on the floor with the daughters and bowed her head in a posture of prayer until the room became silent. The carpenter had taken his last breath.

Quiet weeping ensued, and the priest raised his hand in blessing as he murmured prayers for the dead. The daughters' shoulders slumped, and Aelia put one arm 'round each of them, then stood and embraced the weeping wife, until she caught sight of Mathieu, standing near the door of the shop.

Using the back of her hand, she wiped tears from her cheeks. "Have you come for your first *heriot,* Norman?"

"You always manage to think the worst of me, *demoiselle.* Please give the women my condolences and ask the priest to offer Mass for the carpenter every week for a year."

"I will do so, seignior," replied the priest. His perfect French surprised Mathieu.

"Father Ambrosius was my teacher," explained Aelia.

"And Beorn the Carpenter gave you your music," the priest interjected.

"Aye," Aelia whispered, then returned to the grieving women. She kept her eyes on Mathieu while she spoke to them, then pulled her shawl 'round her shoulders and head, and came to the door.

"I need no guard to take me to my room," she said, pushing past him. She strode ahead, moving quickly through the workshop and exiting the building.

He should have let her go. He had just decided 'twas necessary to keep a safe distance between them, but Mathieu could do naught but follow her in the rain, across the muddy ground. With ease, he caught up to her brisk pace.

"I told you, I am all right on my own," Aelia said.

Belying her words, she tripped and would have fallen had Mathieu not caught her arm and steadied her. Rain soaked the shawl that covered her head, and mingled with the tears on her face.

"Allow me to escort you, my lady."

"Are you afraid I might run off in the night, Fitz Autier? Somehow escape your Norman yoke?"

The most prudent thing would be to let her go. On a night like this, only a fool would try to run from warmth and shelter, and Aelia was no fool.

"What did you say to the carpenter's family?" he asked, suspicious of her interchange in the shop. 'Twould behoove her to foment ill feelings and distrust between him and the Saxons. "Did you tell them I demanded payment before the man's body was even cold?"

"No," she whispered.

"What then? That they would have to vacate the premises immediately?"

She shook her head. "I merely gave words of sympathy and told them I was leaving Ingelwald in the morn."

"And that was all?"

Her chin trembled. "I said 'twas unlikely that I will return here…but that they would do well to—to trust you. I told them that you are an honorable man."

Chapter Eleven

It was just past dawn and Mathieu was saddling his horse when the guards brought Aelia's brother to him. "Ah, 'tis Osric the Terrible," he said. The boy's wrists were tied together at his waist, but still he struggled against the guards who had brought him to the stable.

"I prefer my jail, Norman!" the boy cried.

Mathieu buckled his pack and secured it to the saddle. "You will accompany me on my search for a deserter."

Osric spat on the ground. "Let them *all* desert!"

"I assume you know the territory of your father's holding," Mathieu said. His sister did, too. But Mathieu wanted to stay clear of her as long as possible.

"Little use it will be to you."

Mathieu mounted his horse. One of the guards lifted Osric and handed him to Mathieu, but the boy started to scream as though he were being tortured. Mathieu settled him on the saddle before him, then tied his hands to the pommel.

"Do not think of jumping. You will kill or maim yourself."

'Twas no great feat to subdue the small boy, but the sounds of his struggle caught the attention of the person Mathieu least wanted to see.

"What are you doing with Osric?" Aelia cried, running across the grounds toward him. "Where are you taking him?"

The boy screamed and shouted at his sister, but Mathieu quickly restrained him. "Sit still or you will regret it."

Aelia came close, to stand at the horse's side. When she placed one hand upon Osric's leg, Mathieu turned his gaze away toward the gate. He did not wish to see her giving comfort to the little hellion. He would much rather feel her gentle hand upon his own heated skin.

"Where, seignior?"

"On a search detail, *demoiselle*," he said. "The boy will come to no harm…at least not from any of us. What he does to himself will be another matter."

"Please, baron, allow him to remain here with me. I will see that he—"

"He rides with us. Stand aside, *demoiselle*."

Speaking harshly, Mathieu did not spare her a glance, but spurred his horse toward the gate, with seven of his men following. What she thought of him was of no consequence. He had decided to search for Durand before leaving Ingelwald, and if it meant using her brother for his familiarity with the terrain, he would do so. Aelia could have helped him, but Mathieu had no intention of passing the day in close quarters with her. Besides, 'twas necessary to spend time with the boy to assess how disruptive he was going to be when they traveled to London.

Osric eventually wearied of his struggle and limited himself to making derogatory remarks about Normandy and King William. Then he rode quietly for a time, but refused to answer any questions about the terrain or the trails that intersected the road. Mathieu had little experience dealing with children, but he vaguely recalled his own youth, and his vulnerable pride.

"'Tis unfortunate your father did not allow you to explore his lands," Mathieu said, as much to distract himself as to pique Osric's overblown pride. "I should have brought your sister."

"I went about as much as Aelia!" Osric protested. "More!"

"I cannot believe it. Or you would know much about the paths hereabouts."

"That path circles 'round the high side of a ravine," Osric said, pointing to their right. "No one goes up there, unless they're herding sheep."

"And what about here? Surely you've never seen where this one leads."

"Of course I've traveled it. If you follow this path, you'll soon ride through a dense forest."

Mathieu was familiar with the area where his army had camped prior to attacking Ingelwald, and he knew the northern road, since he'd traveled it with Aelia. But with Osric, he discovered much about the western territory and the most likely path Durand had followed. Mathieu split his men into three companies, each group taking a different direction. He warned them to travel cautiously and to beware of ambush. Then he took the western route and rode hard, with the intention of catching up to Durand if the tracks he saw belonged to the scoundrel.

Unfortunately, the night's rain had obscured any sure trail. At midday, there was still no sign of him. Mathieu's small group stopped their horses just inside a copse of trees and dismounted.

"Are you hungry?" he asked Osric.

The boy shrugged. "I could eat."

The men took food and drink from their packs and shared what they had with Osric. He ate quietly and his demeanor seemed to improve, but Mathieu noticed him inching his way toward a dagger that had been left untended on a tree stump. Mathieu allowed Osric to take the dagger and slip it into his trews, and he waited for the boy to try to use the weapon.

The moment came when Mathieu reached for Osric to lift him onto the horse.

In one swift movement, he pulled the knife out and slashed at Mathieu, who dodged the blow and disarmed the boy.

"You were wise to take a weapon suited to your size," Mathieu said, unsurprised by the boy's gumption, "but you must use it more effectively. Raoul, hand me your seax."

'Twas a weapon shorter than a sword, but longer than a knife. The size made it more manageable for the boy, and Mathieu handed it to him, showing him how to hold it.

"I can hold a sword, Norman!"

"I see that, little Saxon," Mathieu said as he hid his smile. The boy's temperament was as fiery as his red hair. All he needed was discipline and training, and he would make a formidable knight one day. "Now, wield it as though you intend me harm."

"I *do* intend you harm," Osric cried as he jabbed once, and then again, though Mathieu easily stepped away from each thrust.

"Here…this is what you must do," Mathieu said.

He had merely intended to demonstrate who was in charge here, but it turned into a lesson of swordsmanship and defense instead, while Raoul and Guilliaume cheered and offered instructions at a safe distance. The lad did his best to injure Mathieu, who actually gave him instruction on how to do it.

'Twas absurd.

But Osric was somewhat more forthcoming afterward.

"Have you ever been to Grantham?" he asked the boy.

"Once," Osric replied grudgingly, "when Fugol the Bold was lord. But I was too young to remember it."

"Then you wouldn't know how far it is."

"Of course I do. 'Tis more than two days' ride."

There were signs that someone had recently gone toward Grantham, but without traveling to that holding, Mathieu could not be certain it had been Durand. "What say you?" he asked Raoul. "Does Durand intend to go all the way to Grantham?"

"'Twould appear so, baron." But he seemed as uncertain as Mathieu.

Between the journey to London and the task of keeping Ingelwald and all its possessions secure, Mathieu could not spare any men to ride to Grantham. He would have to rely on the evidence of his eyes, which indicated that Durand was well and truly gone. Now that the gate was repaired, and with the walls secured, Ingelwald was safe at least from the likes of him.

Mathieu put his horn to his lips and blew it, hoping to gather all the knights who'd ridden out in pursuit of Durand. With luck, most were within range of the sound of the horn, and would waste no more time in their futile search. He turned back toward the hall, and soon Osric was slumped against Mathieu's chest, fast asleep.

As Mathieu held him to keep him from falling, he admitted to a reluctant admiration for the boy. Osric had never given up the fight for his father's land. In his childish way, he still believed he had a chance to wrest Ingelwald from its Norman conquerors.

Osric's small body went limp and Mathieu held him securely as the boy curved his dirty little hands 'round Mathieu's gauntlets as though Mathieu could protect him from the harshness of the world. 'Twas difficult to believe this fragile boy was the same spirited one who'd sneaked into the Norman encampment to assassinate him, who'd set the storehouse afire in order to free the Saxon prisoners, who'd fought so fiercely for Ingel-wald.

Mathieu tightened his hold around the lad to keep him secure, and rode on to Ingelwald.

Aelia pushed herself up from her chair and walked across the great hall to the door once again. Fitz Autier had not yet returned with Osric, and 'twas nearly dusk. Why did their search take so long?

What if there had been another attack like the one north of the waterfall? Would they manage to overcome their assailants this time?

"I think we should go out and look for them," she said to Sir Gilbert.

The man acknowledged her plea with a snort and continued wrapping a clean bandage 'round a Norman's head.

Frustrated by Gilbert's response, Aelia left the hall and went in search of Sir Auvrai. Mayhap he would lead a party of men outside the walls to search for her brother and Fitz Autier. If anything happened to Osric, she did not know how she would survive it. She had already lost so much in the past few months.

She tamped down her worry for the moment and

walked toward the stable, where Auvrai and some of the other Normans were repairing the burned buildings. It seemed no one else was worried about Fitz Autier, or wondered why he had not yet returned. On the contrary, there was an atmosphere of merriment about the estate, with Normans as well as Saxons preparing a feast.

One of the village pigs had fallen into the river and drowned, and Auvrai had given his consent to roast it. 'Twas a ridiculous waste of meat. It should have been carefully butchered and preserved, but these Normans had seen fit to squander their unexpected windfall.

It should be of no concern to Aelia. 'Twas her fate to leave Ingelwald, and these Normans would be left here to starve.

"Aelia!"

"Freya, hello." She took the younger woman's hands, noting her red-rimmed eyes, her barely concealed grief for her father, Beorn. "Are you all right?"

"Aye. As well as can be for now. Thank you for coming to my father's burial. And for last night…I know it eased my father's passing to see you."

"No need to thank me, Freya."

"But we do, my lady. We see the terrible toll these last weeks have had upon you. With your own father gone, and Ingelwald taken from you…" She began to weep in earnest, and Aelia embraced her. "You are in our prayers."

Aelia walked Freya home. She went into the shop and stayed with the carpenter's wife and daughters for a time, remembering the man and the pleasure he'd taken in the music they made with his instruments. The visit was filled with poignant memories, pierced by grief. By the time Aelia left, 'twas almost fully dark and her sorrow lay heavily upon her, but she had no more tears to shed.

As she walked toward the hall, she saw Fitz Autier coming out of the stable, carrying a small, limp body in his arms. Her hand flew to her mouth when she saw the bright red hair and his arm hanging limp at his side. The worst had happened. Osric was dead!

This new grief, enormous and crushing, exploded through Aelia. Her legs went weak and her throat went numb. She could not speak.

"The boy fell asleep on the way back."

She blinked her eyes and looked again as Fitz Autier approached. "A-asleep?"

"Aye, *demoiselle*. What is amiss? Has something happened?"

"No. Naught but your tardiness."

He started walking and Aelia had to hurry to catch up. "Come with me and you can open the door when I carry him in."

Relief poured through Aelia, but it was quickly replaced by anger. How dare he keep Osric out past dark, and leave her worrying hour after hour? "Seignior, you had no right—"

"Is that roasting pork I smell?"

"Where did you take Osric?"

"*Demoiselle,* I ask the questions here."

"You will be lucky to receive any answers. You wore him to exhaustion!"

"He's healthy enough." He carried Osric effortlessly, allowing himself to be distracted at the sight of Saxons milling in the courtyard alongside Normans. "What are they about?"

"One of our pigs drowned," Aelia replied, her anger unabated. "You gave permission to waste it on a feast."

He said naught, but continued toward the servants' quarters, where the prisoners were kept.

"Let him return to the hall for the night. I will keep him with me."

"No."

"But, seignior—"

He pushed past the guard, who opened the door to let him inside. She'd known perfectly well that Fitz Autier would not allow Osric to spend the night in her room, but that knowledge did not ease her frustration. What harm could there be in allowing her brother to stay with her? Especially after the long day she'd spent worrying about his welfare. They would be together all the way to London, would they not?

Angrily, she straightened her brother's pallet, then watched as Fitz Autier lay Osric upon it. He surprised her when he drew a blanket over the boy and secured it near his neck before turning away, but his care did not appease her ire. Why did the man have to be so obstinate? She was defeated, was she not?

Aelia stormed out of the small jail and made her way to the hall, ignoring the gathering in the courtyard. Even so, she could not help but notice the torches that lit the entire perimeter of the yard and the trestle tables that had been assembled. Men and women carried platters of food to the center of it all, where Modig the Butcher carved the meat.

And Aelia could not deny that she was relieved not only for Osric's safety, but Fitz Autier's, too.

She kept walking until she was inside the hall and had climbed the stairs to the solitude of her room. 'Twas appalling to think that she cared what happened to Ingelwald's conqueror. The man was an invader. A Norman raider, and nothing more.

Yet she could not forget how he'd helped her deal with Durand. Or the fact that he had not executed every one of the Saxon men who would not swear fealty to him. He seemed unwilling to do any more damage.

Aelia lay down on her straw bed and closed her eyes, but the sound of music outside, and then a light tap at her door, brought her to her feet again.

'Twas Rowena, carrying a platter of food. "I thought you would be hungry, my lady."

Aelia was touched by the girl's consideration, and in truth, she was famished. She must have forgotten to eat today, with her concern about Osric.

"Come and sit with me," Aelia said.

The girl handed her the lamp upon the floor. "I—I did not want to stay out there. All those Normans…"

Aelia nodded as they sat together, sharing the food. Even though the man who'd attacked Rowena was gone, she could understand the girl's uneasiness around Fitz Autier's men.

"They are dancing," Rowena said. "Our women with the Normans."

"And swilling barrels of ale, no doubt." Aelia went to the window and looked down at the courtyard. She pressed a hand against her chest as if she could hold in the ache as all of Ingelwald came to feast and to make peace with their enemies. It should have been Wallis down there, celebrating his victory over the Normans, she and Osric at his side.

Tears rolled down her cheeks as she listened to the music and watched the dancing commence. Women and men lined up facing one another, taking steps forward and back, to the rhythm of the music. Then they joined hands and moved in a circle, laughing and singing together as if there had been no warfare only days before.

Aelia knew 'twas for the best, but that did not make it hurt any less. When she could watch no more, she started to turn away, but caught sight of Fitz Autier at the edge of the dancing circle. He held a flagon of ale in one hand, and his other arm was circled 'round Nelda's shoulders.

"So, the bastard wants to celebrate?" she muttered.

"I beg your pardon, my lady?"

Aelia picked up the empty platter and walked to the door. "I'm hungrier than I thought. I believe I'll go down and get some more."

Chapter Twelve

If Aelia was not coming down, Mathieu might just as well find a bed and get some rest before morning. 'Twould be a long, hard ride upon the morrow, and he was going to need all his faculties to keep track of the lady and her brother—not just to keep them under guard, but to keep them safe.

He wanted to suffer no more ambushes like the one that had nearly caught them on their excursion north of Ingelwald.

"*Demoiselle,* I am not interested," he said to the young maid as he unwrapped her arm from his neck. He knew she did not understand his words, but he didn't think she could fail to catch his meaning from his actions.

Unfortunately, she did not. She was a comely woman called Nelda, with flashing blue eyes and rich, dark hair. Her clothes were simple like those of Aelia, but Nelda wore the bodice pulled low, and laced it so tightly there was a good possibility she would fall out of it. And while the sight of such a feminine display should have enticed him, it did not.

Mathieu stepped away, but Nelda followed him, taking his arm and pulling it 'round her waist. She seemed to have tentacles as she leaned into him, sliding one hand 'round his neck and pressing her breasts against him while she pulled his head toward hers. "Not tonight," he said, gently taking hold of her arms to push her away.

He looked up at that moment to see that Aelia had come down to the courtyard. She gave him a hard glance, then walked away.

With less care than before, he set Nelda aside and followed Aelia, but she stepped into the crowd of musicians and picked up a lyre. Surrounded by the others, she took no note of him, but appeared wholly engrossed in her music, so Mathieu could not approach her. Nor did he want to.

He owed her no explanations for his actions, and if he chose to dally with one of the housemaids, 'twas his concern alone. Though Nelda did not appeal to him, he could easily find another Saxon woman to ease his lust. He perused the dancers, many of whom were young and comely.

But none tempted him.

He poured another flagon of ale and walked 'round the circle of dancers to where his view of Aelia was unimpeded.

She began to sing, a song whose words were incomprehensible to his Norman ears. He caught the names of "Aethelstan" and "Edmund," but the rest was lost to him.

Yet the Saxons in his midst stopped their dancing and gathered 'round to listen, as if spellbound, to Aelia's voice. 'Twas pure and true, but Mathieu hardly noticed. He watched her elegant throat, the movements of her mouth, the thick lashes of her expressive eyes. Her golden-red hair fell in loose waves across her shoulders, and when her skillful fingers moved over the strings of the lyre, Mathieu could only imagine what other talents they might have.

She continued singing, but changed languages and sang of Norse warriors and their heroic deeds. The song was a familiar one, sung often in Normandy, and Mathieu forced his eyes away from her comely form. He glanced 'round, looking for Nelda, the most likely maid to satisfy his needs. But she had moved on to one of his soldiers, and the two slipped away from the crowd.

Aelia finished her song and the dancing resumed. The atmosphere was convivial, with Saxons and Normans eating and drinking together.

Sir Auvrai's decision to roast the pig had been a good one. They could have used brute force to subjugate the people of Ingelwald, but this banquet brought the Saxons to the Norman table under peaceful conditions. Soon the people would harvest their crops. The craftsmen would lay down their weapons and return to their shops, and life would go on as before.

For all but Aelia and her brother.

Mathieu trained his eyes upon her, gazing past the dancers and those who crowded nearby. Her body seemed to stiffen suddenly, and she turned slightly to glance in his direction.

A sharp frisson of heat burst through him when her eyes met his, and Mathieu took a quick step back. 'Twas a feeling similar to the odd prescience he'd felt when he'd first seen her standing high upon the palisade, just before her arrow had grazed his face.

But the sensation was more intense now. It raged across his chest and into his loins, knocking him off balance.

At the same time, the lyre slid from Aelia's hands but

she managed to recover it before it fell. On her face was an expression of utter confusion, and she stood wavering for a moment before setting down her instrument and hastening away from the other musicians.

Mathieu went in pursuit of her.

Aelia felt dizzy. She slipped out of the crowded courtyard and made her way to the back entrance of the hall, near the bake house. Surely once she was away from Fitz Autier her heart would stop its pounding and her head would clear.

She pulled open the door leading to the kitchen but, before she could step inside, the door slammed closed in front of her. Without turning to look, she knew whose hand had pushed it shut. She felt his arm just above her shoulder, and she was unwilling to turn, reluctant to face him.

She held her breath as he slid his arm 'round her waist and pulled her against his body. He wore no hauberk but, even so, there was no softness to him. His breath was harsh in her ear, but he said no words. Aelia's legs went limp and her heart raced like a poor trapped rabbit, while his touch sent rivers of sensation through her blood.

She stiffened, closing her eyes and clenching her teeth. Naught had changed. He was her enemy, and he was going to take her away from Ingelwald. She would not succumb to the seduction of his touch, to the heat of his lips upon her nape or the play of his fingers at her waist. She had to push away from him, to stop him from making her forget about his contemptible purpose.

But slowly he turned her, and her resolve faltered. He moved forward and she became vaguely aware of the door against her back, of the cool night breeze blowing through her hair.

Mostly, she felt the heat of Fitz Autier's mouth as it came down upon hers. Blood rushed from her head and pooled in her nether regions as he spread open her lips and plunged his tongue inside. He made a low sound that set Aelia's blood afire. She kissed him in return, sliding her hands up his powerful arms, tipping her head back, plundering as he plundered.

His thumbs touched the underside of her breasts, and their tips pebbled and sparked with sensation.

Mayhap this *was* what her mother had foretold. Surely Aelia was not mistaken about the fierce attraction that pulsed between them. Was it possible the Norman was her one true mate?

No.

Aelia pushed away so abruptly she bumped her head against the door at her back, and Fitz Autier staggered. His eyes blazed with an intensity that matched the fire of his kiss, and Aelia shuddered with some ravenous emotion she could not name. She might have spoken if she could have found words....

Instead, she shoved past him and ran.

Mathieu needed a moment to gather his composure. He could not recall the last time he'd ever been so confounded by a woman. Or so aroused.

Mayhap 'twas the full moon that had addled his brain.

He strode away from the courtyard and the hall and any other place where he might possibly encounter Aelia, and soon found himself at the door of the carpenter's shop. Candlelight flickered in the window, so Mathieu knew someone was about. He tapped lightly on the door.

'Twas Father Ambrosius who opened it. "Baron?" The priest lowered his brow. "'Tis an unexpected… honor…"

Unexpected and unwelcome, if Mathieu was not mistaken. He stepped inside anyway, and gave a nod to the carpenter's widow and two daughters, who knelt at prayer in the room just beyond the workshop. They rose to their feet with the interruption, but stood fast and did not approach him.

"Tell them to rest easy, Father," Mathieu said. "I have not come for any nefarious purpose."

The priest turned and spoke to the women, while Mathieu glanced around the shop. What he wanted—no, needed—would be here upon a workbench or in a cupboard.

"My lord, is there some…are you here to collect the death tax?"

"*Heriot?* No. Well, yes." The floor was swept clean and there was no clutter around the work areas. The carpenter's tools had been neatly arranged, and many of them hung from hooks above the workbench. Illuminated by the priest's light, Mathieu saw neat stacks of raw wood, hewn into long planks or left as rough blocks. He was certain there would be a piece suitable for carving.

"Ask the widow if there is a block of fruitwood here," he said to the priest.

Father Ambrosius asked the question, and the woman nodded, then picked up a lamp and beckoned them to follow her outside. She went 'round to the back of the shop and pushed open the door of a wooden shed. Mathieu took the lamp from her and went inside.

The carpenter had stored finished pieces here, as well as raw materials. Mathieu found several suitable blocks of fruitwood. He chose the pieces he wanted and turned to the widow. *"Heriot,"* he said.

The woman looked from Mathieu to the priest, frowning with puzzlement. The two spoke quietly together for a moment before the priest turned to Mathieu. "My lord, are we to understand that this—these pieces of wood—are to be the widow's payment of *heriot?"*

Mathieu nodded. "Aye. Along with a carving knife and a gouge or two."

They looked astonished, and rightly so. But this was what Mathieu needed most, and it was more valuable to him than any other payment the widow could make.

Wood carving would distract him from thoughts he should not be having about Aelia, and keep his mind and hands well occupied in his leisure time when they journeyed south. 'Twas a pastime he'd developed while passing the nerve-wracking hours before battle, or whiling away the time at court when too little was expected of him. He had developed some skill at the craft and intended to carve a betrothal gift for Lady Clarise. 'Twould keep his mind aptly focused upon the woman who was to be his bride.

The widow picked up a leather cloth, into which her husband's tools had been safely rolled, and pressed it to her chest. Holding back her tears, she handed it to Mathieu.

"Tell her I offer my sympathies. Beorn was a very skilled man and Ingelwald is poorer for his loss."

Mathieu left the carpenter's shop and considered the carving he would make for Lady Clarise, and immediately felt calmer. Soon he would wed the beautiful Norman lady and would never think of Aelia again, never feel such an unreasonable lack of control with a woman again.

He stopped in the stable where the traveling packs had been made ready for the journey, and left the wood and tools there. Then he walked to the servants' quarters, where the Saxon prisoners were being held.

"Robert," he said to one of the guards, "fetch the boy called Halig. I'll speak to him out here."

A moment later, the boy who'd attacked him upon the stairs was hauled out of his small prison. He was sullen and unkempt, and was obviously not interested in speaking to Mathieu.

"Your lady travels to London upon the morrow," he said to the boy. "I will need someone whose task is to protect her upon the road."

"What of Normans? Can they not?"

"Aye. But you've shown yourself particularly loyal to the lady. I would trust you to perform the duty better than most."

Halig's throat moved as he swallowed thickly. Clearly, 'twas an impossible task Mathieu had asked of him—to take Aelia to her fate in London, which would allow him to be close to the lady, and possibly ensure her safety when they reached their destination.

Mathieu intended to see to that himself, but an extra sword, one that was devoted primarily to Aelia's well-being on the road, was all but necessary. Since he could spare only eight Norman knights for the journey, he had decided to see if Halig would be a suitable guard for the lady.

The lad gave a curt nod.

"I will accept your vow of fealty," Mathieu stated.

"No."

"It is what I require, boy. If you cannot give your word to be loyal to me and follow my orders, then you will remain imprisoned here until I decide what to do with you. Do you understand me?"

A myriad of emotions crossed the lad's face, but Mathieu had no doubt that he would kneel to him. His loyalty to Aelia ran too deep to evade this duty.

Aelia was awake long before dawn. She sat upon the floor of her chamber, leaning against the wall, watching Rowena sleep. The girl did not feel safe anywhere, even with her assailant gone, so Aelia had given the maid her bed. 'Twas not as though she could sleep, anyway.

She was leaving Ingelwald today.

A lump in Aelia's throat prevented her from swallowing back her tears. She let them flow until her throat was raw and her head pounded, then wiped the moisture from her face and went to the window.

The remnants of the Norman's feast were visible below, as well as a number of Fitz Autier's warriors, who were slumbering upon the benches. A few of Ingelwald's maids slept alongside them.

She took one last look 'round the room where she'd slept every night of her twenty years, and remembered her days as a child here. Her mother used to come to this room and sit beside her, telling her the tales of Saxon heroes. Aelia enjoyed the stories of her mother's younger days, when she'd fallen in love with her husband.

Though Wallis had been chosen for Elena, when she'd first seen him she'd felt a shattering awareness of him, with the bone-deep knowledge that she'd met her one true mate.

Aelia was sure she herself had not yet experienced such a sensation, if she ever would. She had not felt it when she'd first met Selwyn, nor any other Saxon warrior. Mayhap 'twas her fate never to know the feeling her mother described. Surely 'twas not the odd awareness engendered by the sight of Fitz Autier. She had to remind herself that all she felt on sight of her conqueror and captor was revulsion.

The day dawned cool and bright as Aelia descended the stone stairs and walked to the gate the Normans had destroyed, then repaired. 'Twas open, but guarded, though the knights said naught as she passed through to the section of Ingelwald that lay outside the walls.

The people had brought their livestock inside during the Norman attacks, all but Erlina, who had run out in the midst of the battle, wielding a small knife.

Aelia had wanted to hate the Normans for Erlina's death, but even her own Saxon warriors had said the old woman's fate could not have been prevented. Someone should have seen to her safety within the walls, but they had all failed her. Even Aelia.

Deeply, she breathed in the smells of autumn, the thick, rich earth that would soon give up its bounty.

The church was directly ahead of Aelia and she raised her shawl to cover her head before going inside. Very little light filtered in through the tall, narrow windows, and Father Ambrosius had lit only the candles on the altar. But Aelia could see the bowed heads of many worshippers who knelt before the altar as the priest said Mass.

Aelia approached the altar and knelt, praying silently for the strength to survive the journey ahead. She did not like to admit to fear, but there were many dangerous miles between Ingelwald and London, and she did not know what lay ahead for her and Osric.

Fitz Autier would only say they were prisoners of the crown, at the mercy of his king. At best, it meant that she and Osric would soon become slaves of the Normans.

At worst, it meant she and Osric would be killed.

She closed her eyes tightly and prayed that the Norman king would see fit to spare their lives. When her prayer was done and she looked up, she met the deep blue eyes of Fitz Autier.

He was a fair distance away, kneeling opposite her among several of his soldiers and various Saxons, but there was no mistaking the cool intensity of his stare.

Aelia knew it must be fatigue that made her susceptible to that hard scowl, and she looked away to concentrate fully upon the Mass. But every muscle, every bone of her body was aware of him, and her skin seemed to burn wherever his eyes touched her.

When she approached the altar to receive communion, Aelia felt Fitz Autier behind her. Before God and all the people gathered here for worship, he touched the small of her back as if he had every right to do so.

He stepped up beside her and stood before Father Ambrosius, who paused in the Communion ritual to invoke a special blessing. Then he spoke to Fitz Autier. "My son, is it truly necessary for you to take Lady Aelia to London?"

The question seemed to startle Fitz Autier, who cleared his throat before responding. "Aye, Father. 'Tis the king's order."

"Then I admonish you to keep her safe, for her life is precious to us at Ingelwald."

Chapter Thirteen

"**Y**ou will ride with me," Mathieu said to Osric, whose behavior was just as deplorable as when they'd started out the day before. Aelia spoke to the boy and he quieted, although his squirming in the saddle continued.

Mathieu rode to the head of the procession, leaving orders that Aelia and her guard, Halig, were to remain halfway back. He had extracted Halig's vow of fealty, and had no reason to doubt the young man's integrity. But Aelia had made him no promises. If she chose to ride off, Halig would follow.

And who knew what would happen then?

"Have a safe journey, baron," said Auvrai. "All will be ready for your wife when you return."

Before he could answer, Aelia kicked her heels into her horse's flanks and rode toward the gate. 'Twas closed, and Mathieu knew his men would not open it until he arrived and gave the order. "Two months, Auvrai. I intend to be back before winter."

"Aye."

Mathieu's men followed him to the gate, where he

joined Aelia and Halig. They rode out amid the good wishes of the Norman soldiers posted there and on the walls, but Mathieu felt the icy wall of silence that emanated from the lady as she left her home.

The day was fine and they covered the miles rapidly. Mathieu ignored Aelia's pique, aware that it was due to Auvrai's words. She believed he had a wife.

"Are you going to starve us, Norman?" asked Osric at midmorning.

"Are you hungry, little Saxon?"

They halted beside a low rock wall bordering a ripe field of barley. Mathieu watched Aelia unhook her pack from her saddle and walk away from their group. She did not look in his direction, but followed the rock wall until she reached a small stand of trees and stepped out of sight. He would give her all the privacy she required—unless she took longer than he thought was strictly necessary.

"Shall I...is it your wish that I go with her?" Halig asked.

Mathieu shook his head. "Leave her alone for now." He handed Osric a water skin and the boy drank while Mathieu took food from the pack and set it on the rock ledge. Then he moved away, keeping one eye in the direction Aelia had gone.

"I want to practice with Sir Raoul's sword again," Osric said. "Will you show me how to spear my opponent?"

"On one condition," Mathieu replied, glad to have a reason to stop pacing the ground while he waited for Aelia to return. "You must promise never to use your technique on me or any of my men."

The boy crossed his arms over his puny chest. "How can you make me promise this? You are my enemy! I will do all—"

"Then there's no need to continue this discussion."

Mathieu resumed his pacing, glancing toward the trees again, but he saw no sign of Aelia.

Osric scrambled 'round in front of Mathieu, obstructing his path. "I will promise! Norman, I said I promise not to hurt your men with my skill."

"Your word, little Saxon. You stand by it as a man of honor?"

"Of course. Now show me."

Mathieu borrowed Raoul's seax again and handed it to Osric. "'Twould suit you better to keep your distance from any battle."

"I am no coward, Fitz Autier!"

"While you are small, 'twould be a better strategy to stay clear of a hand-to-hand contest. Learn to use a bow."

"I can already shoot," Osric said as he lunged with his weapon.

Mathieu stepped away. "Do you see? 'Tis unlikely you would ever overcome a full-grown man at close quarters."

"What if I come upon him in sleep?"

Mathieu laughed. "Then you would not need this instruction. You would only have to strike between the ribs."

"Or across the throat…"

Mathieu thought of the thin slice across Aelia's pretty neck that had come so close to taking her life. He shuddered at the thought of what would have happened had he not been there to protect her. "Aye."

"I want to be ready in case we are attacked."

"We travel with eight seasoned warriors and a Saxon cavalier, boy," Mathieu said, looking to the trees again. "You'll have no need to fight."

"But I—"

"Stay here."

* * *

Aelia sat on the ground with her back against the wall. She tipped her head up, letting the sun shine upon her face, drying her tears.

Leaving Ingelwald was the most difficult thing she'd ever done. As the Normans had packed up the horses and made ready for travel, Aelia had walked across the grounds, stopping at every shop and every cottage, burning the sights of home into her memory, for that was all she would ever have of it.

Learning of Fitz Autier's wife had been the final insult. He had demeaned Aelia by treating her as a cheap giglet, making advances and stirring her blood as if he were free to do so. As if he did not have a Norman wife waiting for him in…

Was she in London? Aelia's blood rushed from her head when she understood Fitz Autier's urgency to return there. He had a woman waiting for him.

"What's the delay?"

Fitz Autier's voice startled Aelia and she pushed away from the wall, gathering her saddle pack in her arms. "Time to go, I suppose."

"Have you broken your fast?"

"I'm not hungry."

"You will be by the time we stop again. You should eat now."

"I have no stomach for food, Fitz Autier."

She kept her face averted and pushed past him, heading away from the trees and into the clearing where Osric and the knights awaited her.

Fitz Autier grabbed her arm and stopped her. "I won't have you making yourself ill."

"'Tis no concern of yours." She tried unsuccessfully to shrug his hand off.

"Aye, it is. We have a long way to go and I'll brook no delays."

Aelia glared at him, unwilling to admit that whatever drew her to him had not abated just because she knew he was wed. "Let me take my brother and go." Her voice was little more than a whisper, and Aelia despised the pleading tone of it.

"You know I cannot."

"Give us two horses and we will ride to Thrydburgh. Lord Cælin will give us—"

Fitz Autier grabbed her upper arms. "Aelia. Thrydburgh is no more. 'Tis a Norman holding."

"I suppose you were part of that conquest."

"No. But I would have been if the king had ordered me there."

He held her tight, but Aelia could not tell if 'twas his firm grasp that hurt, or the pain in her soul. Everything was wrong about this journey, but she could do naught to stop it.

"What will happen to us in London? To Osric and me?"

A muscle in his jaw flexed once and he squeezed her arms before suddenly releasing her. "'Tis up to King William."

"What is he likely to do? What has been done with other Saxon prisoners?"

"It's time to leave." He started walking away, but Aelia followed.

"He will put us to death, won't he?"

He turned and faced her, his expression fierce, the gash across his cheek taut with fury. "God's blood, woman, do you think I would take you all the way to London to be killed?"

"What then? Will we be sent to Normandy as slaves?"

Aelia watched as he shoved the fingers of one hand through his hair, a gesture she'd seen before when he was annoyed. "No. 'Tis likely he will give you to one of his knights in marriage."

Aelia took a deep shuddering breath and strode away from him. "I will *never* wed a Norman."

She walked through the trees to the clearing and stumbled when she saw Osric mounting Fitz Autier's horse from the wall. He grabbed hold of the reins as the horse burst into a gallop while Aelia stood stunned, watching. He headed north, back toward Ingelwald, and the horse was moving too fast for Osric to control it. It would not be possible for him to keep his seat. He was going to fall!

Fitz Autier pushed past her and dashed toward his men, who had been taken by surprise and were clambering to their feet to get to their horses. Fitz Autier shouted some orders as he quickly mounted Aelia's mare and went after Osric.

Aelia could not move. She stood with her hand pressed to her mouth, watching as Osric rode out of sight with the Norman baron behind him.

"Lady Aelia…" Sir Raoul took her arm and led her back to the group. "I have orders to hold you here."

"My brother," she whispered.

"Is a terror, but the baron will catch him and bring him back."

Aelia could not be so sure. If Osric was thrown from the wildly galloping horse before Fitz Autier could get to him, the fall could easily kill him.

"Can we not follow them? I promise to—"

"No, my lady. The baron's orders were clear."

The boy would be lucky to survive this latest escapade. Mathieu did not know why he didn't just let

Osric's recklessness take its natural course and kill him. But he recalled a few embarrassing incidents in his own youth and was grateful now for the guidance of the older, patient knight who had seen potential in him and helped to mold him into an honest, chivalrous warrior.

Beyond that, Mathieu would spare Aelia the anguish of losing her brother now. She'd lost her father and her home, and when they reached London, there could be no doubt Osric would be taken from her. 'Twould be soon enough for that final blow.

The boy was dead ahead, but he had no control of the horse. The reins had slipped out of his hands, and his feet dangled high above the stirrups. He was desperately holding on to the pommel with both hands, but Mathieu could see that he was having difficulty at that. A hedge-row lay directly across their path, and Osric would never be able to hold on when the horse jumped over it.

Mathieu leaned forward and urged his own mount to an even greater speed, and when he was nearly abreast of Osric, he dug his heels into the mare's sides for the final burst he needed to reach him. He lunged for the reins, which hung loose, but the movement of both horses made it impossible to grab them.

"Osric!"

The boy did not look to the side, but Mathieu could see that he'd heard him.

"Quickly, boy! I'm going to grab hold of you 'round your waist! When I do, throw your weight toward me!"

They were moving fast, rapidly approaching the hedgerow. Mathieu veered east, forcing the gelding to do the same, but he had to be careful not to cause the horse to lose its footing.

He leaned over, reaching out to take hold of Osric's tunic. "Lean toward me!"

When the boy did so, Mathieu got a firm grip around his middle and eased him to the side of the saddle. Osric slipped and would have fallen if Mathieu's grasp had not been so sure. "Take hold of my arm!"

As soon as Osric grabbed him, Mathieu pulled him off the gelding. He slowed Aelia's mare, but the other animal galloped on, leaving the boy dangling at Mathieu's side. He lifted him into the saddle as the riderless gelding reached the hedgerow and leaped over it. But there was a terrible crash and a sickening screech as the steed lost its footing and fell.

Osric pressed his trembling body against Mathieu. The boy's breathing was quick and shaky, but it stopped suddenly. "Where is he?"

Mathieu sat still and let his own breathing slow to normal and his anger simmer to a low burn. He would like to throttle the child, but decided upon a far greater punishment. He rode to the hedgerow, where the whimpers of the injured horse were audible. Then he rode on, looking for a break in the hedge. When he found it, he dismounted and pulled Osric down with him. Holding the boy by the scruff of his tunic, Mathieu walked to the place where the animal lay writhing in pain, its front legs broken.

"What are you going to do?"

"Not me. You," Mathieu said. "You are going to deal with the havoc you wrought."

"Me? It's…it's just a horse. It's—"

"Take responsibility for what you've done, boy!" Mathieu's anger seethed. He drew his sword and handed it to Osric. "Place the tip here."

"No. I…I—"

"You can run a fine steed to its death—the least you can do is see that its death is quick and painless."

Osric paled, but Mathieu did not relent. Only the rough breathing of the horse and its occasional whimpers broke the silence.

"Here."

Trembling, the boy did as he was ordered, but Mathieu also placed his hands upon the hilt to add his strength to the stroke that would be needed to kill the horse.

"Now."

Osric shuddered but did what was required, dealing a quick death blow to the suffering animal. When 'twas done, he dropped the sword and whirled to face Mathieu. His cheeks were covered with tears, but he shouted as if *he* had every right to be angry. "What was that for? You made me kill a perfectly good horse!"

Mathieu took Osric by the shoulders and turned him to face the gelding, hoping the boy felt as sick as he did. "Look at those legs. Broken right through the skin! Do you think that horse would be lying here now if you had not tried to make a bloody run for it? Do you think *you* would still be alive if you'd made the jump?"

He could not imagine having to return to Aelia with the news that her brother was dead. Even now, 'twas likely Raoul had had to physically restrain her to keep her from following her brother's path.

"There will be harsh consequences for your actions."

"You are not my father, Norman, to mete out punishment!" the boy cried, but there was less bluster in his tone, and he seemed almost contrite.

"I'm the only authority you know, boy," Mathieu said, his voice low and dangerous. "Until we reach London, you are under my jurisdiction and you will not make a single move without my approval."

"You can't—"

"Aye, I can. And I do." He gave the boy a shove toward the break in the hedge. "Move."

Mathieu tossed Osric onto the back of Aelia's mare and mounted behind him. Then he turned toward to the road and retraced the path they'd followed so frantically only a short while before.

"You would have left your sister to face King William alone?" he asked.

His anger had not abated, and he hadn't yet decided upon an apt punishment, but he intended to start by shaming the boy for deserting his sister.

"I left Halig to see to her."

"You are the son of Wallis, but you left your sister in the care of a man who is not even a thane?"

"He—"

"The son of a lord does not shirk his duty."

"But I—"

"Ran away like a coward."

"I am no coward!"

"Your family has indulged you long enough. In my company, you will learn discipline."

"I'm not—"

"Enough."

Mathieu was surprised but grateful when Osric held his tongue. 'Twas not like him to give up the last word, but he rode back to the others in silence while Mathieu controlled his fury.

He saw Aelia first. Her apprehension was demonstrated by her tense posture, and when she caught sight of them, she broke into a run.

But Mathieu was unmoved by the worry she obviously felt.

"Osric!" she cried. Her face was flushed with exertion by the time she reached them. "Where is the gelding?"

"Dead." When Osric continued to hold his tongue, Mathieu said the word. He slowed their pace to allow Aelia to walk beside them.

"What happened?"

Osric crossed his arms over his chest.

"Tell her," Mathieu said.

"Osric?" Aelia reached up and placed her hand upon her brother's knee.

"It fell," he finally stated.

"Fell? How?"

"Jumping a hedgerow."

Aelia put a hand to her breast and stood still. She looked so dismayed that Mathieu would have dismounted and taken her in his arms if he had not been so angry.

And promised to Lady Clarise. Both conditions made any connection with Lady Aelia impossible.

"How…somehow you escaped unscathed." Her voice was strained and flat.

"The Norman pulled me off just before the jump."

"The fall killed it?"

"No. Fitz Autier made me cut its throat."

Aelia's knees went weak and she fell behind as the mare carrying Osric and the Norman baron continued toward the group of knights waiting at the wall.

She had never seen Fitz Autier so angry, and he had every right to be. Yet it did not appear that he had taken out his ire upon Osric. Surely some punishment was in order, but Aelia would not stand idly by if he chose to whip her brother. Osric was surprisingly quiet as Fitz Autier bound his hands with a length of rope and handed him up to Sir Raoul's horse.

There was little doubt that Fitz Autier had saved her

brother's life. He had put his own life in danger by riding at breakneck speed to catch Osric before the fatal jump, then pulling him off the runaway horse. It had been a dangerous task, one that few horsemen could have accomplished. She owed him a debt of gratitude, but words of thanks caught in her throat when she thought of his disrespect for her.

Fitz Autier handed Aelia's pack to Sir Gerrard, then tied his own to the mare's saddle. "Mount up," he said to Aelia.

"I will ride with Halig."

"Leaving me to deal with more Saxon antics? I think not, *demoiselle*."

She had no choice but to put her foot in the stirrup. He placed his hands upon her waist and lifted her up, then climbed into the saddle behind her. She was flanked by his legs and his arms as he gathered the reins and rode to the southern path.

"I…I apologize for Osric's behavior. He—"

"I do not accept," Fitz Autier said. "You have made excuses for him for too long. *He* will be the one to take responsibility for his actions, as well as the punishment. Likely 'twill be the first time for him."

Chapter Fourteen

Mathieu had no intention of relenting. The boy would rub down all the horses and feed them before he was allowed to eat and sleep. And he would do this every night until they reached London.

It came as no surprise when Aelia left her own meal to help him.

"Aelia." He caught her arm and stopped her before she could move away from the small fire at the center of their camp.

"He's too small to do such work," she protested as he directed her back to her place.

It would have surprised Mathieu if Osric tried to run off again. The boy was foolish, but not stupid. He knew how close he'd come to death, and was unlikely to try such a stunt again.

Besides, the men had removed all the saddles before turning their horses over to his dubious care, and they were too heavy for him to lift.

"He's going to fall."

"Why? Has he never climbed onto a boulder before?" Mathieu knew his casual tone infuriated Aelia more than she already was.

"You are treating him cruelly."

Mathieu looked 'round at his men. "What do you think? Am I a cruel master?"

"No, my lord."

"'Tis no more than the boy deserves."

"What do you think, Halig?" Mathieu asked.

The Saxon lad gave a furtive look toward Aelia, then replied quietly. "My father would whip me for what Osric did."

Mathieu felt Aelia stiffen beside him, but he continued eating.

"Shall we set up tents tonight?" Gerrard asked Mathieu.

He intended to keep Aelia and Osric separated, but he would not allow Aelia to sleep in a tent alone. 'Twould be too easy for her to slip out under one of the canvas sides and cause some kind of mischief.

"No. We'll sleep in the open."

He dreaded the night when he would be compelled to set up tents. As long as they slept outside among the men, Mathieu would not be so tempted to touch Aelia, to kiss her mouth, to make love to her as his body had been demanding for days. But he could not leave her unattended in a tent. Someone would have to sleep with her.

He stood abruptly and left the circle.

Picking up his pack, he took out the wood-carving tools and the thick block of wood that he'd taken from Beorn's widow. He kicked a heavy log close to the fire and sat down with his back against it, then lay the wood across his lap and started to carve. 'Twas the best distraction to keep from thinking of the nights he would likely have to spend with Aelia.

As the first Norman lord of Ingelwald, he had decided upon a mighty stag for the symbol of his house. He would carve a crest using this image of strength, speed and endurance, and present it to Lady Clarise when they wed, as a symbol of all that he was, of all that he possessed.

In the flickering firelight, he gave his full attention to his work, carving the shallow lines that would guide his hand when he made the deeper gouges in the wood. He would not give a moment's thought to the tears Aelia had tried to hide from him, or the way her body had fit so snugly against his as they'd ridden to this place.

She had been near exhaustion when they'd arrived at the sheltered spot, but still, she'd begged him to allow her to help Osric with the tasks he'd been assigned.

"I've finished."

Mathieu looked up at Osric, small and filthy, his shoulders sagging with such weariness he was barely able to stand. Yet his tone remained belligerent. He crossed his arms over his chest and waited for Mathieu to respond.

"There's food…." Mathieu nodded toward the opposite side of the fire, where Raoul and the others sat. They'd finished eating, and Aelia was leaning against the trunk of a tree, trying to fight sleep, but nodding just the same.

The boy said nothing more, but turned and joined the men, taking what food they offered. Mathieu finished his own work for the night, wrapped the wood in a piece of leather and put away his tools. Then he laid a fur pelt near the fire and dropped a woolen blanket upon it.

Aelia had slid down and was sleeping soundly on the ground when he went to get her. He crouched beside her and turned away to speak quietly to his men. "Gerrard, see that the horses are secured. Raoul, when the boy has eaten, bind him to you for the night. I'll take the first watch. Gerrard, you're next."

"No! I won't try to run away."

Mathieu ignored the boy.

He touched Aelia's shoulder, but she did not awaken. He lifted her and carried her to the far side of the fire, where he laid her upon the pelt, then covered her with the blanket. His hands lingered longer than they should have, securing the cover over her shoulders, sliding down her arms.

When she turned her head, Mathieu caught a glimpse of the wound in her neck, the cut that had so very nearly taken her life. He'd brought some of Auvrai's salve, and reached for it now, rubbing a small amount onto the reddened gash in Aelia's flesh.

She opened her eyes and looked up at him, though her gaze was clouded with sleep. She raised one arm and reached for him, sliding her fingers through the hair behind his ear. Her lips parted slightly and she peered intently into his eyes.

Mathieu couldn't breathe. Though he knew Aelia was not fully awake, the slight touch of her hand aroused him to a point of pain. He closed his eyes and turned his head enough to feel her fingers caress his ear, before regaining some semblance of control. He took hold of her hand and lowered it to the ground, then covered her again.

She turned to her side and drifted off once more, and Mathieu took a deep breath. He went back to the log where he'd sat before, while his men made beds for themselves and settled in for the night. Even Osric remained quiet, too tired to protest being tied to Raoul.

Then Mathieu stretched out his legs and prepared to keep watch over her—and everyone else—well into the night.

Each day passed much like the one before it, until the fourth day, when Fitz Autier seemed more alert than usual. More wary.

"What is it?" Aelia asked. "What's wrong?"

"Gerrard!" he called.

The knight came abreast of them as they approached a rocky decline in the trail. 'Twas so steep they would have to dismount in order to climb down. "Stay here with Roger and Guilliaume."

"Aye, baron."

Aelia leaned to one side to look behind them, past Fitz Autier. There was naught but trees and the craggy terrain they'd navigated all day. "Is someone there?"

"Keep watch until dusk, then follow us," Fitz Autier said to Gerrard.

"Is someone out there?"

"Just being cautious," he replied, although Aelia did not quite believe him. He helped her dismount, and when he unsheathed his sword, the other men did the same.

Even Osric remained quiet as the men led the horses down the escarpment, and Aelia realized their path was a vulnerable one, out in the open, where an attack would be difficult to repel. Though they had had no trouble on the road so far, Aelia knew the men in her escort were always alert and ready for a hostile encounter.

Yet this was different.

She asked no more questions, but walked on beside Fitz Autier until they reached the bottom of the path and made their way into dense woods.

At nightfall, when Gerrard and the others reached

camp, they reported having seen nothing untoward. "But we brought these." They held up several rabbits they'd killed, and the men soon dressed them and started roasting them on spits over the fire.

But Aelia noticed that Fitz Autier did not relax, even though he must have been weary, since it had been his turn to keep watch for part of the previous night. He paced the perimeter of the camp, and when it began to rain, ordered tents to be set up. By that time, Osric had already completed his duties with the horses and fallen asleep under a tree.

The Norman baron went down on one knee beside the boy and spoke quietly to him. Osric awoke and sat up, his calm, acquiescent attitude surprising Aelia. Clearly, Fitz Autier intended to keep the boy too tired to perpetrate any mischief.

Usually, he kept her apart from her brother, too. But tonight he guided Osric to Aelia's side.

"Stay beside your sister and eat," he said. "There will be no moving about tonight."

"Why? What is it?" she asked.

Fitz Autier shook his head. "'Tis naught but normal caution," he said, then strode away in the rain.

He'd been quiet all day, riding so close behind her upon her mare. She'd felt his breath in her hair and upon her ear, but even that slight contact had made her own breath catch and her loins ache.

For days she'd sat close to him, colliding with his body with every move—with his hard thighs, or the warm metal of the hauberk against his chest—and she thought of his kiss, and remembered how he'd managed to make her melt even when he was asleep.

Aelia did not know how much longer she would be able to travel like this—at such close quarters all day, then watching his skilled hands carve a shape into the block of wood he unwrapped from a soft piece of leather each evening.

He had a wife awaiting him somewhere, in London, perhaps, and 'twas possible Aelia would meet her there.

The thought of such an encounter gave her pause. Aelia found herself troubled by thoughts of Fitz Autier and the unknown woman who was his wife, the woman who had the right to touch him whenever and however she liked, the woman who slept beside him.

When Osric finished eating, he crawled into the tent where he would spend the night, although Aelia was certain Fitz Autier did not trust him enough to allow him to sleep unattended. One of the Norman soldiers would certainly be assigned to guard him.

Aelia finally retreated into her own tent in order to escape Fitz Autier and all the confusing emotions he made her feel. She knew he had no more regard for her than he did for Nelda, the Ingelwald woman who shared her favors with any man who pleased her, else he would not have made such improper advances toward her.

But she could not forget his kiss…or his touch.

The night was cool with the rain, and Aelia wrapped herself in a blanket and tried to sleep. But Fitz Autier's restlessness had affected her, too, and she lay awake listening to the patter of rain upon the canvas shelter, letting her thoughts drift until Fitz Autier opened the flap of the tent and crawled inside.

She sat up abruptly. "You cannot come in here!"

Ignoring her, he rolled up his blanket and lay his head upon it. "I have only a few hours, *demoiselle,*" he said as he settled in.

She could feel the heat of his body through her blanket and her clothes, and 'twas all she could do to refrain from sliding close to him to share his warmth.

"Lie down and take your rest. Tomorrow will be a long day indeed, if this rain keeps up."

Aelia knew 'twas pointless to argue. "I thought you took your turn on guard duty last night."

"We're doubling up tonight."

"Why? What's happened?"

"Nothing. I just…follow my instincts, and they're warning me to be particularly cautious."

They lay still for a long interval, but Aelia knew he was not asleep. She wondered if his heart pounded as hard as hers in the darkness. "Have you any children?"

The question was but a whisper, but it sounded loud and strident in Aelia's ears.

He did not reply at first, and Aelia wondered if she'd been mistaken about his being asleep. She nearly hoped she was.

"'Twould be best if we did not discuss this."

The questions had been burning in her heart for days.

"You would have made me your mistress," she whispered. "You kissed me. Touched me. Treated me the way a wedded man would treat a…a harlot."

He lay perfectly still, not even breathing. A long moment passed without his answer, and when Aelia would have spoken again, he suddenly shifted and pressed his hand against her mouth to quiet her.

He moved in complete silence, and pressed his lips to her ear, whispering almost inaudibly, "Stay still."

He knelt and reached the tent flap, silently pushing it open just a sliver. Then Aelia heard it: a stealthy footstep upon the wet ground. She would not have noticed it had Fitz Autier not alerted her to listen. He pressed something hard and cold into her hand, and Aelia realized 'twas his knife. As he looked outside, he reached behind him and picked up his sword, then eased his way out.

Aelia followed him, watching in the firelight as he moved quietly around the campsite. No one else was about.

Not even the men who were assigned the first watch.

Fitz Autier headed east, into the trees, and was quickly out of sight. Aelia heard a noise behind her and turned abruptly, but she could see no one. Naught lurked in the darkness in any direction.

She heard a rustling in the trees north of her, but when she whirled to look, the disturbance stopped.

Her dagger did not reassure her. Keeping her eyes on the surrounding darkness, she stepped quietly to the closest tent and pulled up the flap, just as she heard the clash of swords ring out in the distance. "Help! Come quickly!"

Aelia did not wait for the men to scramble from their tents, but followed the sounds of battle alone. Soon, though, all the Normans were armed and surging into the woods, where Fitz Autier fought an armored assailant in the flickering light of their fire. The men spread out, and Aelia believed they would go to their leader's assistance. Instead, they slipped into the darkness of the trees, while he fought alone. Only Halig and Sir Gerrard stayed with her.

Fitz Autier's attacker wore hauberk and helm, and wielded a broadsword like a seasoned soldier—like the man who had cut down her father in battle. Aelia narrowed her eyes and watched the man as he fought Fitz Autier. She could not be mistaken. The helm was that of her father's killer, and he wielded his sword in the same manner.

Fitz Autier had no such protection for his head, and

his opponent swung his sword in a deadly motion that would have cleaved his skull from his shoulders had he not dodged in time. 'Twas the exact maneuver that had taken her father's life.

All at once, Aelia felt sick and faint. She leaned against a stout oak and pressed one hand to her abdomen as she watched Fitz Autier fight for his life.

"There are eight of us, Durand," he shouted. "Do you hope to defeat us all?"

"Your count is off, *bastard!*"

'Twas Durand? The man who had violated Rowena?

"Do something!" Aelia cried.

"He can deal with this rogue, Lady Aelia," said Gerrard.

"But—"

Osric insinuated himself between Aelia and Halig, just as Fitz Autier took the offensive, holding his broadsword with both hands and hacking at the other man. The assailant backed up several paces, but managed to get in a blow with the broad side of his blade, catching Fitz Autier on his shoulder, knocking his sword from his hands.

Even then, Fitz Autier did not yield, nor did any of his men move in to assist him. Aelia cried out, but could do naught but stand by, watching silently while he dodged the warrior's thrusts, moving quickly and agilely.

"I'll beat you without a weapon, Durand!" he taunted, pulling away from another thrust of the sword. "You're no man, but a coward, a molester of young girls. Come on."

"Why does he mock him?" Aelia cried in a harsh whisper, twisting the wool of her skirt in her hands. "'Twill only anger him and make him the more vicious."

"Worry not, my lady," said Gerrard.

"Don't be an ass, Aelia," said Osric. "Fitz Autier is the superior warrior."

Aelia hardly heard her brother's insult. Her mouth was as dry as sand and her heart pounded as she watched the battle continue. Fitz Autier moved well, his powerful body dodging every thrust of the blade, but he could not retreat indefinitely. Durand, if that's who it was, would soon make a killing stab.

"What if there are others out there? What if—"

"Raoul and the rest of our men are making sure there are no others. All will be well, Lady Aelia." Gerrard took Osric by the chin and turned the boy to face him. "As for you, boy, you will speak with respect to your elders, particularly your lady sister."

Ignoring the rain and the rough terrain, Aelia lifted her skirts and ran to a place where she was better able to watch. It seemed an interminable length of time that Fitz Autier parried the warrior's thrusts, dodging blow after blow. Breathing heavily, the two men grunted with exertion, but neither yielded, and Aelia thought of all Fitz Autier's injuries—the gash in his side, the cut on his face, the countless other wounds she'd seen when he'd climbed out of the pool behind the waterfall. She swallowed the lump in her throat, pressing one hand against her breast and praying silently that he would somehow prevail.

Fitz Autier made a sudden move that knocked his opponent to the ground. He lunged and picked up his sword as Durand managed to push himself to his knees and jab once again.

"On your feet, Durand!" Fitz Autier shouted. "I will kill you fairly!"

"Not likely, *bastard!*"

He started slashing, but Fitz Autier parried skillfully,

then turned to the offensive. 'Twas his own thrusts and jabs that caused Durand to move backward, awkwardly avoiding the obstacles that would trip him. The knight gave one mighty swing of his sword meant to spike Fitz Autier, but 'twas the baron who dealt the fatal blow, finding Durand's vulnerable spot and spearing him through.

All was silent in the woods for a moment as Fitz Autier stood over Durand's body, holding his sword at his side. His men came to him from their positions in the woods. "He did some damage to Osbern and Hugh," said Raoul, though it sounded to Aelia as though he were speaking through a long, deep tunnel. "But they'll live."

"There were no others," said Sir Guatier, his voice also strangely distant. "Durand came alone."

"Catch her!" she heard Raoul say, just as everything went black.

Mathieu moved quickly, taking Aelia from Halig, who had managed to catch her before she hit the ground. Mathieu did not think about why 'twas so important that he be the one to carry her out of the woods, but took her to the campsite and lowered her into the tent, out of the rain.

"I'll need a water skin," he said. "And a clean cloth."

"She'll be all right," said Osric.

"Which will not be the same for you unless you get to your tent with Raoul," Mathieu said. "Now."

"You bested him, even without your sword!"

"No...he disarmed me, but I managed to hold out until I could retrieve my sword."

"But—"

"Go."

The boy grumbled, but left promptly, as did the rest of the men, all but Halig.

"I would learn, seignior…. I wish to train and become a knight…like you."

Mathieu took no pride in the way he'd fought. He'd nearly allowed his fatigue to get the better of him. Durand should never have gotten so close. "Aye," he said wearily. "When we return to Ingelwald, I'll see that you are given the chance."

He checked on Hugh and Osbern, both of whom had sustained injuries to their heads. It seemed that Durand had sneaked up and attacked each of them from behind, delivering a blow to the skull that could have killed them. Fortunately, both men survived, but 'twas possible they would be unable to ride upon the morrow.

Disgusted with the night's turn of events, Mathieu pulled off his hauberk, then crawled into the tent and closed the flap. All day, he'd been plagued with a feeling of being watched. He should have thought of Durand, and because he had not anticipated an attack from the disgruntled knight, Hugh and Osbern had paid dearly for his oversight.

He poured water on a clean cloth and wiped Aelia's face with it. She made a quiet sound and turned her head away.

"Aelia." He washed her face again to rouse her. Her clothes were soaked through. 'Twas certain she could not spend the night this way.

"Uh…cold."

"Aye, it is. Wake up."

She opened her eyes. "What happened?"

"You fainted."

She sat up abruptly and would have fallen to the

ground again had Mathieu not caught her shoulders and lowered her gently. "I did not faint."

"All right, you didn't faint." He tossed the rag into a corner and lay upon his own pelt, as far from her as possible. 'Twas absurd to think she'd been concerned for his well-being, anyway. She could barely tolerate him.

They had hardly spoken to each other in the four days since they'd left Ingelwald—not at all since he'd pulled her brother from the runaway gelding's back.

"Was it Durand?"

"Aye. I sensed him following us all day."

"You knew it was Durand?"

He shook his head. "Someone. One man, not a group."

She lay quietly for a while, but he soon felt her shivering, and heard her teeth begin to chatter. "Durand killed my father."

"Aye." He turned and looked at her in the faint light of the fire. Though he could not see her well, he knew every one of her features, from her gently arched brows, to the hint of a cleft in her chin. He knew that her mouth tasted of sweet berries and her skin was taut and sleek.

Arousal, hard and unmerciful, hit him.

"You knew?"

"I'd heard talk. Was that why you fainted? Because you realized 'twas Durand who killed Wallis?"

"I've never fainted."

"Then mayhap you were worried about me."

"Certainly not. I do not care what happens to a Frenchwoman's husband."

Chapter Fifteen

But Aelia did. She could not deny it had been terrifying to watch Fitz Autier face Durand without a sword. What she felt had naught to do with gratitude for saving Osric's life, or for killing Durand. 'Twas a frightening magnetism that drew her to Mathieu Fitz Autier, and it had more to do with his touch, his kiss.

Aelia realized she was shivering, and resisted the urge to draw closer to his warmth. She knew his touch would heat her icy skin, but she was no harlot. Fitz Autier not only belonged to another, he was still Aelia's enemy. The only reason he'd come into the tent with her was to assure that she did not try to sneak away, to take Osric and run from him.

She gathered her blanket around her and tried to stop shaking.

"Thank you for avenging my f-father's death tonight, seignior," she said. "My debt to you g-grows."

It would have been better to make some gross insult, or even walk away from him. She would have left the tent to sleep outside if he'd let her, but she knew he would not. He would bind her wrists and ankles and tie her to him if she tried to leave him.

But he was too close. His shoulders occupied an inordinate amount of space, and Aelia remembered all too well how strong and solid his chest felt when she leaned against him on horseback, and the way his muscular arms encircled her as they rode.

But he was her adversary. She should feel no comfort in his presence.

Yet when he turned to her, bringing his face much too close to hers, Aelia could not back away. There was no room within the tent for retreat, nor did she want to, especially when he cupped her cheek with his hand and touched his lips to hers.

Aelia tried to remember why this was impossible, but she could not think coherently, not when his lips moved over hers. She sighed and he deepened the kiss, parting her lips and surging inside. He seduced her mouth with his tongue and teeth as he pulled out the laces that held her kirtle closed, then spread the bodice.

Aelia melted when he uttered a low growl and cupped her breast through the thin linen of her chemise. His lips trailed a path of fire down her neck and to her chest, and when his tongue touched one sensitive nipple, her breath caught.

Whatever she'd felt on that first night with him was naught compared to this. With one move, he took hold of the chemise and tore it away, so that she was completely bared to him. She felt the roughness of his whiskers upon her tender skin, and the pull of his mouth upon her breast. Aelia arched her back and slid her hands through Fitz Autier's hair, holding his head in place.

He licked and sucked one nipple while he teased and tortured the other with his fingers. She wanted him to ease the tension that stretched from her breasts to her womb, to touch her as no man had ever done before.

Selwyn would never have been able to make her blood burn this way. She had never had the desire to kiss him, to slide her hands across his back or touch his bare skin. Only this Norman had the power to make her forget herself.

But not for long. She pushed him away and sat up abruptly, fumbling with the edges of her torn chemise, trying to cover her body.

Fitz Autier thrust himself up to his knees, and in the dim light, Aelia saw him dig his fingers through his hair. "Good Christ, I must be out of my mind," he said.

He stayed crouched in the small space for a moment, then shoved the flap aside and started to leave. Instead, he turned and handed her his blanket. A moment later, he was gone.

Without thinking, she pulled Fitz Autier's blanket over her shoulders and lay down, feeling numb both in body and in mind. She shivered with cold, only this time the chill was inside her.

By morning, the rain had abated, but the mood in camp was somber. Durand's vicious blow to Sir Osbern's head made him too ill to travel.

"That rogue, Durand, must have cracked Osbern's skull," said Gerrard. "At least Hugh seems all right."

"Osbern will be, too," replied Raoul. "I've seen men with worse wounds who recovered after a few days."

Aelia could not allow herself to care what happened to any of these Normans. She and Osric were their prisoners, no matter how kindly they treated her.

"Where is my brother?" she asked the two knights.

"With the baron."

"Why?" She could not imagine what Osric had done now. "What is amiss?"

"I would not worry about him," said Raoul. He picked up a large canvas satchel and handed it to her. "The baron left this for you."

She took it, but was more concerned about Osric, gone away somewhere with Fitz Autier, than she was about the contents of the pack. "Where did Fitz Autier take my brother?"

"To the horses," Raoul said. "I believe the baron is inspecting—"

Aelia did not wait to hear the rest. Clearly, Osric was in trouble again, and 'twas up to her to protect him. She hurried away toward the edge of camp, where they'd strung the horses together. But neither Osric nor Fitz Autier were there. Nor were the horses.

She moved quickly through the trees until she came to a fallow field, and came to a dead stop at the sight before her.

The horses had been hobbled and left to wander in the field to graze. Standing out in the open were Osric and Fitz Autier, facing one another with swords crossed.

Aelia's heart dropped to her knees until she heard Fitz Autier's words.

"No, little Saxon," he said. "You should have taken advantage there and thrust. Try it again."

Aelia was certain her eyes deceived her. 'Twas not possible that Fitz Autier was teaching swordsmanship to Osric. Yet her eyes did not lie.

Bewildered, she watched Fitz Autier parry each of Osric's thrusts, then demonstrate better techniques for maiming his enemy. "If he wears armor and helm, you must use your speed, for that is your strength while you are still small."

Aelia lowered herself upon a broken branch at the edge of the wood, watching unobserved, as Fitz Autier taught Osric the rudiments of battle. They laughed together, and at one point, Fitz Autier even ruffled Osric's red hair.

Aelia took hold of the dead wood underneath her and held on while her world shifted. Her brother could not possibly have made an ally of Fitz Autier. He'd been at odds with the Normans, especially their leader, ever since Ingelwald had been conquered. The baron had been right about Osric. He had behaved rashly, undisciplined and heedless of the consequences of his actions.

Was it possible that Fitz Autier had forgiven him all that—and that Osric was actually taking a lesson from the Norman?

No. Aelia's heart sank when she realized 'twas more likely Osric had figured out how to gain Fitz Autier's trust. That way, he could get his hands on a weapon and—

Aelia jumped to her feet as Fitz Autier knocked Osric to the ground. But rather than lashing out in anger, her brother merely laughed. Their combat was all in fun.

"You'll never best me in this manner, little Saxon," Fitz Autier said. The Norman's tone was different, as was the expression on his face. He looked younger, and more relaxed, than Aelia had ever seen him.

"I wager I'll win the next match, Norman!"

"You have nothing of value to wager, little Saxon."

"Aye, I do—a good word for you with my sister!"

Osric's statement took Aelia's breath away. She watched Fitz Autier lower his hand to Osric and help him up as his expression changed from jovial and insouciant to serious. "What makes you think I want your sister's favor?"

"Ha! Though I might not be fully grown, I've seen how you look at her."

Fitz Autier walked away and bent down to retrieve Osric's sword. Aelia waited for him to deny Osric's words, but he said naught about it as he handed the weapon to the boy. "And what would be your prize if you won?"

"Aelia's dagger," Osric said without hesitation. "I would return it to her."

"Agreed."

She covered her mouth with her hand. Raw emotion welled within her chest—love for her brother, confusion over what she felt for Fitz Autier. He was her enemy, yet he'd protected her, saved her life. What he made her feel was beyond her comprehension, and she was afraid to examine it too closely. She feared it meant she felt something other than hatred for the Norman.

Fitz Autier waited for Osric to make the first slash, but dodged the blow and delivered one of his own. Aelia felt no fear for her brother; 'twas obvious that the baron used a mere fraction of his strength as he cut and jabbed at Osric. He gave instructions to the boy as they parried, and Aelia sensed an unusual connection between them.

But she did not have a chance to ponder that thought as a ragged group of travelers came into sight at the far edge of the field. There was only one man among them, along with two women and three children. As they came closer, Aelia could see that one of the women carried an infant, too.

Fitz Autier pushed Osric behind him as he took a stance indicating he was ready for battle. Aelia noticed then that he had his horn slung over his shoulder, so he could call for help if 'twas needed, but he said something quietly to Osric, then addressed the intruders.

They seemed not to understand him.

Aelia rose to her feet as they came closer. Fitz Autier addressed them again, but they replied in English. They were Saxons. Unarmed, filthy and weary, they were as haggard and woebegone as anyone Aelia had ever seen. The children's eyes were hollow and dull, and none of them spoke.

Fitz Autier bent slightly to Osric again, though he never took his eyes from the group of Saxons as he told the boy what to say.

"Who are you?" Osric asked them.

"I am Cuthbert of Bruenwald," the man replied. "Our fields were burned, our cottage destroyed, my shop overrun. We have no place... My children are starving." Warily, the Saxon watched Fitz Autier as he spoke, though he had to know his words would not be understood by the warrior who stood with his sword drawn before him. "This is my wife, Odelia, my sister, Wilda."

Osric translated.

"He had a shop? What is his trade?"

"I am a woodworker," he replied.

"Tell him to come with us to camp," Fitz Autier said. "Say they are welcome to a meal."

Osric followed Fitz Autier's instructions, and the group fell into step behind the Norman leader.

Mathieu let Osric lead the way, and followed behind the beggarly Saxons. It did not surprise him to see Aelia awaiting them in the woods, but the unmerciful punch of arousal that hit him at the sight of her was unprecedented. He knew her taste and the feel of her breast in his hand.

And he wanted more.

She did not meet his eyes, and the hint of a blush colored her cheeks when the group joined her. Yet she had no reason to feel embarrassed. She had been right to stop his advances the night before.

She would never know how difficult it had been for him to leave her there in the tent, so beautiful and so aroused. But he was beyond the point of slaking his lust with her, only to hand her over to King William to do with her as he pleased.

Even the boy had become something more than just a captive. He was a bright lad, and anxious to learn all that Mathieu could teach him. Mathieu closed his hands into fists and walked behind the Saxons, keeping his eyes averted from Aelia's comely form as she joined the group and began conversing with them. He was damned if he would allow his dealings with this Saxon beauty to cloud his judgment—or let whispers of an alliance with Aelia of Ingelwald to reach the king's ears, or Simon de Vilot's.

"Cuthbert wants to know if he can travel with us," Osric said. "He doubts he can keep his family safe much longer."

"Ask him where he is headed."

"North," Aelia said, speaking directly to Mathieu for the first time. "They hoped to find a Saxon holding that is safe from Normans." She held the Saxon infant close to her breast, caressing its head, murmuring soft words. With its silvery-blond curls, it might have been mistaken for Aelia's own child, the one she would have in a year or two, after King William married her to a Norman knight.

Mathieu moved ahead of her and led them into camp. Osbern still lay near the fire, conscious, but in pain. The gash on the back of his head needed sewing, but they had not brought any thread or needles. Instead, they'd wrapped a cloth 'round his head and bade him to lie quietly by the fire.

Mathieu did not know how long 'twould take before the man stopped retching every time he moved. His injury was going to hold them there indefinitely, but Mathieu was suddenly impatient to be traveling again. The sooner he got Aelia to London, the better.

After a short conversation with one of the Saxon women, Aelia turned to Mathieu. "Wilda was a healer in their village. I told her what happened to Sir Osbern, and she says she can make a potion to ease his malaise."

Mathieu stopped pacing. "Do you know of such potions?"

"Aye," Aelia said. "A decoction of tree bark is said to ease pain."

Mathieu nodded at the woman, but spoke to Aelia. "See that she does him no harm. Guatier, bring your bow and come with me." He picked up Osbern's bow and stalked out of camp, leaving Raoul in charge.

'Twas unlikely there would be a better time to hunt, and Mathieu intended to take advantage of it. He would decide later what was to be done about Osbern if he was not ready to travel upon the morrow.

He and Guatier collected their horses, saddled them and rode far afield until they found a likely spot to scare up a wild pig or some other game. They hobbled the horses, slung their bows over their shoulders and found a tree to climb and wait for their prey.

They settled themselves upon branches that were high enough to keep them away from danger, yet provided a good perch from which to shoot. Mathieu hoped it would take all day. He did not want to return to camp, where Aelia would be mothering the Saxon child.

Mathieu gazed out at the woods and tried to banish

Aelia from his mind. He did not want to think about her, or the way he'd left her the previous night. He did not want to think about turning her over to the king.

Wilda seemed to be a healer of some skill, Aelia thought. Only an hour after Osbern had drunk the woman's potion, he was able to sit up without pain, though he did not do much else. Aelia bathed his head with cool cloths, and gave him sips of water as he recovered. The rest of their Norman guards took turns sleeping or playing at dice, while at least one of them remained alert and on watch. Halig hovered nearby, but he was not trustful of the other Saxons, and so he remained guarded.

The newcomers were quiet in camp, wary of the Norman warriors, seemingly uncertain of Aelia's and Osric's positions here, and unnerved by Halig's warlike devotion to Aelia. Without a doubt they made an odd party of travelers.

Aelia opened the satchel Raoul had given her earlier, and found clothes for the two women, to replace the rags they wore. There was naught for Cuthbert, but Odelia and Aelia managed to fit the children with cloth from a tunic that Guilliaume gave her, saying it no longer suited him.

Aelia discovered her recorder hidden deep within the satchel, and wondered at Fitz Autier's reason for bringing it. Had he done it out of kindness?

She pulled the instrument out, caressed it, and remembered the hours she'd spent watching Beorn carve it just for her, then learning from his wife how to make music with it. She felt a sharp stab of homesickness, and put the recorder, as well as her sad memories, away.

Fitz Autier remained absent all afternoon, but Osbern's head seemed to improve with every hour. Aelia did not doubt that they would return to the road upon the morrow.

"Will you continue north?" Aelia asked Odelia. She took the woman's bairn and held it on her lap, while the other three children stayed close to their mother. They did not smile, or try to run off and play. 'Twas a sign of the war-torn times.

Odelia shook her head. "'Tis dangerous to travel, and winter will soon be upon us. I…I do not know what will happen to us."

"No doubt we will camp here at least another night," Aelia said. "I am certain Fitz Autier will allow you to remain with us until we leave."

The Saxon woman paled. "Fitz Autier? That is the demon Fitz Autier?"

"He's—"

"We heard of his atrocities, Aelia. We cannot stay here among—"

"No, Odelia, you don't understand."

"He burned Ingelwald to the ground and killed all the men."

"That is untrue. Ingelwald was never—"

"Aye, it is. Riders came into Bruenwald," Odelia said as she started to gather her few belongings together. She took the infant from Aelia's arms. Her husband, noting Odelia's agitation, joined them. "The riders told us Fitz Autier butchered Ingelwald's lord and lady, and hung their bodies—"

"Odelia, stop. *I* am the lady of Ingelwald."

"Come with us!" Odelia said. "We can go away now, while the demon is away hunting. We'll find a place to hide."

"Please. 'Tis true Fitz Autier conquered Ingelwald, but there were no atrocities. He butchered no one."

"The baron is Fitz Autier?" asked Cuthbert. He kept his voice low, taking care not to frighten the children. 'Twas clear to Aelia that Fitz Autier's ruthless reputation was known to all—not just in the lands he conquered. Yet she knew 'twas inaccurate. He'd tried to deal peacefully with Selwyn, trading her and Osric for a truce. He had only gone to battle when her Saxon betrothed had refused to submit to him.

"But it is said, all over the countryside, that he is a ruthless mercenary, a killer of women and children."

"He killed no women or children at Ingelwald," Aelia said. "He dealt fairly and honestly with my people. I assure you, Fitz Autier will not harm you. He will see that you and your children are well fed, and then allow you to go on your way."

Aelia knew this was true. Mathieu Fitz Autier might be a ferocious warrior, but he was no killer of the innocent. He was undeserving of his ruthless reputation, although it seemed that tales of his barbaric victories were being spread intentionally. Likely it worked to intimidate Saxon leaders into surrendering their lands with less trouble.

In frustration, she turned away from Odelia and walked through the woods toward the field where they'd first laid eyes upon the Saxon travelers. Aelia did not know why she cared what these people thought of Fitz Autier. He had been less than fair with her, taking her from her home and everything that was familiar, and making her feel things no honorable woman should feel for another woman's husband.

Chapter Sixteen

Mathieu was greeted with wary looks from the Saxons when he returned. The two women were not wearing the same rags as when he'd last seen them, and Mathieu had no doubt that what they now wore were the clothes he'd brought for Aelia. And she was likely wearing the same green kirtle that was worn and tattered from their days upon the road…and his rough handling of it the previous night.

Mathieu blew out a deep breath. At least Osbern looked better. 'Twas likely they would be able to continue on their way in the morning.

"Henri and Guilliaume, go and help Guatier with the meat," he said.

"You killed a deer?" asked Osric.

"No, a boar. A small one, but there will be plenty of food."

"I want to go, too, baron," the boy said.

Osric had not posed it as a respectful request, but at least he'd called him "baron" instead of spitting out his name disdainfully, as was his habit. 'Twas progress.

Mathieu nodded, glancing 'round the camp for Aelia.

"Aye," he said to Osric. "But you are under Guatier's command. If you cause any trouble, I give him leave to bind your hands and feet and drag you back here behind his horse."

"I will not trouble anyone," Osric said. "When was the last time I—"

"Enough. You have permission. Now tell me, where is your sister?"

The boy shrugged. "She was here a moment ago."

Mathieu had not seen her on the way back to camp, so he went searching in the direction of the field where they had met the Saxon family earlier in the day.

'Twas not safe for her to wander alone. She had to realize that there were others displaced by war, and not all would be as benign as Cuthbert's family. Men like Durand, for example.

"Are you looking for me, seignior?"

He looked 'round, but did not see her until he glanced up into the trees. There she sat, perched in an ancient oak, sitting upon a high limb. She was barely visible in her dark green clothes.

"Do you need help to come down?"

"I'm safer up here."

"Do you doubt I can protect you?"

She shook her head. "From an outside intruder, aye..."

He threw one leg over the pommel of his horse and slid to the ground. "But not from myself?"

"You are the one who said it, seignior."

'Twas best to let Aelia continue to believe he was already wed, since he seemed to lose all discipline when he was close to her. Even now, he had a nearly irresistible urge to climb up after her.

"You gave your clothing away," he said.

She nodded and started to climb down. "They had greater need than I."

"Until now," he muttered when he heard something tear. "Are you certain you don't need help?"

The view was enticing as Aelia pushed her skirts aside to descend. Mathieu could not turn away. Unbidden, a picture of her without those skirts came to his mind, and he realized he must look away if he was to avoid repeating his mistake of the night before.

He had only come to assure her safety, not to seduce her.

She swung down to the lowest branch and sat upon it, her hips about level with his shoulders. He reined in the urge to slide his hands 'round her waist to help her descend, and turned away as she dropped down.

"Was your hunt successful?" she asked.

He nodded. "We'll have food enough to feed the Saxons—and send them on their way with meat."

"That is generous of you."

He watched her brush the dirt from the back of her gown. "I'm thinking of sending them to Ingelwald. Is there another carpenter there, now that Beorn is dead?"

Aelia stopped abruptly and frowned up at him. "You would send strangers to my home?" Her voice was ominously unsteady. "You take Osric and me away from Ingelwald, yet these Saxons—unknown to you until today—will have your consent to go there?"

Her eyes filled with tears, but she said no more. She backed away from him, then started to run through the trees.

Mathieu caught up to her quickly, grabbed her arm and spun her 'round to face him. A crystal tear slid down her cheek, but he refused to be swayed by it. His heart had been hardened by years of warfare. He cared for naught but the spoils of war.

"Do not run from me, *demoiselle!* None of us knows what danger lurks within these woods."

"What do you care what happens to me?"

She slapped his hand away from her arm and turned from him. He could not help but note the shaky movement of her shoulders as she took a deep breath.

"I have yet to fail in my duty to the king. I will not do so today." He took hold of her once again and led her back to the place where he'd left his horse.

She did not speak, but maintained a tenuous silence until they reached the camp. Mathieu told himself 'twas better this way. If she stayed angry and distant, he would not be so tempted to take her back into the woods and lay her upon the soft moss, where he would kiss her tears away and make her forget her name and the reason for going to London.

Aelia would never be able to get Osric to leave with her, not with his belly full of boar meat and beans. While he sat with Fitz Autier, imitating the baron by carving some nonsense into a piece of wood, Aelia paced the edges of camp, trying to decide what to do.

She did not begrudge Cuthbert and his family a place at Ingelwald. On the contrary, they were more than welcome to make a home for themselves there. But Aelia wanted to return there, too. She missed her home and everyone familiar to her. Even Nelda.

And Aelia could not bear to spend another day with Fitz Autier, the bastard knight who thought of her as nothing more than a task to perform for the Norman king.

Would she be able to steal a horse during the night?

Osbern was sure to sleep soundly, as would Sir Hugh. That left only six knights and Fitz Autier to impede her. Surely Halig was still loyal and would help her.

"Aelia, look what I made!" Osric held up the block of wood he'd been carving. He'd sat next to the Norman baron, working alongside him as if they were brothers. Or father and son.

When had their animosity for each other cooled?

In the past few days, Osric had lost his belligerence for the Normans. Had Aelia not seen it with her own eyes, she would never have believed Fitz Autier was teaching her brother how to handle a sword, or giving him patient instructions on carving a figure from a block of wood.

She did not understand why Osric's attitude had softened. Fitz Autier had not let up on the boy—the discipline and punishments continued. Osric was still required to take care of the horses each night before seeing to his own needs, and perform many other tasks as they traveled. This afternoon, he'd even helped the men carve the pig and hang the sacks of meat from a tree in the distance in order to avoid attracting predators.

He was one of them now.

Fitz Autier's long legs were stretched out before him as he carved, the muscles relaxed, his feet crossed at the ankles. But Aelia knew he was not at ease. His body and mind were alert as always, watching and listening for anything that threatened their small group.

"'Tis a fine carving, Osric," Aelia said absently.

"No, you haven't really looked," Osric said, rising to his knees. "Come closer. It's a horse. See?"

Reluctantly, Aelia approached her brother and reached for the block of wood that he'd carved into the vague shape of a horse. She could not help but notice the work Fitz Autier had done on his own piece. She did not want to look at it or even acknowledge it, but could not deny that it was beautiful. The Norman had an artist's eye and a master's skill.

He'd carved the head and antlers of a powerful deer, making it appear as if the animal was emerging from the wood. 'Twas an accurate likeness of a virile beast, almost a symbol of Fitz Autier's own potency.

She slid her fingers over the wooden horse in her hand and swallowed. "I like it very much, Osric."

"Look at what the baron has made!"

"Aye. I see."

"'Tis to be the crest of his house. A mighty stag."

"*His* house, Osric?" Her voice was taut. "'Tis *our* land!" She turned to Fitz Autier. "Where will you hang it, baron? In my father's hall? Upon the gate? Mayhap 'twill grace the wall above your bed!"

She whirled and stormed away as tears of anger threatened to blind her.

Mathieu did not believe Aelia had gotten much sleep. She'd given up her tent to the children, and laid her blanket out to take her rest underneath the spreading boughs of a pine near the edge of camp. He watched her awaken, her body stretching, her eyes opening, awareness dawning.

Her posture stiffened as soon as she remembered her situation, and she glanced 'round, finally catching sight of him. Their eyes met, but she soon turned away, as if burned by his glance.

He could easily imagine slipping his legs between hers and pulling her close. He would warm her chilled body with his kisses, and heat her blood with his caress.

Looking for a diversion, he pushed himself to his feet

and walked away from camp. First he checked the
horses, as was his habit, then walked to the tree where
the meat had been stored for future use. 'Twas the same
tree Aelia had climbed the day before, the place where
he'd watched her descend from one limb to the next.

He shook his head to get her out of it, then walked
much farther afield, until he came to the small stream
near the place where they'd shot yesterday's boar. He
ripped off his tunic, knelt beside the water, scooping
some to wash his face and head, sluicing it over his
chest.

He had never spent so much thought on one woman.
Could he toss her down, spread her legs, use her and be
done with her once and for all?

Whipping his head back to shake off the water, he
started toward camp again with purpose in his stride. He
would not be the first conqueror to take his pleasure
with a captive. He had no use for her objections—or
even his own. He was fooling himself to think he was
a better man than his half brothers or his father, who
took whatever wenches they desired and damned the
consequences.

Mathieu's anticipation grew as he crossed the field
and entered the trees at the perimeter of the camp. He
could take her away from the group, carry her back to
the water's edge, where there was a mossy bank. There,
they would lie together in privacy until he had appeased
the fierce need that burned within him.

Saxon voices met his ears, and when he entered
camp, he saw that Osric and the English travelers were
deep in discussion. Aelia stood well beyond the fire,
gathering her belongings with Sir Guatier's assistance,
while Henri shook the leaves from her blanket and
folded it for her. The other men saddled and packed the

horses, ignoring the argument between Cuthbert and Osric. Their attention was on Aelia.

Mathieu turned away from the woman, placed his hands upon his hips and spoke to Osric. "What is it?" he growled.

The boy looked up at him. "They want Aelia and me to leave here and go with them."

"No."

Aelia called over to him in a dismissive tone. "I already told them you would not let us go."

Mathieu speared her with a glance. She did not stop what she was doing, or look up from the blanket she was folding. She'd braided her hair into a long, thick plait that brushed her hips, and had put on a new kirtle and bliaut. 'Twas the color of some flower Mathieu had noticed growing wild in the fields, and it brought out the blush in her cheeks, the only outward sign of her anger.

His muscles clenched at the sight of her, at the sound of her voice. He looked away, gritting his teeth. "You are my prisoners, by God."

A crash sounded in Aelia's vicinity, but Mathieu did not glance her way to see what caused it. She was not the only angry one here.

His men hurried to help her, and Mathieu knew there would be no bedding the woman. Every one of his warriors—and Halig—had become her champion. None would stand idly by if he dragged her off to the river.

As if he would. He *was* a better man than his father.

"Tell these Saxons," he said to Osric, as Raoul brought his horse 'round, "that they are welcome to go to Ingelwald."

"To Ingelwald? But that's—"

"*My* holding. I have need of a carpenter there."

He mounted up and spoke to Raoul. "Break camp.

Bring the prisoners and follow me on the southern road."

"Baron?"

"I will see you at noon."

"But Lady Aelia—"

"Don't leave her alone with the boy."

He kicked his heels into the mare's sides and rode out toward the road that led south. To London.

Chapter Seventeen

Fitz Autier had said it intentionally. He'd wanted to hurt her.

And he'd succeeded.

He was sending Cuthbert and his family to her home, while she had no choice but to leave it forever.

It made her too ill to eat, and nearly too ill to ride.

Sir Guatier managed to keep her secure in front of him, while Osric rode with Henri. Halig, as usual, stayed close by.

"How much longer will it be until we reach London?" Aelia asked. She was glad she rode with Guatier, since he was more talkative than the other men. 'Twas not so easy to hate him, even though he was a Norman.

"Another week at least, if all goes well. But I think the baron will want to stay a night or two at Rushton."

"Why?"

Guatier shrugged. "The Norman lord of Rushton is an old friend of Fitz Autier."

They rode in silence for a time, but the question that burned hottest in Aelia's mind soon came out. "Does Fitz Autier's wife await him in London?"

"His wife?"

"Aye."

"The baron is unmarried."

Aelia did not know how she kept her body from reacting to Guatier's statement, even as her mind careened in shock. She took a deep breath. "Sir Auvrai spoke of the baron's wife."

Guatier shook his head. "I heard talk of a betrothal, but I'm certain I would know if the baron had wed before we left Rouen. Or London."

Aelia was disgusted with herself for caring whether the man was married or not. His lack of a wife changed naught.

Yet there was an unrelenting connection between them—whether he was arguing with her or kissing her. 'Twas unconscionable for him to have allowed her to keep believing he had a wife. How many hours had she wondered about the woman, and whether or not he had children?

"Baron Mathieu has the king's favor. 'Tis said that he will marry well," the knight stated.

Aelia wanted to hear no more, so she kept her silence, and Guatier did the same as they continued their journey south. It began to rain steadily, and they stopped long enough to pull cloaks over their clothes.

They finally stopped for a meal after Osric complained of hunger, but the only sign that Fitz Autier had passed this way was a strip of leather Raoul found hanging from a low bough that bordered the narrow road.

"He's gone on," said Raoul.

"Is he…is everything all right?" Aelia asked Raoul. "I mean…there does not seem to be any trouble…."

"No. 'Tis a sign for us to go on."

"You have such signals already arranged?"

"Aye. Had anything been amiss, he would have dropped a spur."

The day grew colder as they rode, due to a chilling, autumn wind that blustered down from the north and cut through their wet cloaks, and the rain, which became even heavier. Guatier blocked the worst of it with his body, but Aelia found herself shivering until she could almost hear her bones rattling.

The night was going to be a misery, even worse than today. Aelia did not know how they would make a fire to warm themselves, and the small canvas tents would provide little protection against the penetrating wet. She wished Fitz Autier was with them so she could castigate him for taking her away from Ingelwald, only to die of exposure to the elements.

They continued on for hours, with Raoul setting a faster pace after the horses had had a short respite. Aelia started talking, to take her mind off her chattering teeth and hands that were so cold she could hardly move her fingers. "Is it always like this for you Norman soldiers?"

"Like what?" Guatier asked. "Cold and wet?"

"And on horseback day after day."

"No, my lady," he replied. "The baron gives us leave to do as we will when we're not under his orders."

"I doubt that occurs very often."

"Aye, well, not much since we came to England with King William. But we have our freedom often enough."

"What do you do?"

"Er…"

"Something unsavory, then?"

"Mayhap in a maiden's opinion, my lady."

"Drinking?"

"Aye."

"Wenching?"

"Some."

She shivered. The cold was becoming unbearable. "Will we stop soon?"

"I do not know, my lady. Sir Raoul is in charge."

Aelia wrinkled her nose. "I smell smoke."

She heard Guatier sniff behind her. "I believe you're right."

"Ride up to Raoul and ask him if we might stop awhile and warm ourselves near this fire."

Aelia no sooner asked this than they turned a curve in the road and came upon a manor house that had seen better times. There was a stable and another smaller building nearby, along with four small cottages.

Aelia did not care who owned the house. She could only think of the warmth she would find inside.

As they rode up to the main entrance, two men stepped outside. One was Fitz Autier, and Aelia's temper flared when she saw him. She averted her eyes and allowed Guatier to help her down. Her legs failed her with her first step, but her knight escort was quick to keep her from falling. She felt Fitz Autier's eyes upon her and cursed the weakness of her legs while he watched.

"Henri, take the horses to the stable," he said. "Raoul, get the boy inside. A hot meal will soon be served, and there are rooms for us all." With that, he turned and went inside.

Aelia did not hesitate to follow him, but she was greeted by the matron of the house before she could get to the fire. "Lady Aelia?"

"Aye."

"I am the innkeeper's wife, Diera," she said, leading her away from the men. "We speak little of the French tongue—only enough to know how many of you were coming, and that you and your small brother would be needing warmth."

"Aye. We're chilled to the bone."

"Our best chamber has been made ready for you," Diera said. "There's a fire blazing and a hot bath awaiting you."

"May God bless you, Diera," Aelia said as she followed the woman up the stairs. They were joined by two young girls, who were introduced as Eda and May, the woman's daughters. "Do you know where they've taken my brother?"

"To the hearth in the common room. We will serve the men their supper there. Do you wish to take yours below stairs with them, or would you prefer it in your room?"

Diera pushed open the door to a chamber where a fire blazed cozily upon the hearth, even as the rain lashed brutally against the narrow windowpanes. Aelia shuddered at the sight, but warmed again when her eyes lit upon the bed, with its thick hangings pushed back to reveal a soft feather mattress within.

'Twas the large tub of steaming water standing in the center of the room that made Aelia decide to forgo supper with the Normans.

Besides, she had no desire to see Fitz Autier until her temper receded again.

"Have you any dry clothes?" the proprietress asked.

"Not likely," Aelia replied. "My only other kirtle is in a canvas satchel that was probably soaked in the rain. I have nothing else."

Diera clucked her tongue. "Come and take off what you're wearing. I'll see that it dries while Eda and May help you with your bath and bed."

With the aid of the Saxon girls, Aelia peeled off her

wet things. The chamber was warm, but she shivered until she got into the bath and submerged herself in the hot water.

Using steel tongs, Eda took several hot bricks from the fire and slipped them into cloth sleeves. She then placed the bricks under the heavy covers of the bed to warm it, while May lit a number of tapers all over the room to give more light.

Diera returned soon, carrying a tray laden with food—a hot potage as well as bread and cheese, and a crock of mulled wine, which she placed upon a table beside the tub. As May scrubbed her back and Diera poured her a cup of the warm wine, Aelia sighed with pleasure. She had thought never to feel such comfort again.

"'Tis enough," she said. "And I thank you. Just let me repose here in the water awhile, and then I shall eat and go to bed."

"Are you certain there is no more we can do for you? Baron Mathieu has paid handsomely for the use of the inn. We're to see to everything."

Aelia shook her head lazily. "Just leave the drying cloth nearby." She was content. She had barely given thought to Fitz Autier and his lies, or to her fate once she reached London. For this short span of time, her spirit was comforted.

May pointed to a bucket of hot water beside the tub. "Here is rinse water, my lady. Use it when you are through, and we'll take the tub away in the morn."

Aelia sighed and smiled as the three women left her to her pleasure.

For the first time since arriving at the inn, Mathieu rested easily. The tension in his limbs loosened and he sat down, leaning back on the bench facing the staircase to await the meal.

And Aelia.

Another kind of tension took over when he thought of her, of the way she'd fallen against Guatier when she'd dismounted. Mathieu had come close to reaching for her, but 'twas clear she was still angry. He had hurt her—had done it intentionally, too. And the ploy had worked well. She wanted naught to do with him.

When Osric clambered over and leaned against Mathieu sleepily, he wondered if the boy would be able to stay awake long enough to eat. He had to remember that Osric was still a child, though he had the will of a grown man.

Mathieu looked up at Raoul, who had discarded his wet cloak to come and sit near the fire. "I trust your ride here was uneventful?"

"Aye," replied the knight. "Except for the cold and rain, 'twas without incident."

"Lady Aelia shook with cold all afternoon," said Guatier, who peeled away his hauberk as he approached.

Mathieu looked up sharply. "Did she not have a cloak?"

"Aye. And I gave her mine, as well. But she seemed chilled through."

He glanced to the stairs once again, but there was no sign of her. "Was she ill?"

Guatier shrugged. "I could not say, baron. Only that she was cold. Shivering."

The women of the house started bringing platters of food to the common room, along with pitchers of ale. The men were warm now, and were starting to fill their bellies, but Osric had fallen asleep. Mathieu roused him enough to feed him a few bites of food, then lifted him up and handed him to one of the men to carry upstairs to bed.

"Knock on Lady Aelia's door and tell her it is my wish that she join us." He only wanted to assure himself that she was healthy. She'd looked pale when she'd arrived at the inn.

"Aye, baron," said Henri as he left with the boy.

Waiting for Aelia became tedious, so Mathieu sat down and began to eat. But he did not enjoy his food as he should.

He listened to the wind howling and the rain pelting the windows, and wondered what had happened to the fair autumn weather they'd enjoyed for the early days of their journey. The harsh turn was difficult even for seasoned soldiers. He did not think the lady and her brother would fare so well.

He wanted to see her.

Henri descended the stairs and found an empty chair. He took a seat and began to eat.

Mathieu glanced at the stairs, then at Henri. "Where is she?"

"Sorry, baron," said Henri. "She said she's not coming down."

"Did you tell her 'twas my request that she join us?"

"Aye." The man raised his hand to his mouth and coughed. "She, er…declined."

The woman still had the power to infuriate him. Mathieu thought he'd burned out his anger and frustration during the long day's ride, but he was mistaken. "Raoul," he said. "Go up and tell the lady 'tis my order that she join us."

Mathieu sat down again and poured a cup of wine. He took a sip and forced himself to relax once again while he waited for her. He would not allow her to see his agitation.

"Baron?"

"What is it?" he barked at Halig, and stopped drumming his fingers on the table.

"If my lady has fatigue…mayhap she should stay, er…sleep." The boy's accent had improved, if not his grammar. And certainly not the sentiment.

"I am in command here, and everyone—women and children included—would do well to understand that."

Halig said no more, and when Raoul came down the stairs alone, pulling his collar from his neck, Mathieu knew what he would say before he'd even opened his mouth. Aelia had defied him.

"My lord…"

Mathieu stood. His blood burned with anger. He did not speak, but took to the stairs himself. She had disobeyed him. Before all his men, she had mocked him.

He stalked to the end of the hall, where he knew her room was located, lifted the latch and shoved the door open.

The room was bathed in soft, flickering light, and Aelia stood in the midst of it, in a tub of water that rose slightly higher than her knees. She held a bucket over her head, allowing the water to pour over her naked body.

Mathieu stood rooted to the floor. His anger left him, only to be replaced by something wholly different, yet fierce and primal. The door swung closed behind him, and with the water splashing over her head, she did not hear him.

He had an unimpeded view of her flank, a smooth expanse of feminine curves, marred by a purple bruise on the side of her hip. There were multiple yellowing bruises on her ribs and arms, but they did not diminish the beauty of her form.

Or his raw desire.

All at once she turned and shrieked, startled by the sight of him. She tried to cover herself, but what she left bare was all the more enticing.

"Out!"

Mathieu closed the distance between them as she crouched and seemed to consider whether 'twould be better to sit down in the tub, or grab the drying cloth that was draped on a nearby chair. She reached for it and nearly fell, but Mathieu caught her.

Careful of her bruises, he took hold of her arms, watching her throat move as she swallowed nervously. Her lips parted as he held her and drew her close.

"You are so beautiful…." he whispered.

"You must leave." Her voice was soft, uncertain.

"Must?"

She shivered and he reached for the cloth. He slipped it 'round her shoulders and slid his hands down her back.

"Please don't."

She continued to tremble as he caressed her. His nostrils flared with the scent of her freshly washed skin and the sight of her lustrous green eyes. He was beyond mild arousal, and more than ready to lay her upon the bed and take his pleasure.

He lifted her into his arms and felt her stiffen against him. "Fear not," he said as his lips brushed her temple. He carried her to the bed and let her slide to the floor. "'Twill be as much your pleasure as mine."

"Do all slaves enjoy the attentions of their masters?"

He ignored her question and pressed the drying cloth to her hair, blotting up the moisture. Then he pulled it 'round her back, drying her there. She stood still, with her eyes closed, and allowed him to tend her as he looked his fill. He slid the cloth slowly and gently across her shoulders, then down to her hips, using it to pull her close. He lowered his head once again, and kissed her.

"You taste of wine," he whispered against her mouth. 'Twas all he could do to keep from trembling like an untried lad. He raised her cup and sipped from it, then held it to her lips, but she turned away.

"You have not eaten."

"I have no hunger."

"I do," he said. "I want you."

She bowed her head and took a deep, shuddering breath. "Do what you will, seignior. I am at your command."

"I have never commanded a woman to submit to me," he said. His throat felt raw as he said it, but not nearly as raw as his nerves.

"I am your prisoner. Your slave. I will do what is required," she said. "I only ask that you…be patient with me, as this is my first… I—I have never…"

Her breath came out in a shuddering rush of air and when Mathieu saw her tears, he released her arms. He dropped the drying cloth, clenching his hands into tight fists. 'Twas not at all how he'd envisioned their lovemaking.

"You are no slave."

She looked up at him, her body naked but for the curtain of damp hair that draped her back. "Then I have a choice here?"

He silenced her with his mouth upon hers. She started to pull away, but Mathieu was unrelenting. He stroked her lips and parted them with his tongue.

A moment later, he pulled away. "There will come a day, Aelia, when you will have no wish to refuse me."

* * *

That day had already come.

Aelia stood silent and shivering in her chamber as the door closed behind Fitz Autier. She shut her eyes and sank onto the bed, pulling its blanket 'round her.

What had she done?

She'd sent away the man whose very presence made her body hum with a force she could not name. 'Twas more than anything her mother had foretold. Though Aelia felt the same shocking awareness whenever Fitz Autier was near, some other, equally potent force drew her to him.

She lay quietly for a long time, half listening to the comings and goings in the corridor outside her door, until all was finally still and she could think.

Naught that was said about the man was true. He was no barbarian butcher. Fitz Autier had spared as many lives as possible at Ingelwald, and begun to rebuild and restore her father's holding, allowing the people to return to their work and their homes. He'd even spared the lives of the Saxons they'd met the day before, sending them to safety at Ingelwald when he could have left them to their wanderings. He'd been patient with Osric when another Norman might have killed the boy and been done with him after the incident with the horse.

Instead, the baron had devised a punishment that was severe but not harsh. And in so doing, Osric had learned to value the steeds that carried them over miles of rough terrain every day. Aelia's brother was maturing.

And Aelia feared she was falling in love with Mathieu Fitz Autier.

She ached with the need for his touch, and her body still trembled with the power of his kiss. She'd wanted more, but she could not merely submit to him as his captive. She was no harlot.

Pulling the blanket tightly 'round herself, she lay back upon the bed and curled into a ball. She'd rejected the one man she would ever love.

Soon they would reach London and he would turn her over to his king, who would have her wed a Norman warrior. And Aelia would have no choice in the matter.

Would Fitz Autier care?

Why should he, when he was destined to marry a Norman woman and take her back to Ingelwald? 'Twas a rich holding, and now that he possessed it, he had no use for Aelia.

And what would happen to Osric? Fitz Autier had never said what he intended to do with the boy. Would she be separated from him? Aelia sat up abruptly. She would never allow it. Osric was just a small boy. He needed her.

She climbed out of the bed and slipped on the thick chemise that had been left for her, then tied the laces at the neck. 'Twas an adequate enough covering and would have to do, since she had no other.

Taking a candle to light her way, she lifted the latch on her chamber door and slipped out into the gallery. 'Twas dark and quiet, and it seemed that no one was about. She did not know which of the rooms was Osric's, and she was reluctant to begin tapping upon doors to find out. Instead, she headed toward the common room, in hopes of finding Sir Guatier, or mayhap Diera, who could tell her where to find her brother.

As she descended the stairs, she saw that there was little light in the common room, likely only that coming from the fire in the grate. The room was silent and it seemed that no one was about until she heard the creak of wood and a muted groan. Curious, Aelia lifted her candle and entered the room.

One man lounged in a chair, with his feet propped upon one of the tables. Two pitchers sat upon the same table, and another dangled from his fingers, precariously close to the floor.

"Seignior," Aelia said.

"Ah, 'tis the fair Aelia." Mathieu Fitz Autier slurred his words as he raised his cup of ale and drank. Aelia had never seen him so relaxed. So inebriated.

She looked about the room and saw no one else, no one to help her get him up the stairs and into his bed.

"Baron, 'tis late." The pitchers on the table were empty, and she managed to catch the one in his hand before it slipped from his fingers. At least there was a bit more ale in that one, but it was clear Fitz Autier had imbibed too much. He would give her no answers about Osric tonight. "Mayhap you should go to your room," she said, placing her hand gently upon his shoulder.

"Alone? No. I crave the company of a fair maid tonight."

"You need sleep."

"But not jus' any fair maid," he said, taking her hand and pressing a kiss to its palm. "There is only one whose lips I would taste...."

Aelia's heart beat faster, but she knew 'twas the drink talking. She could not believe anything he said in this state.

Taking hold of his arm, she tried to pull him up from the chair, but he did not budge. He gathered a lock of her hair and pressed it to his face. "Smells like wildflowers."

"The soap was scented," she said, extricating her hair from his hand. "Can you stand?"

"'Course I can."

"Come on, then."

"Is that an invitation?"

"No, seignior, I only—"

He made a deceptively quick move and managed to pull Aelia into his lap. "You have the most amazing mouth."

She tried to get up, but he had a firm grasp 'round her waist. He tipped his head down and kissed her. 'Twas not a punishing kiss like the one he'd given her before leaving her chamber, but gentle and sweet. "Baron—"

"Mathieu. My name is Mathieu." His voice was soft and seductive, and as he touched his lips to her jaw and her ear, then trailed soft kisses down her throat, Aelia could hardly breathe.

She swallowed. "M-Mathieu…"

"'Tis a sweet sound upon your lips," he said. "So much better than the shock I feel every time I see you."

"Shock?"

"Aye." He nuzzled a particularly sensitive spot below her ear. "When I first laid eyes upon you, I felt the ground shift under my feet."

Aelia pushed away from him. "The ground shifted?" She could hardly think when he fondled her breast through the soft wool of the chemise. "Mathieu, you should stop—"

"No. You are mine. You will never belong to another."

A shimmering pleasure ran through her at his touch, at his words. Had he really felt the same force of recognition that her mother had foretold, or were these just drunken ramblings? How could she push him away if he was truly the one?

"Every time I see you, 'tis as if someone set fire to

my blood." He drew her close and kissed her. His lips stroked hers, his tongue sliding into her mouth, and she did not want to resist him.

Chapter Eighteen

The rain continued for another full day. Unfortunately, Mathieu could not blame his headache or sour mood upon it. He had only a vague recollection of the previous night's debauchery. Without a doubt, he'd consumed too much ale. That was the only reason he had imagined Aelia in the common room with him…sitting in his lap as he kissed and fondled her.

He narrowed his eyes against the faint light coming in through his chamber window. He'd always tolerated his drink well. It must be his preoccupation with Aelia that had addled his brain.

He'd told his men to plan on staying another day if the rain continued. By the sound of it pattering against his window, it had not let up in the least. But one day's delay in the warm comfort of the inn would not be amiss, especially since they journeyed with Aelia and the boy. The two were unaccustomed to the harsh conditions of travel.

A knock at the chamber door drew Mathieu from his bed. He opened it to Osric, who stepped past him into the room. "'Tis late, baron! Will you take me to the stable and practice with swords today?"

The lad's voice stabbed through Mathieu's head and he winced. "Later, boy. Mayhap later."

Then he saw Aelia and had to grab hold of the door-jamb to steady himself. She looked different today.

"Hush, Osric. The baron does not feel well and your chattering only makes it worse." She looked up at him. "I brought you this…the same potion Wilda used on Osbern's headache."

He took the mug she offered and raised it to his lips as he tried to determine what had changed. Her clothes were the same as she'd worn the day before, but they were clean now, as was her face and her hair.

'Twas her eyes that were different.

"Drink it all at once, seignior," she said when he hesitated. "'Twill do no harm, I promise."

He had a most disturbing thought—was it a memory?—of Aelia with her head tilted back as he kissed his way down her throat. Her eyes had been soft then, too.

Mathieu tipped his head back and downed the draught, wincing at its bitter taste. How could he have such a strong memory of Aelia's hands slipping 'round to the back of his neck to caress him, when he knew he'd left her alone in her chamber?

He did not wish to examine too closely the anger that had sent him away from her, but he knew that was the reason he'd overindulged in drink. 'Twas not his habit to drown his frustrations in ale, but last night had been an exception.

"Will you let me practice with Guatier, baron?" Osric asked. "Sir Raoul will surely allow me to use his sword!"

"Go away, Osric, and let the baron rest."

"But I—"

"Now."

Osric started to protest, but Aelia turned him around and took him outside, while Mathieu sat down in a chair and lowered his head into his hands, grateful to be left alone in his misery. It had been years since the last time he'd felt so low.

"Lean back."

Mathieu looked up so suddenly his ears rang.

"Sorry. I did not mean to startle you," said Aelia, who had obviously not left with her brother. She stood behind him and placed her hands upon his shoulders.

"'Twould be best if you left me to suffer in peace."

"The decoction should work soon, but this will help."

"No, I…"

A sorceress could have worked no more potent magic. She kneaded his shoulders and neck, then slid her fingers through his hair to press on the parts of his skull that pounded from the inside out, and the pain eased.

"My father sometimes overindulged," she said softly, "and I helped him this way."

Her touch was too good to be true. Mathieu could have let her continue indefinitely, but reason prevailed, and he stood up and went to the door. "This is a very bad idea," he said, more to himself than to Aelia. 'Twas strange that she was suddenly willing to act as his personal slave.

But his brain wasn't working well enough to figure it out.

Within the hour, however, his head had improved, and he spent much of the day away from the inn—away from Aelia. Most of the men stayed in the common room, playing at dice or chess. Mathieu took his saddle pack to the stable and found a comfortable place to sit and carve. 'Twould settle the restlessness that had plagued him for days.

"Will we be off tomorrow, baron?" asked Osric, who sat beside him, carving his own small statue.

"Aye."

"What if it's still raining?"

"I've never known a warrior deterred by a rain shower."

"Then why are we stopped here?"

Mathieu's knife slipped. "'Twas time for a rest."

"Do your men tire of travel, then?" the boy asked.

"You insult my men. Of course they don't," he said, aware that he was contradicting himself.

"Well, I don't understand—"

Mathieu stood abruptly and went to the open door of the stable. "There are many things you will not understand until you are grown, boy." In spite of the cool autumn air and the constant rain, 'twas warm inside with the heat of all their horses.

Mathieu stood under the lintel and looked across the yard at the inn, a stone-and-timber building with narrow windows in the walls of the upper and lower floors, and wondered if Aelia had joined his men in the common room. Mayhap she craved the company of her fellow Saxons and had joined the innkeeper's family.

"You stopped for my sister," Osric said with a hint of taunting in his tone.

Mathieu gritted his teeth. "We travel at the pace I choose," he said angrily. "If we stop it is with good reason." It galled him that the boy was right and that his motivation was so transparent. Never in his life had Mathieu altered his plans for a woman, and 'twas time he took his duty into account. "We will leave upon the morrow. Regardless of the weather."

* * *

The rain stopped sometime during the night, for which Aelia was grateful, though there was not much else to lift her spirits.

Fitz Autier had stayed away all the previous day. When he'd turned up for supper with Osric in tow, he'd eaten and retired to his chamber, barely sparing her a glance.

Aelia wondered if she'd been mistaken about what she'd heard when he'd rambled in his drunken state. Mayhap all he'd experienced was a surge of anger when he'd first seen her. Or annoyance when he realized he'd been wounded by a *woman* in battle.

The horses were saddled and ready for the road when Aelia went outside, only to find that the baron had ridden ahead, leaving orders for the rest of their party to follow. He stayed far ahead of them for the next two days, barely stopping with them for meals and to sleep.

'Twas clear to everyone that he was avoiding her.

On the third day, they reached a large holding, an estate called Rushton, which had been wrested from its Saxon lord the previous year.

"'Tis a massive place," Guatier said. "Mayhap as large as Ingelwald."

"We stayed here one night when we came north," said Henri.

'Twas now under the command of Baron Roger de Saye, and when they rode up the path that led to the gate, Aelia could see that a vast number of Norman soldiers were garrisoned there.

She quaked at the sight of so many of William's men, many of whom turned to gawk at her as they rode past. Though her escort treated her well, there was no doubt she was merely a prisoner, a captive on her way to her fate at the hand of their king. And all of these Normans knew it.

"What will we do here?" she asked.

"Baron Fitz Autier awaits us," Guatier replied. "'Tis likely we'll spend the night and be on our way again tomorrow."

"Aye," added Henri. "Roger de Saye is an old friend of the baron."

Aelia felt uneasy as they entered through the gate. Soldiers and workmen seemed to be everywhere, and several of the buildings within the walls had only recently been built. The largest of these was a long, low structure that seemed to be the soldiers' quarters.

Accommodations for hundreds.

Near the center of the property was the lord's hall. 'Twas at least three stories high, with a tower that extended even higher. The building was grand, made mostly of stone, and had banners hanging from the highest points.

"There's the baron," Guatier said.

Fitz Autier stepped out of one of the buildings with another man. The two were dressed similarly, in hauberks with their swords at their sides. But there was no comparison beyond that. Mathieu towered over the other man, his shoulders broad, his features starkly handsome. A familiar shudder of attraction flared through Aelia at the sight of him.

He was her captor and she should feel naught but hatred for him. But she could not.

Sir Guatier and the rest of the company dismounted in front of the great hall. As Aelia placed her hands upon Guatier's shoulders to be helped down, she caught sight of Fitz Autier, who glanced at her at the same instant.

Then he looked away, as if she were not of the slightest interest to him.

Aelia's balance faltered and she slipped, but Guatier prevented her from falling, and took her arm. "Is aught amiss, Lady Aelia?"

She shook her head, not trusting her voice, but she had no chance to dwell upon the baron's slight when a matron in a dark brown kirtle and light headgear appeared at the top of the wide wooden staircase that led into the hall and shouted to them.

"This way! This way!" she called impatiently. Flanked by two guards, the woman beckoned Aelia and her escort to enter the hall, then she disappeared inside, expecting them to follow.

Aelia looked in Fitz Autier's direction, but he seemed deeply absorbed in conversation with his companion, and did not glance at her again.

"Who's that?" asked Osric, as wary as Aelia. She half expected him to dig in his heels and demand to speak to the lord here, but Fitz Autier's tutelage had had some effect. Osric was not the same rash child as the boy who'd left Ingelwald.

"I know as much as you." She braced herself and started up the steps, unprepared for whatever awaited her within. Certainly the situation could not be too bad if they were being taken to a chamber within the hall. And 'twas only for one night.

"Why is Fitz Autier not here to see us situated satisfactorily?" Osric asked.

Aelia did not answer, but stepped through the doorway into Rushton's great hall. She had always taken great pride in the grandeur of her father's hall, but Rushton's main room was massive, with furnishings that took her breath away.

A large table with at least sixteen chairs dominated the space, and two maids worked at dusting and polishing them. Two more women swept the floor, while another two spread fresh rushes. There were men setting up trestle tables adjacent to the main table, while others carried in firewood and set it on the hearth.

Aelia was so absorbed by the activity in the hall, she was startled to see the woman in brown standing imperiously, with her hands upon her hips, waiting for them with obvious annoyance.

Aelia put her palm upon Osric's shoulder and followed her to the far end of the hall, to the massive fireplace where a young woman awaited them.

Her age was close to Aelia's, but her bearing was that of one much older, and Aelia realized she must be the lady of Rushton. Garbed in a richly embroidered gown of deep blue, she had beautiful dark hair that was partially covered by the sheerest of veils. Thick chains of gold encircled her neck and waist, and colorful jewels adorned several of her fingers. Though her features were comely, her dark brown eyes were cold and assessing. Aelia knew she would need to tread carefully with this one.

"Lady Hélène, these are the Saxons."

The lady tipped her head back slightly and narrowed her eyes. "A ragged pair, are they not?" she said to the matron as her gaze flickered over Aelia's travel-worn clothes.

Aelia blushed at Lady Hélène's rudeness. Clearly, she did not realize she and Osric understood her words.

Osric started to speak, but Aelia gave his shoulder a squeeze, hoping he would understand the need to keep silent. They had an advantage in their knowledge of the Norman tongue, and Aelia did not want Lady Hélène to be aware of it. At least, not until Aelia knew what was in store for them here.

"I will have her serve as my lady's maid, before tonight's festivities."

"Oh, but my lady—"

"I would enjoy having a Saxon slave," said Hélène. "A high-born woman who should be able to anticipate my needs. Not like these ignorant peasants Sir Bernard keeps sending to me."

The older woman bowed in acquiescence, then called to one of the men. "Beauvais, take this urchin to the stables." Then she made a gesture indicating Aelia was to follow her.

"Go with him, Osric," Aelia said. "'Tis likely you will see Raoul there with the other men."

"But what about you?"

Aelia looked into the eyes of the haughty Lady Hélène as she spoke to her brother. "I'll survive."

"What's got you so restless, Mathieu?" asked Roger de Saye. "Planning to go to battle again?"

Mathieu shook his head. "I hope to be finished with warring."

"Aye. Now that you've got Ingelwald. And Lady Clarise. Have you had any word from the lady since you left London?"

"No."

They left the overheated armorer's shop with its fires raging and the clang of hammers upon steel, and stepped into the fading light of the cool afternoon.

"Well, I suppose that should be no surprise. We've had no travelers stopping at Rushton since you were here last, much to my wife's lament."

De Saye had done much with Rushton in the year since he'd taken possession of the Saxon holding. He'd enlarged the hall, expanded the walls and added space to house the large number of knights who protected these lands. Many of the improvements were changes Mathieu would have to implement at Ingelwald to accommodate all his knights and to make the holding secure.

Mathieu walked across the grounds with Roger, inspecting the new buildings and discussing his plans for administering the estate. He concentrated fully upon Roger's words, aware that he would learn much from his friend's experience.

But when his own knights entered through Rushton's gates, Mathieu could not keep from searching their number for Lady Aelia.

"Your men, no?" asked Roger.

He nodded as his friend spoke of the accommodations for his men. Aelia rode in the midst of them, cloaked in Mathieu's black mantle. Seated upon Sir Guatier's battle horse, she looked small and weary. Guatier leaned forward and spoke into her ear.

Roger glanced at Mathieu's expression when it became clear he wasn't listening to him. "Is aught amiss?"

Mathieu braced himself against the torrent of sensations brought on by the sight of her. "No...you were saying?"

Roger frowned. "You looked as if you just swallowed a bad herring, Mathieu. Are you sure—"

"Certain." He cleared his throat and turned away from Aelia and the men surrounding her. "What were you saying about the knights' quarters?"

"You're sure you want to keep the Saxon boy with your men, Mathieu?"

"Aye."

"And Wallis's daughter?" Roger asked. "She'll be secure in a guest chamber?"

"She is resigned to go to London. We'll have no trouble from her."

Mathieu glanced in her direction once again and caught sight of her as she stumbled, but he knew better than to go to her, or watch as she ascended the stairs to the great hall.

"I've worked up a good thirst," said Roger. "I say we stop in the wine shop before going back to the hall."

Mathieu ducked under the lintel of the tavern and followed Roger. They took seats near the fire and soon a bushy-bearded Saxon brought a couple of mugs to them. He was followed by a young serving maid, who set a plate of bread and cheese upon their table.

"She's a beauty, is she not?"

Mathieu looked up at the girl, who smiled and posed before him with her hands upon her hips and her breasts thrust forward. She ran her tongue over her lips in a blatant invitation. "Saxon?" Mathieu asked.

"Aye. The old man will not stand in your way if you'd care to take her upstairs."

She was comely enough to tempt any man, but Mathieu was unmoved by her beauty, or her willingness to assuage his lust. He lifted his cup, but the memory of his last bout with too much ale made his stomach quake.

"'Twould take the edge off your journey, Mathieu. Do you some good," Roger said as he took a long swallow of his own ale.

"I'll decline for tonight," he said, setting his cup aside. "'Tis nearly time to rejoin your lady wife in the hall."

Roger laughed aloud. "I'm sure I misheard you, old friend."

Mathieu muttered under his breath. There was no good explanation for his lack of interest in the Saxon woman. "It's been a long day." It had to be fatigue.

Roger clapped his mug onto the table and wiped his mouth. "Then mayhap I'll do the honors myself," he said as he stood, taking the girl by the hand and heading for the stairs. "Don't wait for me."

"Aye," Mathieu said with a shrug. "If the maid is willing…"

Roger paused and laughed ruefully. "I forget myself," he said, releasing the lass. "There is much more to show you, and then we shall return to the hall together."

They walked to the gates as Roger explained what additional fortifications he'd made to them and the walls. "I don't really expect trouble from the east," he said, "but Hélène is still apprehensive here, so far from…well, from Rouen, to be honest. She did not care for London, and this land is remote…."

"Your wife is not content at Rushton?" asked Mathieu. He did not understand how the woman could be dissatisfied with her husband's holding. 'Twas a much richer estate than the meager property Roger had held in Normandy. And here in England, he had no overlord but the king himself.

King William had made him a baron. 'Twas not unlike Mathieu's own reward—plentiful lands and a beautiful, noble wife. He and Mathieu were the new lords of the realm and would build their houses in unison.

"Women," said Roger, shaking his head. "They like their comforts, their entertainments. Hélène is far from her mother and her friends. And—" he shrugged "—she prefers them to me. To Rushton."

"No doubt she'll soon become accustomed to England. And you." Mathieu hoped for no less with Clarise.

"Well, she's happy now, overseeing preparations for

a fete in your honor. As I said, 'tis not often we have guests here."

Mathieu scowled. He was in no mood for a celebration, but when they returned to the hall after dark, he discovered that Roger's wife had indeed organized a grand feast.

The lady greeted him warmly, taking his arm to lead him to a table where bowls of fresh water had been set out for hand-washing. Roger followed them, and beckoned a footman to come and take their hauberks. When that task was completed, Roger urged Mathieu to take Lady Hélène's hand and join the throng in the great hall.

The lady was beautiful, dressed in a rich gown of some fabric that flowed seductively about her legs as she walked. Her hair was dressed simply, and partially covered by a veil with small, sparkling beads sewn into it. She was as elegant as he remembered Lady Clarise to be, yet Roger had considered swiving the serving maid at the tavern. By the wench's reaction 'twas clear Roger frequented the place often.

Mathieu did not dwell on his puzzlement over it as they entered the great hall and Roger's highest-ranking retainers and a few women greeted them. Servants were busy lighting the candles upon the dais, and some served ale or wine to all who were present. Minstrels stood near the hearth tuning their instruments, but there was no sign of Mathieu's men.

Or his Saxon captives.

'Twas no wonder Hélène had not adjusted to Rushton. There were very few ladies about, and every one of Roger's soldiers seemed the raw and randy sort. Their warriors' skills had not been in use for too long, and they were raucous and undisciplined, drinking too much and behaving like louts in the great hall.

"Come, have some wine," said Lady Hélène, turning her back to them.

Mathieu took a goblet from her. "Where are my men?"

"I'm sure they'll be here presently," the lady replied.

"And my prisoners?"

Lady Hélène turned a brilliant smile upon him. "They've been dealt with, so you needn't trouble yourself with them tonight, baron."

Her words should have put him at ease, but they did not. "You found a secure chamber for Lady Aelia?"

"Of course. She will stay in my chamber tonight. 'Tis not often a high-born woman comes to Rushton."

Her words made Mathieu inexplicably uneasy.

"What will happen to your prisoners when you arrive in London?" Hélène asked.

"I do not—"

"Likely the same as what the king did with the Wessex Saxons," said Sir Bernard, Roger's chief retainer. "He'll have them stripped naked and driven through town."

"As I recall, they were pelted with cabbages and the like," added Roger with a laugh. "'Twas amusing to watch."

"The meal is about to be served," said Hélène, placing her hand upon Roger's. "If you will escort me to the dais, husband."

The lady sat between Roger and Mathieu, and Mathieu's men arrived shortly. Each one made his bow to their hosts, then found a seat at one of the tables near the dais, as the musicians played a lively melody. Platters of food were set before them, and Mathieu could not help but wonder how Aelia fared, locked away.

Yet he did not ask.

"How do you find Ingelwald, baron?" Hélène asked. "Will you need to make many improvements, as my husband has done here?"

"Aye," he replied. "The gates and walls sustained damage in battle. And the hall is primitive. It needs to be enlarged and improved, but beyond that, I'll leave it to my wife to decide."

"Ah, yes…Clarise de Vilot—she is my cousin, you know."

Mathieu nearly choked on his wine, and he did not know whether 'twas due to Lady Hélène's words, or the sight of Aelia, wearing an apron like the commonest of maids, serving platters of food to Roger's men.

Chapter Nineteen

Mathieu nearly shot out of his chair to go after Aelia, but grabbed hold of the table to steady himself instead. He reminded himself that she was his prisoner, nothing more.

He blew out a breath and calmed down. "I assumed you had confined Lady Aelia to her chamber," he said to Hélène.

The lady laughed. "She is a slave, is she not? And I had need of additional help tonight."

"My lady, you overstep your bounds."

Hélène's cheeks flushed with color, whether in embarrassment or anger, Mathieu could not tell. "She is merely a Saxon, my lord. Likely to be hanged with her brother when King William sees them."

Mathieu clenched his teeth. 'Twas unseemly to make anything of the way she was treated. Hélène was correct. Aelia was no more than a Saxon slave, and subject to the whims of the Norman nobility, whatever they may be, though he found that he no longer cared quite so much for the company of his Norman peers.

'Twould be best to turn his attention to the acrobats who jumped and tumbled adroitly before the dais and let Aelia do whatever she was bade. Yet Mathieu could not take his eyes from her, watching as she moved among the tables with trays of food, pitchers of ale.

Mathieu sipped sparingly of his wine as Roger freely imbibed, laughing and clapping at the antics of the entertainers. Hélène sat back in her chair and watched dispassionately, as if it would suit her just as well to leave the company and retire.

"Where is the Saxon boy?" Mathieu asked the lady as Aelia left the hall.

"In the stables…sweeping floors, I imagine."

"'Tis a recipe for trouble," Mathieu muttered.

"I beg your pardon, my lord?" Hélène said.

"'Tis naught."

Aelia never looked toward the dais. No doubt she knew he was there, but she refused to glance toward the table where all the Norman nobles sat. He took note of his men, sitting at a nearby table, perhaps vaguely aware of Aelia's role as a serving maid, but most certainly unaware of Osric's location. They should know better than to leave the boy to his own devices here.

Mathieu's attention was drawn by an outburst of laughter in the crowd of men to his left. He glanced toward them and took note of a blond serving maid who was the brunt of their joke. Her long braid swayed as she pushed their hands away, but they grabbed at her and prodded her unmercifully.

She suddenly dropped the tray she carried, then turned and ran. 'Twas Aelia.

Lady Hélène tittered with laughter and beckoned a few of Rushton's soldiers to come to her.

"The Saxon prisoner seems to think she is above

serving our men," Hélène said. "Go find her, and show her what her place is."

Roger roared with laughter, then kissed his wife's hand. "Well done, my sweet."

With tears of anger clouding Aelia's vision, she ran through the cold until she reached the stable, but when she called to Osric, he did not answer. There was naught he could do to help her, but 'twould be a comfort just to see him.

She would not think of the Norman bastard, Fitz Autier, who had abandoned her. She did not care that he sat upon the dais beside Lady Hélène, listening to the Norman woman's patter, and doing naught to rectify what had been done to Aelia. She shouldn't have expected him to intercede for her. 'Twas clear he denied what he felt when he saw her, refused to acknowledge any connection between them.

Her one decent kirtle had been taken from her, and now she wore a rough, woolen rag given her by the old woman who followed Hélène's every move. Aelia had been required to assist Hélène in dressing for her fete, and had been sent to the kitchens to assist the other Saxon servants in preparing for the Norman festivities.

'Twas not so terrible a fate. She should not feel like weeping just because Mathieu Fitz Autier had not corrected her situation. There could be no more denying she was naught but a slave.

Wagons and saddles, harnesses and other equipment were stored in the next building. Aelia looked for a lamp and called Osric's name once again. She heard a voice behind her, but 'twas not her brother's.

"There she is," said a man at the far end of the corridor.

Three Normans staggered toward her, one carrying a torch. Aelia backed into the building and shoved the door shut in their faces. She hurried to the rear of the structure, but smashed her knee on something and could only stagger in pain as the three men sang drunkenly outside.

The door crashed open on its hinges and the Normans shoved their way in, laughing and staggering. Aelia retreated, hoping she would be able to find a door or window to escape the drunken louts. If they were inebriated enough, she should be able to get away from them.

But she could find no other door.

"Thought you'd evade us?" asked the tallest one, who swayed the most as he walked.

Aelia pretended not to understand him, and kept moving, feeling her way along the wall, searching for a shuttered window. But the men stalked her purposefully.

"You're going to enjoy this," said the one with the torch. He'd tossed it in the dirt in order to free his hands, then joined the game with his comrades. For that was what it was: a game to them. She was to be used and discarded the way Durand had used Rowena.

The men flanked her sides, and one of them grabbed her arm to spin her 'round and off balance. Another one yanked her toward him. Aelia swung a fist and caught him under his eye. He howled and knocked her to the floor.

The others laughed noisily as she kicked and pummeled him, desperately trying to push him away. "That's it—pull off her skirts, Herve!"

She managed to turn over and start crawling on her hands and knees, but one of them grabbed her ankle and pulled her back. "No!" she cried, kicking again.

She reminded herself she'd been in more dangerous situations in recent months—she still had the wound in her neck as evidence. Somehow, she was going to survive this.

Their hands were on her clothes now, and one of them suddenly tore her gown from her legs. She screamed, though she knew her cries were of no avail. Surely no one would be able to hear them, and there was no one to know—or care—where she was.

The flickering torchlight cast them in shadows, and Aelia imagined them as demons biting and tearing, hurting her as they tore her kirtle from her body. All that was left was the threadbare chemise given her by Lady Hélène's servant.

"Look what we've got here!" said one of them with a laugh.

As drunk as they were, the men were surprisingly determined against her struggles. They pinned down her hands, but when Herve flattened himself on top of her, panic gave her a sudden burst of strength and she managed to free one arm.

She shoved Herve and slammed her knee into his groin. He howled in pain, and when he rolled to his side, Aelia pulled his dagger from the sheath in his belt, slashing the first man who touched her.

"She cut me!" the Norman howled as she scrambled to her feet, brandishing the knife.

While Herve rolled on the floor, whimpering, the man she'd stabbed stood frowning at her in shock as the wound in his hand dripped blood.

Keeping the knife in front of her, and her distance from the attacker who remained unscathed, Aelia made her way to the door. The man made a sudden move to seize her, but she jabbed at him. He dodged away from her, taking a step back.

Aelia kept her eyes trained upon him as she backed through the doorway. But when she stepped outside, an obstacle blocked her path. 'Twas a wall of muscle and bone—another Norman.

"I've got you, Aelia," Mathieu said, taking hold of her upper arms as much to steady her as to restrain his urge to destroy the three imbeciles who had ripped off her clothing and cornered her in this dark building.

Her skin was cold and she was shivering, but he felt a great shuddering sigh escape her as he pulled her back against his body. He did not insult her by asking her to release the knife, but set her behind him and faced her attackers, while she kept hold of the back of his belt.

"I'll see you whipped."

"Baron, she would have gutted me!"

"She unmanned me!"

"'Tis no defenseless maid who stands before us, my lord," said the third man, the only one unscathed. "Her reaction was much too exaggerated for our horseplay. The whore doesn't understand innocent fun!"

Mathieu backhanded the buffoon, splitting his lip and knocking him to the floor. "You three will present yourselves to your baron," he said in a low and dangerous tone. "Tell him you assaulted my prisoner and—"

"But 'twas Lady Hélène who gave us the nod."

"Said we were to put the Saxon wench in her place!" another added.

Aelia gave a mad shriek and lunged, but Mathieu caught her and lifted her into his arms. As angry as he was, he had to get her—and himself—away from these three before either of them committed murder.

The knife fell from Aelia's hands when he tossed her over his shoulder. She kicked and pummeled him as he carried her to the hall and up the first staircase they encountered. He gave her a sharp pat on her bottom. "Kick me again, *demoiselle,* and I'll be forced to do violence."

He was close enough to it already.

Her struggling did not stop, but when Mathieu reached the door to the chamber that had been given him, he kicked it open and strode in, dropping Aelia unceremoniously to the floor.

"You had no right!"

"Not to let you kill those men? Aye, I had the duty."

She tried to shove past him, but he barred her path. A fire had already been started in the grate, and Mathieu saw her clearly for the first time in its flickering light. She wore naught but a sheer linen chemise that was torn and stained, and the scrape at her shoulder had started to bleed again. She looked like a warrior princess, fierce and proud.

"Duty!" She quivered with anger.

"Do you know what Roger de Saye would have done had you killed one of his men?" He shook her once, then pulled her into his embrace. "*Gesu,* Aelia…"

His mouth came down hard upon hers, but she resisted, pulling away from him even as she kept a death grip on his tunic. She turned her head, though her hands remained closed upon his chest. "I don't want this, Norman!"

"Neither do I!"

She did not release him. With fire in her eyes, she pulled his head toward hers, and kissed him with a fierceness that took his breath away. He tipped his head to deepen the contact, tasting her anger and her passion.

He broke the kiss and leaned his forehead against hers as he caught his breath. "You belong to no other, Aelia."

She fisted her fingers in his hair, and Mathieu felt the flutter of her pulse in her throat, the quickening of her breathing, and knew that her arousal matched his own. But he had no intention of rushing this lovemaking. His lust had burned too hot, and for too long. He would woo her, and seduce her until her nerves were as taut as bow strings.

Like his.

Her taste was intoxicating, more sensuous than any kiss he'd shared with more experienced women.

She began to untie the laces at the neck of his tunic, tugging the sherte away from his chest. Mathieu pulled it over his head, then slipped the torn chemise from her shoulders and lowered his mouth to her breast. The nipple responded to his tongue, tightening into a hard pebble. She made a soft moan and slipped her fingers 'round to his nape, holding his head in place as he slid his hands down her belly, to the very heat of her.

She was hot and moist, the hard bud of her arousal ready for his touch. Her knees buckled when he caressed the spot, but she placed her hands upon his shoulders and steadied herself against his intimate touch.

Mathieu turned his attention to her other breast, sucking and licking until she whimpered with need. It aroused him to know he was the only one who had touched her this way. He was the only one who'd roused her to the peak of desire, and he would carry her over the edge. He would own her, heart, body and soul.

Taking her hand, he pressed it against the front of his braies and shuddered with the painful pleasure of her touch. She was untutored and hesitant, but before night's end, she would know about pleasing him, and learn the limits of her own pleasure.

Her eyes glittered in the firelight and she gazed up

at him heatedly. Mathieu was certain he had never seen anyone so beautiful.

Or so beguilingly innocent. She trembled with nervousness.

"No need to fear me, *ma belle,*" he whispered.

"I am not afraid of you, seignior." She showed it by opening the belt that held his braies, and pushing them down his legs with his hose. But when he was fully naked, her eyes widened and she began to tremble again.

Mathieu did not give her time to think, but lifted her in his arms and carried her to the bed, gently placing her in the center of it.

"So beautiful." He kissed her then, deeply, as he slid one hand down her body, from her throat to her thighs. He'd never felt anything so soft or so fine as her skin.

He traced slow kisses down her neck, then pressed his mouth to the tip of each breast. Encircling her waist with his hands, Mathieu felt her flesh quiver at his touch.

She took his head in her grasp and guided him back to her mouth for her kiss. Though she was untutored in lovemaking, she'd learned from their earlier encounters.

And more.

Her tongue was hot and sweet as it darted into his mouth. She raked her nails over his shoulders, then down to his hips, pressing his body tightly against her as she moved restlessly upon the mattress. Mathieu took one of her hands and placed it upon the hard shaft of his arousal.

"Touch me, Aelia."

She closed her hand around him, and when he groaned, pulled her hand away. "I hurt you?"

"No."

Gingerly, she tried it again, and Mathieu placed his hand over hers, guiding her, showing her how to please him.

Her breath quickened as she made him burn, his flesh seething, pulsing with need. He pressed his mouth to her breast once again, sucking, laving the nipple with his tongue. He wanted to be inside her—now. Yet her pleasure was as important as his own.

He wanted her aching for him as badly as he throbbed for her.

He arched suddenly, then pressed his lips over her skin, skimming to her belly and below. When he kissed the heat of her, she gasped and opened to him.

"Mathieu…" Her voice was low and husky, and the sound of his name upon her lips burned a path to his heart.

"Aye. Say it again. My name."

"Mathieu!"

She was hot and moist—ready for him.

He shifted his body, slipping between her sleek thighs as she clutched at his shoulders. He was huge and impatient, and wanted naught but to possess her. Placing his hands on either side of her head, he kissed her deeply as he eased into her, unwilling to cause more pain than necessary.

But she made a sudden move, and Mathieu found himself buried deep within her, sheathed so tightly he thought his heart would burst.

When she made a small sound, Mathieu released her lips. "Aelia…"

"More." She sighed and wrapped her legs 'round his waist. Her gaze burned into his, searing him with her passion, her desire. Never had this act seemed so intimate, so intense. 'Twas as if she had become part of his body…and his soul.

Her hands framed his face and he closed his eyes, turning into her touch, kissing her palm. She let her hands slide back to his shoulders and chest, finding his nipples fully erect and anxious for her touch. Mathieu nearly came out of his skin when she brushed them with her fingertips.

He plunged deeply and Aelia arched beneath him, crying out as spasms of pleasure overcame her. He felt his own release, a fiercely pulsing completion that was incomparable.

Mathieu eased his weight off her, but did not withdraw. Kissing her, he rolled to his side, taking her with him.

She fit him as though she were made for him.

"Are you all right?"

"Aye," she said, her voice barely more than a sigh.

'Twas good that *someone* here was all right, Mathieu thought. Because he certainly was not.

Aelia awoke sometime during the night to find there was no light coming in through the window and the fire had burned low. She did not know how long she'd slept.

Nor did she care.

She lay on her side with Mathieu curled against her back, her head pillowed upon his arm, her heart in his hands.

She had never wanted to care for him. More than anything, Aelia had wanted to hate Mathieu Fitz Autier for taking Ingelwald from her.

Instead, she had fallen in love with him.

He sighed, his breath ruffling the hair at her ear. She shivered, and he pulled her tightly against him, shifting his leg until it rested between her own. Then he whispered her name in sleep.

Naught in her life was certain, only what she felt for Mathieu.

He moved against her, his free hand cupping her breast, teasing the nipple. Aelia's breath caught in her throat when he shifted his attention to the sensitive place where her legs joined.

"Mmm. So sweet," he murmured in her ear.

He nuzzled her neck, then pushed her hair aside to press his lips down the exquisitely sensitive ridge of her spine.

Aelia turned to him. So many questions burned in her throat, but she could not bear to ask them now, not when he touched her this way.

He made love to her slowly and gently, each touch intended to give her more pleasure than his last. He kissed her and lingered wherever it seemed to please her most, and showed her how it felt to be cherished. With his eyes locked upon hers, he showed her a depth of intimacy with each thrust, with every caress.

"You were made for me, *ma belle.*"

And Aelia knew it was true.

When 'twas over, and he lay imbedded deep within her, her muscles still tense with the last shudders of her release, he kissed her with such tenderness that Aelia felt another kind of release. It could only be the ecstasy of their spirits fusing as one.

Yet she doubted the reality of what she felt when Mathieu suddenly left the bed. In the dim light, Aelia saw him jab his fingers through his hair before tossing another piece of wood on the fire. She felt at a loss, awkward and alone.

"While you slept, I had someone gather your belongings," he said without turning to face her. "'Tis nearly dawn and we need to leave Rushton."

The rose-colored kirtle that had been taken from her lay across a wooden bench, with her shoes placed neatly below it. When Mathieu began to clothe himself, Aelia arose from the bed and did the same, feeling cold and abandoned. He was no longer her attentive lover, but a warrior with an assignment.

"Will Osric and the men be ready?" she asked, pulling on her own chemise. The torn rag she'd been given was nowhere to be seen.

Mathieu sat on the bed and drew on his boots. "No. Raoul and the others will bring him and follow shortly. The sooner we leave here the better it will suit me."

"Why? Has something—"

"No. No more than Roger's lady sending his vassals to accost you." He stood and strapped on his sword. "Or putting you in rags to serve his men."

Aelia took a shuddering breath of relief when he turned her and pulled her kirtle over her head, pushing her hair aside to reach the laces. "Hurry. 'Tis almost dawn."

Chapter Twenty

'Twas surely a breach of courtesy to leave this way, but Mathieu thought it much less than the insult to Aelia.

He was partly to blame for what had happened to her. He had neglected to disabuse Roger and his wife of their mistaken impression that Aelia would be turned over to William's men to be used as a slave. He had opened the door for their mistreatment.

Mathieu's anger simmered just below the surface. He was determined to be the one to decide Aelia's fate. Certainly 'twas not to be raped by three drunken soldiers in a dark and abandoned corner of Roger de Saye's estate.

Sometime while Aelia slept, Mathieu had decided to leave Rushton before dawn. He'd left their bed and gone in search of Raoul, giving him instructions to gather Aelia's clothes and the rest of their belongings so they'd be ready to depart before first light.

'Twas so early when Mathieu and Aelia rode through the gate that the only person they saw was the guard, who let them pass without question. Mathieu pulled

Aelia close to his chest as they headed toward the southern road.

She tipped her head slightly to the side and he leaned forward and kissed her ear. It would have been much preferable to spend these early morning hours in bed, but it seemed a far better course to get Aelia away from Hélène and Roger.

And he was not ready to make any explanations for his actions the night before.

The sun crept up over the horizon and brightened the day, though 'twas a chilly morn. The weather suited Mathieu's purpose, though, giving him good reason to hold Aelia close. He inhaled her scent and felt her soft curves against his body, and wished they were closer to the end of their day's ride rather than the beginning.

At midday, they stopped in a copse of trees to break their fast. Mathieu deemed the site safe, since there was no sign of any recent travelers in the area. He spread his blanket upon the ground, where they sat to take a short rest and consume a small meal.

Aelia was quiet, her eyes skittering away from his when he looked at her, and a delightful blush coloring her cheeks. Mathieu leaned toward her, taking a wisp of her hair between his fingers. "You are very beautiful."

Aelia brushed his hand away. "You embarrass me, my lord."

"'Twas not my intention to make you uncomfortable, Aelia," he said. He did not understand this need to be so close to her, to touch her. He'd never required the companionship of women, but it was different with her.

"My brother has changed since we left Ingelwald," she said, clearly anxious to switch the subject.

Mathieu nodded. "He needed discipline. I merely provided it."

"We indulged him. After Godwin died, my father and I…mayhap we protected Osric too much. Allowed him too much freedom." She looked toward some point in the distance as she spoke, her voice quiet. Mathieu could not change what had happened to her family. He did not even know if he could protect her now. "You were right about him."

"Osric is still young. But now he understands there are consequences to his actions."

They fell silent with those words. Osric was not the only one who had to live with the consequences of what he'd done.

Mathieu looked at Aelia. He wanted her. He could taste her, feel the soft slide of her skin against his, hear her cries of pleasure. Even now, after the hours he'd spent through the night making love to her, he still wanted her as he'd craved no other woman.

She'd lost none of her nobility in the days since Ingelwald's defeat, not even when she'd been forced to wear rags and serve Rushton's rowdy troops. William's conquest had stolen nearly everything from her, and Mathieu had finished the task himself, taking her from her home and her people.

But he felt no guilt for his actions. He was a soldier in William's service and had done as he'd been commanded, reaping the reward for his victory.

He leaned toward Aelia and touched his thumb to the corner of her mouth, just as her tongue darted out to catch a crumb of bread. A burst of heat shot through him at that slight contact and he cupped her face before touching his lips to hers.

He had to be out of his mind, continuing this liaison

when there was no future in it. He would return to Ingelwald without her, and there was no point in encouraging her affections…her hope.

Her expression of raw desire was shattered by confusion when he withdrew abruptly. It should not have mattered.

"'Tis time we were on our way," he said, his voice harsh to his own ears. "I want to make camp before the rain comes."

Aelia did not understand the distance Mathieu put between them. They continued riding south, but he did not hold her. His lips never touched her ear or the back of her neck, as they'd done all through the morn. 'Twas as if last night had never occurred. As if Aelia had not given herself—body and soul—to him.

She had to be mistaken. More likely, he was being vigilant as they traveled without an escort. Mayhap he'd seen something suspicious to make him more alert, as he'd been when Durand had followed them. She asked him.

"No. No sign of any other recent travelers."

Aelia took a deep breath and tamped down the ache that had developed in the middle of her chest.

"I wonder if Osric and your men are far behind," she said in an effort to counter the uncomfortable silence that had risen between them.

"At least a couple of hours, if not more."

Aelia moistened her lips. "Will Osric be allowed to stay with me when we get to London?"

He said naught at first, and Aelia was about to ask again when he replied, "I do not know what William will decide."

"But until he decides…what do you think—"

"Aelia, I am not privy to the king's thoughts. I cannot say what will happen."

She turned to look at him, to plead for a scrap of reassurance, but saw that his expression was hard and unyielding. "'Tis clear you have no siblings, else you would have more—"

"I have two brothers," he replied. "Two who are legitimate, anyway."

"There might be others?"

"I suppose so. My father availed himself of any woman in the household, willing or not."

The bitterness in his tone took her aback, and Aelia wondered if his own mother had been one of those women, an unwilling one. 'Twas well known that Mathieu was a bastard...

And he clearly had little regard for the two brothers he'd mentioned.

"Your family was different from mine."

"Aye. Without a doubt." His voice was harsh, his expression tense.

"What of your mother? Does she await your return?"

"She's dead."

"I'm sorry."

"No need for regrets. 'Twas a long time ago."

"How old were you when you lost her?"

"Seven years." There was no hesitation, no doubt in his voice. Yet it sounded to Aelia as though he recalled it as if it had happened yesterday.

"I remember when my mother died," she said. "'Twas the same day Osric was born."

Mathieu gave no reaction beyond the flexing of a muscle in his cheek.

"Was your father... What happened to you after your mother died?"

"I found myself in a great deal of trouble. Often. And when my father realized what a little warrior I was, he sent me away to Cartaret to be trained as a soldier."

Aelia smiled. "You liked to fight?"

"My father's sons—my brothers—enjoyed making my life a misery. And I enjoyed making them pay."

'Twas no wonder he did not understand her allegiance to Osric.

"Turn 'round, Aelia, while we make this crossing."

She did as she was told, and felt him slide his arms around her waist, holding her securely as they forded a shallow, but swiftly flowing river. It had a rocky bottom that was likely to be slick, and Aelia had to raise her feet to avoid having them soaked. But their mount was sure-footed, and they reached the other side safely.

All but Aelia's heart.

Something had changed in Mathieu's demeanor. He held her as a captor holds a prisoner—not the way a man holds his lover.

Aelia realized what she should have known from the beginning. She understood with sudden clarity why he'd ignored her plight at Rushton's feast the previous night, and had only come for her when she had not returned to the great hall.

She was no special captive, en route to King William in London. She was merely Fitz Autier's possession, a Saxon with no rights, no privileges. She was a fool to think her feelings for the Norman baron were returned beyond the man's interest in bed play. There was no true tenderness in him.

They stopped before dusk, yet the rain was still far off.

"We'll make camp here," he said, dismounting, then

helping her down. They had barely spoken since the river crossing, which only reaffirmed Aelia's new understanding of her situation.

She felt ill, and wished for the comfort and security of home…yet she had no home. She was in no better condition than Cuthbert and his family, wandering the countryside, uncertain of their future. She and Osric had no family, no friends.

And when Mathieu Fitz Autier turned her over to the king's men in London, her isolation from all that was familiar would be complete. He would wed his Norman bride and return with her to Ingelwald, while Aelia…

"Take hold of this rope," Fitz Autier said. He was hanging a leather tarpaulin like a roof over an open space, so that when the rain came, they would have a place to sit, and the fire would not die.

Aelia felt numb as she worked alongside him. Their conversation was sparse, consisting only of the instructions Mathieu gave her. There were no tender words or loving caresses between them.

'Twas as if she had imagined the intimacies of the previous night, and during their morning's ride. Had he actually kissed her ear and nuzzled her neck as they rode? Had he not slid his arms 'round her, fondled her affectionately?

Choking on her misjudgment and all its consequences, Aelia left the site where Fitz Autier worked, stumbling away to gather her composure in private, unwilling to shed any tears for him.

Or at least, none for him to see.

She heard him call to her, but ignored his summons as she wandered some distance from their campsite. She came upon a pond surrounded by willow trees, with low branches that dipped into the pool. There, she sat upon an old, weathered log and wept until she had no more tears to shed.

Mathieu gazed in the direction Aelia had gone and wondered if 'twas yet time to go and fetch her back. Standing with his hands perched upon his hips, he perceived no danger in the vicinity. She would be all right.

At least for now. He did not know how she would fare once they reached London.

He added a few sticks to the fire he'd started to ward off the chill of the early evening, and wondered when Raoul and the others would arrive. 'Twould be much better not to be alone with Aelia now, not while she was so clearly in need of reassurances he could not give.

Mathieu was not without influence with the king. Surely William would take Mathieu's counsel and choose an apt husband for Aelia, rather than sending her to Rouen, or elsewhere, to serve in some distant household.

Now that so many Normans were in possession of modest estates here, one of them would make a suitable husband. And Mathieu intended to choose one for Aelia.

He started to rearrange the logs on the fire and suddenly dropped a burning ember he'd mistakenly picked up. Cursing viciously, he took his water skin from his saddle and poured the soothing liquid over the burn, but felt no relief. How could he, when he would soon be compelled to turn Aelia over to King William, who would give her to another man?

The blistering of his hand was echoed in his gut. The afternoon had been interminable. Aelia had almost succeeded in masking the pain he'd dealt her, but he knew her too well. His disregard had hurt her badly.

Mathieu tossed down the water skin and strode away from camp, in the direction Aelia had taken. He could not stand to see the confusion and hurt he'd put in her eyes.

Gesu. She belonged to him, and Mathieu was not going to give her up to any other man. Aelia was his captive, and on that basis, he would argue that she should remain with him.

Her path was clearly visible through the tall grass. Mathieu followed it until he reached a large pond, where he found her sitting upon a thick log, with her face in her hands. She stood abruptly when she saw him, quickly turning her back to him. But he did not miss her quaking shoulders, or the sob that escaped her lips.

"Aelia."

"Go away," she said, her voice thick with emotion. "I—I'll return shortly."

She started to walk on, but Mathieu caught up to her, placing his hands upon her shoulders and pulling her into his chest. "Don't go."

"Please, Mathieu… I—"

"Don't go," he repeated. He slipped his hands across her chest, above her breasts. Her head fit just under his chin, and he pulled her into his embrace. Still, he felt her shuddering breaths, her stiff posture against him.

"I understand what you must do…." she said. "I beg you to release me. Let me take Osric and—"

Swiftly, he changed positions, suddenly standing before her, clasping her body to his. He brought his head down and slanted his mouth against hers, marking her as his own.

He swept her into his arms and laid her down upon

Chapter Twenty-One

$\sim\!\!\sim\!\!\sim\!\!\sim$

Aelia felt shaken when they returned to camp. She'd thought there would be naught to compare to Mathieu's intensity the night before, but she was wrong. He'd made love to her by the pond with a fierce possessiveness that rocked her soul. She must have been mistaken about his indifference that afternoon.

She felt her body quake even now, just looking at him.

Wincing with discomfort, she moved to sit by the fire. Mathieu took her hands and came down upon one knee before her. "I hurt you," he said.

Aelia leaned toward him and kissed him with all the love in her heart. "You could not hurt me, Mathieu. I…I am merely unused to such sport."

He touched her face, running his fingers across her mouth, her cheeks. "I did not take time to shave this morn. My beard was too rough for you."

His usually clean-shaven face was dark with the stubble of whiskers, but they had caused Aelia no pain. She closed her eyes and relished his gentle caress.

Surely his bristly mood this afternoon had been

brought about by talk of his family, and his mother's death. Aelia would remember in future not to mention them, for they clearly brought him unease.

She covered his hands with hers and drew them to her breast. "I love you," she said, looking into his deep blue eyes. "When first I saw you, even as I loosed my arrow against you, I knew that you would change my life."

She touched the reddened track across his cheek. "I am sorry for this…and for—"

"Listen," he said, abruptly turning away. "Riders."

He stood and took her by the hand, leading her to a concealed place away from the light of the fire. "Wait here," he said, drawing his sword.

Fortunately, Aelia had little chance to fear for Mathieu's life, for the shouts from his men announced the identity of the intruders before they rode into camp. Raoul came first, with Osric perched upon the saddle before him. The rest of the men followed, all but Halig, Guilliaume, and Foque.

They dismounted and greeted one another. Mathieu asked about the missing men. "They became ill after the feast," one knight announced.

Which left them only six men in their escort, and two did not appear in good health. Both were pale and gaunt. Hugh and Guatier wasted no time, but pulled down their saddle packs and made beds under the tarpaulin near the fire.

"I think 'twas the quail they ate, baron."

"Please do not speak of it," Hugh said, groaning from within his blankets.

Aelia came out from the shadows and took her brother by the shoulders. He had a scab on his lower lip and a bruised eye. "Osric, you are well?"

"Aye," he said, shrugging away from her. "I ate no quail. They kept me prisoner in the stable, mucking out manure."

Aelia looked up at Raoul, who turned away, unsaddling his horse, giving orders to the men. 'Twas as if he intentionally avoided speaking to her.

"Did you see any sign of travelers?" Fitz Autier asked.

"No, Baron," Raoul replied. "'Twas an uneventful day."

"Still, I want two of us on guard at all times. Osbern and Henri. Unpack your gear and take the first watch."

Since the newcomers carried the bulk of their food and supplies, they set up camp under the tarp and went about preparing a meal. Raoul, whose manner was usually cordial, was terse and decidedly unfriendly. Even Osric was quiet.

Aelia felt drained. She was physically exhausted, and there was much left unsaid between her and Mathieu. Mayhap when he joined her in their tent...

She finished the simple meal, then rose from her place and left the group, picking up a blanket to arrange inside her tent. When their bed was prepared, Aelia walked alone to the pond, taking a few minutes of privacy before retiring. Rain clouds still approached, but the moon was nearly full, and Aelia easily found her way down the path she and Mathieu had made earlier.

There was no confusion about the way she felt for him, but she was uneasy. Whether 'twas due to Raoul and the other men's different demeanor...or the knowledge that Mathieu's fierce lovemaking had changed naught between them...

She filled her water skin and headed back toward camp, stopping short when she heard voices arguing in

hushed tones. Two men stood near the horses, oblivi-
ous to her presence.

"You've always counted me among your friends,
Mathieu," said Sir Raoul. "And I must speak frankly to
you now. Your insult to Roger de Saye will come to
plague you someday."

"'Tis my own affair, Raoul."

"Your leman's contentment has more import than an
affront to a powerful baron?"

"She is *my* slave, Raoul. *My* leman." Aelia's heart
thudded in her throat at his words. "My actions are
none of your concern."

"That's where you are wrong, Mathieu. King William will take her from you. You know as well as I that
he will send her to Rouen after he displays her as his
vanquished enemy. He—"

Raoul's words were cut short by a sharp scream in
the night, and the sound of swords striking swords.

Half-blinded by tears welling in her eyes, Aelia ran
toward camp in search of Osric.

Men on horseback, at least a dozen of them, invaded
the camp, swooping down like hawks on their prey.
Mathieu's men met them with swords drawn, but they
were no match against the Danish attackers, with their
axes and blades. Mathieu and Raoul joined in the fray,
but Aelia could see no sign of Osric.

"Aelia! Run!"

The invaders trampled the tents, shouting in their
unfamiliar tongue as they parried against Mathieu's
men, and nearly crushed Hugh and Guatier with their
horses' hooves before the two men could move.

Aelia could not follow Mathieu's order to run away,
not without her brother. Not while Mathieu battled
against so many foes. She cried out when Henri fell, and

again when Gerrard's blood spilled on the ground beneath him. She watched in horror as Mathieu pulled one man down and speared him with his sword. Relentless, he went after another as the rest of his Norman warriors fought for their lives.

"Osric!" she cried, even more terrified now. These Normans had seemed indestructible before. Now, as they fought for their lives against the brutal Dane warriors, she feared for them.

For Mathieu's life.

She could not think about what she'd overheard a few moments ago. 'Twas most important to find Osric, and then she could get the two of them away from the fray. She kept to the perimeter of the battle, running from tree to shrub, searching frantically for her brother as the rain finally began to fall.

"Get away, Aelia! We have no chance here!" Mathieu shouted.

Hugh and Guatier were barely able to stand, but they drew swords and fought bravely against thrice their number. The horses churned up the ground, making a muddy mess in the rain. Aelia tripped over her sodden skirts, but managed somehow to stay on her feet. She suddenly heard Osric's voice calling out a youthful battle cry. Her heart dropped when she saw him standing among the mounted Danes, wielding the short sword he'd used when he'd taken instruction from Mathieu.

She could not get to him through the mass of horses and warriors.

Aelia trembled as she watched her small brother thrust his blade upward, somehow managing to unseat his target. She lost sight of Osric as the man fell, and started toward him. But one of the Danes took note of her, turning his horse and riding in her direction. Aelia ran into the dark woods, hoping to find a place to hide among the trees.

The Dane laughed, clearly understanding the futility of her move. He swooped down and grabbed her, lifted her up and tossed her across his horse.

Aelia screamed and struggled to get away, but she was no match for the barbarian's strength. He rode back into the melee, shouting to his companions, pulling Aelia up by her hair as if to show them what he'd captured.

"Mathieu!" she cried, futilely. She reached for her knife, but the Dane knocked it from her hand, then struck her.

She caught sight of Mathieu, just as his assailant landed a massive blow. Crying out with despair, she watched him fall. They'd killed him. The savages had murdered Mathieu.

Aelia fought to get down, to go to him, but the barbarian held her in place, bruising her arms and legs. When the Dane struck her again, Aelia was too shattered, too dazed to continue the struggle.

Mathieu pushed himself up off the ground and shook his head to clear it. 'Twas dark, and all was quiet. The fire had gone out in the rain and—

Gesu. Aelia!

He'd seen her carried off by one of the Dane bastards. When his eyes finally adjusted to the darkness, he saw bodies all 'round him. His men. Danes.

Where was the boy?

More important, how was he going to get Aelia back?

Quickly, he got the fire going again, ignoring the blood that oozed from a gash on the top of his head, and the burning pain in his left shoulder. When there was enough light, he set about the grim task of checking his men for signs of life.

Only Raoul and Osbern survived, and Osbern was unlikely to live very long with the injuries he'd sustained. Mathieu wrapped a cloth 'round the man's wrist, where his hand had been severed, and spoke gravely to Raoul. "See if you can find Osric. He must be here among the dead."

He did all he could to make Osbern comfortable, then joined Raoul in the search for Osric. Mathieu had seen the boy join the battle, wielding Raoul's seax just as he'd been instructed, using his small size and his speed to harry the enemy. He was afraid the lad's overconfidence had gotten him killed.

They found him half concealed under the body of one of the Danes, unconscious but otherwise unhurt. Mathieu roused him.

"Aelia," he said. "Where is my sister?"

"They took her," Mathieu replied.

"Most of the horses are gone, Mathieu," said Raoul. "There are only three here. One belonged to the Danes."

Mathieu picked up his sword and sheathed it. "Stay here with Osbern. When you are able, take Osric and continue south. Get him to London. I'm going after Aelia."

"You cannot," said Raoul, watching as Mathieu grasped the reins of the Dane's horse, which was already saddled, and laden with bulging packs. "You are wounded yourself, and she is gone. There is naught you can do for her."

Mathieu mounted.

"She is a slave, Mathieu. 'Tis a waste of—"

"Tell King William what transpired here. Ask him to

keep Osric in his household. The boy will make a formidable warrior someday."

Mathieu dug in his heels and rode out of camp, following the path the Danes must have taken. He moved slowly, straining his eyes to see signs of their trail.

He wiped blood from his face and felt for the bump on his head, wincing when he found it. There was pain in his left shoulder, too, but Mathieu thought his hauberk had deflected the worst of the blow.

Eight Danes lay dead in camp, but Mathieu did not know how many had survived, how many were in the party that had carried Aelia away. They had left a clear trail, trampling down the low grass on the forest floor.

He followed for hours, carefully watching the trail they'd left, unwilling to lose track of them on a time-wasting detour. His strategy was effective until he reached a swiftly flowing river. Had they gone north or south along the riverbank, or had they crossed the stream?

Dismounting, Mathieu saw tracks in the muddy bank. In spite of the rain, he could tell that several horses had gathered here. And it looked as though this was where they'd entered the river.

Mathieu muttered a curse. Crossing the rain-swollen river was much too dangerous in the dark. He did not know how deep it was, nor could he see exactly how fast the current flowed.

He shuddered at the thought of Aelia being carried across.

He unclenched his teeth. He could not think of all the things that might have already happened to her. He had to believe they'd reached the opposite bank and that she was still on the trail with her captors, alive and well.

Assuming the Danes had already made this crossing

once, Mathieu entered the water. He was wet from the rain, so the additional soaking meant naught. But the current was strong, and the river deeper than he liked. Still, he went forward, urging his horse on, even when the water reached his thighs.

In the shadowy light, Mathieu could see the far bank. 'Twas a struggle for his horse to keep its footing against the strong current, but Mathieu held on, fixing his eye on a landmark so he would not lose his way. He tightened his legs 'round his mount to increase his control, and leaned forward, badgering the animal to keep moving.

But the horse faltered and lost its balance, hurling Mathieu into the rushing water.

The weight of his chain mail dragged him down, and the current tossed him in every direction. He fought to unfasten his sword belt and the cumbersome hauberk, and when he finally dropped the heavy metal, he was able to surface.

There was no doubt he'd been carried some distance downstream. With powerful strokes, he fought the current, swimming toward the far side, unwilling to give up his pursuit of Aelia.

Numb with cold, his injured shoulder burning with every stroke, he struggled to get to the far bank, and finally crawled onto firm land. The terrain was somewhat more open now, which would make it easier for Mathieu to search for tracks, but he had no idea how far he'd been carried downstream.

He started walking back along the bank, thankful he still had his boots, for he had no doubt it was going to be a long walk. Soon the sound of birdsong filled the air, and a sudden, loud snort that made Mathieu turn abruptly.

'Twas the horse he thought he'd lost.

It seemed hours before his mount took the first few steps toward Mathieu, who remained unmoving, until the beast stood only a few yards away. Then Mathieu started speaking quietly to the animal, careful not to frighten it again, but mindful of Aelia's plight.

As soon as he could, Mathieu took hold of the reins and led the animal behind him as he continued looking for signs of the Danish riders.

It was several more minutes before he found what he searched for. Far upstream was an area of tall weeds that had recently been trampled. Mathieu mounted the horse and followed where the hoofprints led, certain these were the tracks of the Danes who had abducted Aelia.

As the sun rose, he was able to spur the horse to a faster pace, following the trail with much more ease. The Danes were overconfident. They had not taken care to cover their trail, certain they'd left no one alive in the Norman camp. Mathieu was going to use their arrogant attitude against them, and slip Aelia out of their grasp before they knew she was gone.

Chapter Twenty-Two

Aelia's brutal captor pulled her off his horse and shoved her to the ground, laughing and shouting to the others. They had stopped only once during the night's long ride, and that was to salvage Aelia from the river they'd crossed so recklessly in the faint light of a washed out moon.

She had let herself fall into the rushing water, hardly caring whether or not she survived. 'Twas pointless to go on, only to become a slave to these barbaric Danes. Mathieu was dead, and Osric, too. They'd killed every one of the Normans in camp.

To her great dismay, one of the Danes had hauled her out of the water. And now she was to become their sport.

They were at the base of a steep incline, with high cliffs all around them. One of the Danes yawned and stretched, then began to gather wood for a fire.

Aelia tried to scramble away into the nearby trees, but one of her captors grabbed her.

"Where do you think I would go?" she demanded indignantly. She shook off his hand, crossed her arms over her chest and continued speaking, even though she knew they could not understand her words. Perhaps they would be able to grasp her intention. "I require a few minutes privacy, you swine."

"Swine?" One of the men scowled down at her.

"Privacy."

Aelia turned and walked a short distance into the woods, indifferent to whatever they might say or do to her. But the Danes just laughed and allowed her to leave.

She felt numb. Hollow inside.

She had told Mathieu of her love, and when he'd spoken of her to Raoul, he'd called her his slave. His mistress.

With tears in her eyes, she tripped over a rock and fell, landing hard on the heels of her hands. She did not get up, but remained where she lay, curled upon the ground.

Aelia's love for Mathieu had not changed, in spite of what he'd said to Raoul. She could not bear to think of his death at the hands of the barbarians who awaited her. Nor could she allow herself to consider what had happened to Osric.

She heard them coming for her, and decided she would never submit. They might violate her body, but she was going to see that each of them suffered for it, and for the slaughter of the Norman soldiers, of Osric…of Mathieu.

She picked up a rock that fit in the palm of her hand, and slipped it into her bodice. Then she searched for a twig or small branch with a sharp end. They'd taken her knife, but she was not going to be entirely defenseless when they confronted her.

Two of the brutes came for her, taking hold of her

arms and pulling her back to the place where the others waited, their horses unsaddled and tethered, and a fire burning. The small clearing resembled the kind of area where Mathieu established camp when they stopped each night, with a fire blazing in the center. But instead of laying out blankets and food, these men opened their packs and dumped out the contents near the fire.

They were clearly pleased with the goods they'd looted. Cups of silver, bronze bowls embedded with jewels, necklaces, daggers…and Aelia knew she was part of the spoils. The Danes pawed through their booty, laughing and shouting to each other. They repacked their stolen goods, tossing their packs aside when Aelia came into their midst.

When the leader grabbed her and started to take her away, one of the other Danes challenged him, grasping his arm and spinning him 'round. An argument ensued, and then a fight. Suddenly released by the tall Dane, Aelia lost her balance and fell, but she cracked his skull with her rock before crawling away from the commotion when the rest of the men joined the altercation.

There had to be a place to hide.

Mathieu lost track of them on a rocky plain.

But Aelia's captors had been heading steadily east, so he continued in the same direction. 'Twas nearly noon and he had not stopped since his near disaster in the river. He'd shoved aside the gold and bronze objects in the saddle pack and dug out what food there was. Then he'd strapped on the ax that had been tied to the saddle. He was much more proficient with a sword, but his own lay at the bottom of the river. The ax would have to do.

The smell of wood smoke attracted him to the edge of an embankment. He dismounted and looked down into the dell below, and noted that there was, indeed, smoke rising above the trees. He hoped the Danes believed there would be no one to follow them. 'Twould mean they'd actually stopped to make camp.

Mathieu descended, making as little noise as possible. He tied his horse at the base of the hill, and went forward on foot, keeping to the trees, out of sight. He soon heard shouts, and the sounds of a scuffle. It seemed members of the raiding party were fighting over their plunder...or over Aelia.

With even more urgency than before, Mathieu raised his ax and prepared himself for battle. He approached the camp cautiously, prepared to slay anyone who kept him from her.

When he entered the clearing, no one was there. Yet, spread upon the ground, were some of the spoils of these barbarians' raids. Mathieu kicked away the inconsequential items and picked up a dagger, shoving it into his boot. Then he grabbed a sword in place of the ax he carried, and slipped back into the trees.

He went directly to their horses and turned them loose—all but one, which he mounted. Then he headed toward the melee happening several yards away.

Mathieu took them by surprise, all seven Danes, spearing two of them before the bastards could locate and draw their weapons against him. Searching the area for Aelia, he met all who tried to unseat him, slaying them before they could do any harm.

Where was she? Had she been lost along the way...in the river, perhaps?

No! He would not even entertain such a thought. Aelia was not lost to him.

One of the Danes tried to pull him from the horse, but Mathieu put his foot in the man's chest and shoved him to the ground.

"Mathieu, behind you!"

He had no chance to rejoice at the sound of Aelia's voice, but quickly turned and dispatched the warrior who attacked him from that quarter. Three raiders remained standing—until Aelia knocked one of them on the head with a rock. The man fell as Mathieu rode toward her.

She reached up as he grabbed for her, pulling her onto the horse's rump. She straddled the gelding, then held Mathieu tightly 'round his waist, pressing her face to his back, and he rode away through the trees as the Danes shouted, scrambling to find their horses.

Her body trembled against his, and Mathieu wanted naught but to take her in his arms and hold her, touch her, breathe in her scent, feel her heartbeat against his. But he could not, at least not until they'd put several miles between themselves and the Danes.

Neither of them spoke as they covered the terrain, finally reaching the base of the trail where Mathieu had left his horse. There he dismounted and reached up for Aelia. A moment later she was in his arms, but he felt more shaken than ever before. He'd nearly lost her.

He kissed her soundly, then held her against his chest as she wept. "I thought they'd killed you!" she cried. "I saw you struck down."

"I am not so easy to kill."

"But Osric—"

"Is alive and on his way to London with Raoul."

She nearly collapsed then, but Mathieu held her tightly. "He fought like a Saxon warrior. Aelia, are you unhurt?"

She nodded, and he brushed tears from her dirty face. "A few new scrapes, I suppose."

"We must leave," he said. "I scattered their horses, but they'll soon gather them and come after us."

He was reluctant to let her go, but they had no choice but to move on. They mounted the horses and started south, since 'twould take too much time to ride all the way to the peak of the escarpment. Mathieu wanted to be miles ahead when the Danes regrouped. Aelia's fear was only going to carry her so far. She was exhausted, and the new "scrapes" on her body were not insignificant.

He had to get her to a safe place.

Their only obstacle was a shallow stream, which proved to be fortunate. Riding through it for at least a mile to eliminate their tracks, they came upon a rocky terrain where several small rivers met.

The river bed was uneven and treacherous, so Mathieu jumped down into the water, then helped Aelia dismount.

"If the Danes are still following us, we can lose them here. They won't be able to find our tracks when we leave the water."

For good measure, Mathieu reached up to the saddle pack and removed a dagger. He tossed the knife to the far bank in hopes that if the raiders followed them, they would notice it and head in that direction.

"This way."

They continued walking south, but kept to the eastern banks when they finally left the water. Mathieu could see that Aelia was near collapse. They could not go much farther.

He lifted her onto his horse and mounted behind her, pulling her back against his chest. "Sleep awhile, *ma belle*," he said, touching his lips to her forehead. "I'll hold you."

Mathieu had a few more miles in him, but there was no doubt he would also need to stop and rest soon. They crossed a hilly meadow, and soon came upon a dell where a small church lay visible in the distance. 'Twas in the midst of an orchard, and there were several stone-and-timber buildings nearby.

Leading Aelia's horse behind them, Mathieu headed for the place. Aelia awoke when he stopped the horses. "It's an abbey. We'll stop here for the night," he said. Monks gathered 'round when they approached.

Since it was clearly a Saxon holding, Mathieu spoke to them in Latin. "We were attacked by Danes," he explained. "My wife and I escaped, but she is exhausted. Is there a place where we might sleep a few hours?"

"We want no trouble from the Normans," the abbot said.

"We mean you no harm," Mathieu replied. "We ask only for shelter until morning. No one will ever know we were here."

The old man nodded, then spoke to several of the monks. Mathieu jumped down, then reached for Aelia. Her legs gave out, so Mathieu carried her as they followed the brothers to a cottage behind the church. When they pushed open the door and entered, one of the men lit a lamp.

"You can put her here," the second said, pulling down the blankets on the only bed in the room.

"My thanks to you," Mathieu murmured as two other monks carried in the saddle packs.

"We will bring food later," one answered, "but you should tend to your wife now."

"Aye. I'll do that."

They left, closing the door behind them. Mathieu pulled the shutters closed and went to Aelia, who barely stirred when he knelt beside her and removed her shoes. He unlaced her torn and soiled kirtle and slipped it from her body. Once his own clothes had been removed, he climbed in the bed beside her, took her into his arms and held her as she slept.

He'd called her his wife. What he felt for Aelia threatened everything he'd hoped to gain when he'd come to England with William.

He pressed his face to Aelia's hair and wished there were some way to keep her with him.

Every muscle in Aelia's body ached.

She awoke to pain and stiffness in all her bones and muscles. She felt Mathieu's arm over her waist, felt the heat of his body warming her back. She did not know where they were, but it seemed to be a safe place. They were warm and dry, and they were together. At least for now.

She thought it must have been hunger that woke her, for her stomach was making tortured noises. Careful not to wake Mathieu, she slipped out of the bed. Her kirtle had been draped on a nearby chair, and she pulled it over her head and laced it, then went to the hearth to build up the fire.

The two saddle packs lay upon the floor beside the door, and there was a large basket upon the table. She went to the basket first, and found food, along with two flagons—one of ale, one water.

Still weary, Aelia sat down at the table and helped herself to the bread and meat that someone had left for them, while she considered what to do.

She could leave. Osric was long gone. Everything that Aelia valued had been taken from her. She had no home, no family, no friends… There was only Mathieu, who thought of her as his possession. When he reached London, he would wed the woman who'd been chosen for him.

And Aelia would have no place in his life.

Her heart clenched in her chest when she looked at him, sleeping so soundly. He'd ridden all night to rescue her from the Danes, yet he would soon give her up to her enemies when they arrived at their destination.

She trembled at the prospect of leaving him now. She loved him more than she'd ever thought possible. She could not go. She would take whatever remaining time they had together and make the most of it.

Using the bucket of water that had been left for them, Aelia removed her kirtle and washed, recoiling every time she encountered a new bruise or scrape. Then she crawled back into bed with Mathieu.

This time, she intended to disturb him.

She pushed the blanket aside and looked down at his chest. 'Twas broad and heavily muscled, with crisp, dark hair.

She guessed his nipples might be as sensitive as her own. His breath caught when she leaned over and flicked one with her tongue, and there was a distinct reaction in his nether regions.

Aelia's heart fluttered when he responded so dramatically, and she continued laving his nipple as she stroked the hard length of him.

"Aelia."

She felt him touch her nape, and continued licking and sucking his nipple while she learned the size and length of him with her hand. She was new to this kind of play, but when his muscles clenched in reaction to her touch, she knew she pleased him. And herself.

He started to turn to her, but Aelia pressed his shoulder to the mattress, then straddled him. He did not resist. Pouring all her love into her actions, she kissed his lips, then moved her mouth to his throat and chest. She felt the hard muscles of his abdomen contract when she touched her lips there, then moved lower.

She felt as well as heard his sharp intake of breath when she pressed her lips to the smooth, taut tip of his arousal. "Aelia," he gasped.

"Should I stop?"

"No!"

Aelia felt powerful then, and as aroused as Mathieu. She ached with it, and with the desire to make her mark upon him. She grew bolder, encircling him with her tongue, nipping with her teeth. She lowered her body and looked up at him, meeting his eyes, seeing the fever she'd aroused.

He arched under her, and Aelia's blood turned to fire. She became reckless as he surged and grew under her ministrations. He slid his fingers into her hair in a silent plea for her to continue, and Aelia did, until she was weak with her own need.

Mathieu moved suddenly, turning and pinning her beneath him. He positioned his body between her legs. "My beautiful Aelia," he said as he slid into her. She clenched him tightly, throbbing as he plunged deep.

Aelia tried to say his name, but the power of their bond rendered her speechless. He withdrew, then buried himself again, pulling her hips tightly against him. She held on to his arms as he increased their rhythm, the exquisite sensations of their union overpowering her.

Mathieu was not gentle with her. He was a fierce warrior, intent upon conquering her, and he succeeded. He drove deep inside, pushing Aelia to a fiery peak of pleasure. She wrapped her legs 'round his hips as if to anchor him there. When her climax shuddered through her, Mathieu groaned harshly and trembled, finding his own satisfaction.

He raised himself up on one hand and gazed down at her, then lowered his head and kissed her, even as he pulsed within her. Aelia's nerves hummed when he deepened the kiss, and her body shattered again, with another burning wave of pleasure that shook her to the depths of her soul.

Tucking her against him, Mathieu rolled to his side and stroked her hair away from her face. "Did I hurt you?"

"No," she whispered. She knew that was to come later.

"Your hands are scraped raw," he said, bringing one of them to his lips and kissing it. "And you are bruised."

Concern was in his eyes, along with the ebbing flow of passion.

"Mmm." Exhaustion crept up on Aelia again, making her eyelids droop and her body feel heavy.

Mathieu kissed her forehead. "Sleep now."

Aelia took a deep, shuddering breath. "When we go to London, will you promise me something?" she asked sleepily. "I have no wish to marry one of your peers. Will you use your influence with your king and see that I am given to a household that needs no wife?"

Mathieu had no appetite for the food on the table. He'd been sitting near the fire for some time, gazing into the flames, wondering how long he could delay their departure for London. He heard Aelia moving in their bed, and saw her reach for him in her sleep.

When she did not find him, she awoke and sat up.

Gathering the blanket 'round her, she came to him, taking his hand and pressing it to her cheek. "Come back to bed."

"No. Sit here with me awhile." He gathered her onto his lap, touching her hair, stroking her shoulder, until she dozed against him in the warm firelight. She'd been through an ordeal and it wasn't over yet. Mathieu did not know what would happen when they reached London, nor could he say how much influence he would have with William.

There was one thing that Mathieu was certain of. He could not give Aelia to another man. Something happened to him whenever she was near—it felt as though they were two halves of a whole—and Mathieu knew 'twould be impossible to part with her.

"You lost everything," she said. "Even your carving. 'Twas so beautiful."

Her words pleased him. "Aye. The stag was to be the symbol of my house."

"The wood was from Beorn's stores," she remarked quietly. "Father Ambrosius told me you took it as *heriot*."

He nodded and she kissed him softly.

He doubted that he could abide a marriage with Clarise. The woman was barely known to him, and if she was anything like her cousin, Lady Hélène de Saye, Mathieu would rather pass on the nuptials.

He wanted a virtuous wife who would manage his house graciously and fairly. She should understand the laws of the estate, and most of all, be loyal to him. She should make his blood surge with desire when he looked at her, and welcome him to her bed.

He did not want a mistress. Mathieu wanted a lover in his own hall, under his own roof, bearing his lawful heirs.

* * *

The monks found clothes for them. Mathieu did not ask where the holy men had found a woman's kirtle that fit Aelia, nor did he care where his own tunic had come from. 'Twas better than the one he'd been wearing since the night of the Danes' attack, though Aelia had insisted upon borrowing a needle and thread in order to rework it so it fit him.

For three days, they did naught but eat, sleep and make love in the small cottage behind the abbey. They tended each other's wounds and avoided speaking of London, and what awaited them there. Mathieu waited to hear the words again—the words Aelia had said to him before their world had been shattered by the Danes' attack.

But she said naught.

The abbot requested Mathieu's presence on the afternoon of the third day. As a Saxon cleric, the man had concerns about King William's intentions toward the monasteries. Mathieu spent an hour in discussion, reassuring the abbot of the king's piety and faith, and he bestowed upon the abbey a few of the valuables he'd found in the Danes' packs. By the time he left the priory, the sun had come out. Mathieu's mood was light until he returned to the cottage and found it empty.

The fire was cold. There was barely any sign of his occupancy here with Aelia, and the sight of their empty haven made his stomach burn. He stepped outside and saw one of the monks chopping wood nearby. Approaching the man, he asked if he'd seen Lady Aelia.

The monk nodded and pointed to the tree-covered hill behind the cottage. "She went walking, my lord."

Mathieu knew where she must have gone. They'd walked this path together the previous morning, and at the top of the hill was an expansive view of all the sur-rounding lands. 'Twas a restful place.

He followed the path as it climbed uphill through the orchard. When he reached the top, he saw Aelia sitting motionless on the ground, with her back against one of the standing stones that littered the place. Her gaze was on the land below, and she did not notice his presence until he was upon her.

She started when he spoke, rising to her feet and turning her back to him. When she finally faced him, Mathieu's heart cracked. "You've been weeping."

"Don't be daft," she replied with a quick laugh. But her voice sounded thick. Her eyes were reddened, and too moist for Mathieu to be fooled. She pulled her shawl tightly 'round her shoulders. "'Tis only the wind that burned my eyes."

But he knew better. Their time in the small cottage was nearly at an end. And while his own life would go on as he'd planned, Aelia's was drastically different from anything she'd ever conceived.

"Try to catch me!" she called as she took off running.

Mathieu was taken off guard and she got a head start, circling 'round the standing stones, heading for the far end of the hill. He ran after her, but allowed her to elude him time and time again. She laughed and shrieked when he almost caught her, but she lifted her skirts and ran off once more.

She was beautiful, with her bright hair shining in the sunshine and her cheeks tinged pink from the cool air and the exertion of the chase. Mathieu could think of nothing he wanted more.

Only Aelia.

He caught up to her and grabbed the back of her shawl, then pulled her toward him. She came into his arms and pressed her face against his chest, wrapping her arms 'round his waist.

He was not fooled by her jovial manner. 'Twas all a pretense to keep him from knowing she'd been crying all alone up here on the hilltop. Yet there was naught he could say to reassure her. He could not promise that William would allow her to remain unwed, nor could Mathieu promise that he would take care of her.

She was well and truly alone.

"The rain will soon return," he said. He did not—could not—release her just yet. Not when she held on to him as if the wind would blow her away if he let go.

The evening air had turned cold, but Mathieu and Aelia were warm and content in their room. After supper, they sat together by the fire, as was their habit. Aelia closed her eyes and felt the solid strength of Mathieu's chest behind her, and swallowed the lump of raw emotion that formed in her throat. They would leave here upon the morrow, and she would not spoil their last night together with her tears.

It had been bad enough that Mathieu had caught her weeping earlier in the day. 'Twould not happen again.

With a gentle touch, he unfastened the laces of her gown and slid it from her shoulders. He leaned forward and touched his lips to her bared skin.

Aelia closed her eyes and enjoyed the moment, fully aware there would never be another one like it. They had not spoken again of London, or what was going to happen there, and Aelia prayed that Mathieu could prevail upon his king to allow her to remain unmarried.

She could never be another man's wife.

In silence, Mathieu took her to bed and made love to her body as he ravished her heart and soul. Later, she had difficulty falling asleep and keeping her emotions in check, so she was weary the following morning as she mounted the horse she was to ride on the final segment of their journey.

Taking their leave, they bade farewell to the abbot and monks. Aelia wrapped herself tightly in her cloak against the biting wind that swept across the road.

"Tell me about London," she said, hoping to take her mind off the biting wind.

"What do you want to know?"

"I suppose it is like Ingelwald, only larger?"

Mathieu's brows came together for a moment, then he nodded. "Aye. Shops, people… There are many more streets, and large houses."

"But it is no longer a Saxon city."

"No. William is quite visibly king."

"What do you mean?"

"Norman soldiers make their presence known," Mathieu replied. "And the king is building a new fortress near the bank of the river."

He described the markets and the churches, but Aelia could not imagine such grandeur. "Where will we find Osric?"

Mathieu did not respond.

"I *will* be permitted to see him before the king sends me…?" She lowered her head and blinked back tears. "I see."

He reached over and took hold of the reins, stopping the horses. "No. You don't see."

She looked away, biting down on her lip to keep it from trembling.

He muttered something unintelligible and released her horse, and they continued on their way.

Chapter Twenty-Three

Their arrival in London came much too soon for Mathieu. He dismounted in front of the king's hall and was met by a guard.

"King William is away at Barking, my lord."

Mathieu helped Aelia dismount, then approached the guard. "When is he expected back?"

"This evening, baron. There is a feast in honor of—"

"Mathieu!"

"My lord." Mathieu turned to see Robert, Count of Mortain, coming down the steps. As brother to the king, he was richly dressed, but his finery seemed more conspicuous than usual. Mathieu stiffened at the sight of his own father, Autier de Burbage, equally well dressed, swaggering down the staircase as though he'd just returned victorious from battle.

"So…you managed to rescue the Saxon wench. Raoul de Moreton told us of your misfortune with Danish raiders," Autier said.

"Aye," Mathieu replied. "Does it surprise you that I made it back to London?"

"No," said his father. "Only that you wasted your time and your life going after a Saxon woman."

Robert motioned to one of the guards. "Take her to Billingsgate."

Mathieu saw Aelia's expression of panic. "My lord," he stated, addressing Robert, "the lady had hopes of seeing her brother."

"The lad brought here by Raoul?"

Mathieu nodded.

"They will most certainly be reunited," Robert said with a laugh. He patted Mathieu's back and propelled him toward the steps, where a crowd of Norman noblemen had gathered, many of them shouting greetings. Mathieu stopped short and turned to Aelia, even though his father's critical gaze was upon him.

The guard had hold of Aelia's arm, but his treatment was not unduly rough. Still, Mathieu had no intention of letting her go. "Lady Aelia will stay with me."

'Twas Autier's turn to laugh. "I think not, my dear Mathieu. She is the daughter of Wallis, is she not? The king will have his satisfaction for her father's rebellion."

"No! She—"

"Come, Mathieu," said Robert, as two grooms removed the saddle packs and carried them into the hall. "Your peers await you."

"Your pardon, my lord. I'll join you shortly."

Mathieu left the king's brother on the step and caught up to the guard who had started to lead a very subdued Aelia away. Mathieu had no choice but to go with Lord Robert now, and he could not bring Aelia with him. But he would not leave her this way, afraid and uncertain.

Ignoring his father's disapproval, he took hold of her shoulders and looked into her eyes. "All will be well, Aelia. I will find Osric and make this right."

Aelia raised her head, but kept her gaze away from his. Witnessing her struggle for control, Mathieu released her and stepped back. He would not embarrass her here, before all these men, or make their parting any more difficult.

But he would find her as soon as he could get away from the king's hall. King William would have to deal with them together. "You will answer to me for her treatment," he said to the guard, who did not reply.

Robert, Autier and all the men who stood at the top of the stairs observed Mathieu's actions with frank interest. But he offered no explanation when he rejoined them and stepped inside, where it appeared that a celebration of grand proportions was about to take place. Mathieu knew most of the men who had gathered in the hall. Among them were Simon de Vilot, the father of Clarise, and his own brothers, Geoffroi and Thierri.

The enormity of all that had happened hit Mathieu at once. He'd lost the men who'd traveled with him, all but Raoul, and the two who'd remained at Rushton. He'd gained Ingelwald, and the bride of his choice—the lovely Clarise de Vilot. All he had to do was claim her.

But the price was too high if he had to forfeit Aelia.

Billingsgate was not far. As soon as Mathieu had a chance to speak privately with Simon de Vilot, he would leave the hall and go in search of Aelia. Together, they could track down Raoul and Osric.

Then 'twould be necessary to petition King William for permission to wed Aelia. He would have no other wife.

Geoffroi clapped him on his back. "Lord of your own estates now, brother?"

Before he could reply, he heard his father's voice be-

hind him. "I always told William he could count upon
you, my son," he said, a statement that Mathieu knew
was untrue. His father had said naught of him to William, while he touted the prowess of Geoffroi and Thierri at every opportunity. Autier's demeanor was one of
haughty disapproval, even as he complimented him.

Mathieu did not mind. Their distaste for each other
was mutual.

"We must drink to my son, the conqueror of Northumberland!" Autier called out, handing Mathieu a glass.

But Mathieu was uninterested in his father's acco-
lades. The highest lords of the realm drank to Mathieu's
success while he gritted his teeth. Somehow he would
deal with the problem of his agreement with Simon de
Vilot, and take Aelia back to Ingelwald with him. She
would be his lady, and no other.

"May I have a few words with you, Mathieu?" asked
Lord Simon.

Mathieu followed the man into the next room, where
tables were being assembled for the feast. A number of
Norman ladies and noblemen milled about near the fire,
and Mathieu caught sight of Lady Clarise, talking and
laughing in the midst of several young admirers.

Mathieu braced himself to deal with Lord Simon's
anger when he reneged on their agreement. He could
not blame the man, but he would not go through with
the marriage to his daughter.

"Let us go into the anteroom."

A woman's high-pitched laugh caught Mathieu's attention and he looked back at Clarise. When their gazes
met, the lady stopped laughing and her eyes skittered
away nervously. More resolute than ever, Mathieu followed Clarise's father into the next room, but kept his
silence while the man lit several candles on the desk.

"I understand you were attacked by raiders on the road," Simon said, his voice full of concern for the man who would soon be his son-in-law.

Mathieu nodded. "Danes. They've been harrying Norman holdings. 'Tis likely the king will need to deal with them soon."

"How many days' travel was it from Ingelwald to London?"

Mathieu answered this and many other questions as he considered the best way to withdraw from their marriage agreement. He decided the direct approach would be best, but was sidetracked once again by Clarise's father.

"Do you know Martin d'Ivry?" Simon asked.

Mathieu nodded. "Aye. He has served the king nearly as long as I. Didn't I just see him…"

"Aye. Talking with the ladies," said Simon. "King William has given d'Ivry an estate near Windsor."

Mathieu clasped his hands behind his back and paced the length of the desk. "He is fortunate, my lord."

"'Tis very near London."

"So it is," Mathieu replied, barely concealing his impatience.

"Fitz Autier, I have some concerns about my daughter's well-being on a journey all the way to Northumberland. And once there, the isolation of Ingelwald…"

"Aye. 'Tis a far-off place," Mathieu replied, finally understanding the direction of this conversation. He suddenly felt as though a dark cloud had been lifted from his heart and soul. "Ingelwald is remote. The nearest estates are leagues away."

Simon rubbed a hand over his face and looked away. "I am in a quandary, Fitz Autier. You see, my daughter…er, she is loath to live so far from…civilization.

And d'Ivry has offered for her hand. Not to fault him—
he was unaware of our agreement."

"I see," said Mathieu. His relief was palpable. "I understand your concerns, my lord. But you and I had an
understanding, even though no documents were
signed."

"Aye. We did," said Simon. Worry weighed heavily
upon him, from the crease between his brows to the
slope in his shoulders. He looked up at Mathieu. "I
would barter with you, Fitz Autier. King William was
so confident of your victory at Ingelwald, he has already
named you its lord. There can be little else you desire,
but for an old man's peace of mind, try to think of something. I will use all my influence to convince the king
to grant it to you."

Mathieu stopped moving. "Agreed."

Simon sank into a chair. "What then? Name whatever it is."

"Ask the king to grant me one favor, as unconven-
tional as it may be."

Aelia did not understand why the guard had been ordered to take her to a house on the river, rather than Billingsgate—the place where Mathieu thought she'd be.
She found herself more frightened now than she'd been
with the Danes.

The tall Norman lord with dark blue eyes had
changed the first lord's order for some reason, and his
penetrating gaze made her skin crawl. She jerked her
arm from the guard's grip and turned to speak to the
man. "Please, sir," she said, forcing her voice to remain
steady. "Will you see to it that Baron Fitz Autier is told
where they're taking me?"

The richly dressed lord stood silent, looking at her

with frank curiosity. Then he gave a slight shake of his head and muttered a few words that Aelia could barely hear. Her heart shattered when she realized what he said.

"Rid the bastard of his Saxon whore."

The guards took her away before she could react. These Normans had conquered her land, and she knew she could expect no mercy—except from Mathieu—but only if he could find her.

She'd asked the guards about Sir Raoul and Osric, but they did not answer her questions, nor would they agree to take a message to Mathieu. They left her at a grand house, where two more Norman guards locked her into a room.

Aelia struggled against her confinement, pounding on the door and shouting until her voice was hoarse, but no one returned for her. She'd been abandoned; now she was trapped.

The room was empty, but for a chair against the far wall, beside the window. Aelia pushed open the shutters and looked down into the street, but it was no means of escape. She was much too high to jump.

She wrapped her arms 'round her middle and leaned her back against the wall, sliding down until she was sitting on the floor with her knees to her chest. 'Twas hopeless. Mathieu had done what he'd been charged to do—bring her and Osric to London. She was at the king's mercy now. Mathieu didn't even know where to find her.

Aelia did not know how many hours passed while she sat in the cold little room. But guards finally came for her. 'Twas no reprieve. They tied her hands and took her down a dark staircase and out of the house. They crossed a courtyard encircled by a tall fence, and entered a smaller building. From there, she and a dozen other prisoners were loaded into a wagon and driven away from the yard.

With futile desperation, she hoped Mathieu would come for her.

But as the hour came closer to dusk, Aelia and the others arrived at a harbor where the largest boats she had ever seen were docked. And she suddenly knew her fate.

"Is this the sea?" she asked one of her fellow prisoners.

"No. 'Tis the river. But it leads into the sea. They're taking us to France."

Aelia could not breathe. If Mathieu had wanted to find her, wouldn't he have done so before now?

"I cannot go! Let me off," she cried, pushing her way to the gate at the back of the wagon. Mathieu might have forsaken her, but she would not do the same to Osric.

"Get back!" shouted the guard. He shoved her down, but Aelia scrambled to her feet.

"I must find my brother!"

The men unloaded their passengers and led them to the ship.

"Please! I was brought here to see your king. I demand—"

The Norman guards laughed in her face, then pushed her forward. "When the king returns, we'll be sure to tell him you were here."

It was some time before Mathieu was able to take his leave of King William's brother and the rest of the gathering, and he was allowed to go only with his promise to return in time for the fete. He avoided his father and brothers and went directly to Billingsgate in search of Aelia, but she was not there.

"There must be some mistake. I heard Lord Robert's orders to have her brought here!"

"Aye, my lord, but they were changed."

Mathieu's voice became low and dangerous. "Find me someone who knows where Lady Aelia was taken."

All of Billingsgate's knights scrambled to find an answer, but none had seen the lady. They'd only heard rumors of the comely Saxon slave brought by Fitz Autier from the northern country.

Mathieu mounted his horse. Surely Raoul would know where they'd taken her. He would also know where to find Osric.

There was an inn about a mile upriver where Mathieu and his men had lodged weeks ago, before leaving for Northumberland. Raoul had favored one of the Saxon serving maids there, and Mathieu had no doubt that was where he would find the knight.

He rode through the streets, passing several markets as he went in search of Raoul. When he finally reached the inn and went inside the noisy, crowded common room, he found Raoul coming down the main stairs.

Their parting after the Danes' attack had been tense, but they embraced now as brothers. "I need your help," Mathieu said.

"Mathieu, I offer my apologies for all I said. When they took your Saxon lady, I realized—"

"Let's go outside."

They pushed through the crowd and left the inn. Mathieu followed as Raoul circled 'round to the back of the building. "I need your help to find Aelia."

"I knew I should have gone with you. When do we leave?"

"You don't understand," Mathieu said. "She is here in London."

Raoul gave a low whistle. "You caught up to the Danes and rescued her?"

Mathieu nodded. "But Robert de Mortain's guards took her into custody before I could stop them," he said, regretting that he had not spoken up and prevented her detainment right then. "I was a fool to let them take her."

"And defy Lord Robert? Mathieu, you might be on good terms with him, but he *is* the king's brother."

"Where would they have taken her?"

"Billingsgate."

"No. I tried there."

Raoul scratched his head. "Some prisoners are being taken to the king's new fortress on the river, south of here. Mayhap she's there."

Mathieu's sense of relief was fleeting when they arrived at the tower and spoke to the guards. They quickly learned Aelia had never been brought there.

"This is absurd," said Mathieu to the knights on guard. "Lord Robert de Mortain ordered her taken to Billingsgate, yet she is not there. How can I find out who is in charge of the king's prisoners?"

"That would be…your father, my lord," the guard replied. "Baron Autier de Burbage."

"My father?"

"Aye. Lord Autier has had the authority since his arrival in London a fortnight ago."

Mathieu seethed with anger. Clearly, his father had changed Lord Robert's order. For what reason, Mathieu did not know, but he could guess.

He and Raoul returned to their horses. "Where is Osric?" Mathieu asked.

"I kept him with me. He's at the inn with the family who owns the place—they're Saxon."

"Raoul…I have no choice," Mathieu said as his temper boiled. "I must go to my father at the king's hall while you keep looking for Aelia. Take her to Osric and tell her I'll join her as soon as I can."

"Aye, my lord."

Raoul turned into a street heading north, while Mathieu went directly to the grand hall where he'd last seen his father. He knew he had put Raoul in an awkward situation, but it could not be helped. Besides, if Mathieu was not mistaken, he now outranked his father. Ingelwald was greater than any property Autier de Burbage could claim, and so were Mathieu's victories in battle.

Autier had no right to decide Aelia's fate.

Mathieu reached the king's hall, but 'twas not the same composed, sedate crowd that greeted him earlier. William had arrived with a large entourage, and the place was filled with music, noise and jocularity. Mathieu saw the king in the center of it all, a tall figure making his way to the dais. There was clearly some celebration in progress, but Mathieu cared naught. He only wanted to find his father and learn what he had done with Aelia.

The king suddenly called out to Mathieu. "Join me here, Fitz Autier! Lord of Ingelwald!"

Mathieu gritted his teeth. He could not ignore William. For the first time in his recollection, he was being honored above his brothers, but he took no pleasure in it. He made his way through the throng of knights and ladies gathered in the dining hall, and joined the king and his closest advisors upon the dais. The rich bounty he'd found in the Danes' saddle packs lay spread upon a low table nearby.

William silenced the throng and publicly congratulated Mathieu on his victories in Northumberland. "I grant you all of Ingelwald, Mathieu Fitz Autier, and

name you earl," said the king. "I expect a full account-
ing of your properties by the new year."

"Thank you, sire," Mathieu said, searching the crowd
for his father. "You do me great honor."

"Your exploits in Northumberland precede you,"
William continued. "I would honor you above all others tonight. Allow us to grant you a king's favor."

Shooting a quick glance toward Simon de Vilot, who
gave a slight nod, Mathieu spoke directly to the king.
"As I have been released from my betrothal agreement
with Simon de Vilot, I ask only that I be given Aelia of
Ingelwald for my wife."

"A Saxon lady?"

"Aye."

"To bind Ingelwald more closely to you, Mathieu?"

Mathieu agreed. If the king wanted to believe 'twas
diplomacy that dictated his actions, Mathieu would
keep private what he felt for Aelia. 'Twould not be necessary to tell the king that he loved her more than his
own life, although he would certainly do so if the situation demanded. He loved her, and he would tell her so,
as soon as he discovered where his father had sent her.

"You are one of my most able commanders, and now
I count you among my noblest lords, Mathieu of Ingelwald," said William. "I grant you your request. Bring
the lady forth, and wed her now, amid this company."

"Sire, I cannot," Mathieu said. "She is being held as
prisoner…."

"Where? We can send men to rescue her."

"I must find my father, sire, and ask him. He is her
jailer."

Chapter Twenty-Four·

Autier de Burbage did not appreciate the interruption, but the young kitchen maid he'd cornered did not hide her relief. She scampered away as Mathieu and Lord Robert closed in on Autier.

"Where did you send the Saxon woman?" Robert asked.

Autier did not bother to disguise his angry frustration, shooting a furious glance in Mathieu's direction. "I saw how you looked at the wench. I heard what you said. And I merely prevented your disgracing my name with your—"

"Too late, Autier," said Mathieu, grabbing the front of his father's tunic in his fist. "You've done enough disgracing for us both. Where is she?"

"Gone." His expression was smug. "To Normandy."

Mathieu felt the blood drain from his skull. "How?"

"By ship, only a short time ago."

"I know where," said Robert. "Maybe there's still time. Let's go."

Robert gathered several of his men as he and Mathieu retraced their steps through the hall, ordering their horses to be saddled and brought 'round to the front of the building. Then he stepped up to the dais and spoke to the king.

Mathieu did not wait for Robert. His own horse was saddled and waiting outside. He left the crowded hall and mounted up, then quickly headed south, toward the wharf.

He encountered Raoul in the street.

"I could not find her—"

"They're putting her on a ship bound for Normandy."

Raoul muttered a curse and joined Mathieu. They rode to the wharf and saw that there were three ships preparing to set sail.

"Which one?" Raoul asked.

"You take this one," Mathieu said, indicating the first of two ships that looked most ready to sail. "I'll go to the next."

He covered the distance between the two ships and stopped his horse where two men were pulling up the gangplank.

"Stop!" he called as he dismounted. The two sailors gaped up at Mathieu as if they did not understand him.

"Halt! Do you have Saxon prisoners aboard?"

"Aye," said one of the men warily.

Mathieu wore no insignia of his station. Without armor and helm, he had no visible authority with these men. "Who commands this vessel?" he demanded.

"Who might you be, asking all these questions?" asked a sailor of rank.

He stepped onto the plank and crossed to the ship. "I am Mathieu Fitz Autier of King William's court," he said, drawing his sword. There was a crowd of people in the bow, and though Mathieu could not see Aelia among them, he saw that there was a disturbance taking place there.

"You cannot come up here," said one of the men, but Mathieu ignored him, shoving past.

"Aye, he can," called a voice from the dock. 'Twas Count Robert de Mortain, and he was recognized by the ship's hands.

"My lord," Mathieu shouted back to him. "Will you go to the last ship?"

Robert gave him a quick nod and rode away, leaving two men on the dock awaiting Mathieu's command.

He hurried to the far end of the ship and pushed through the crowd of guards and frightened Saxons who were gathered there. "Aelia!" he shouted.

One of the guards was about to whip a prisoner with a leather strap, but Mathieu stayed his hand, and noticed it was Aelia lying facedown upon the wooden planks. "What—?"

"Strike at your own peril," Mathieu said viciously. Her hands were tied, but she rolled over and held them over her head to ward off the blows, and 'twas all Mathieu could do to refrain from taking the whip from the Norman guard and seeing how he liked its bite.

Instead, he leaned over Aelia and said her name.

She lay perfectly still.

"Aelia, I've come for you."

Her shoulders heaved once, and Mathieu took hold of her and gently turned her. His relief was just as great as when he'd taken her from the Danes. "Aelia."

He cut the ropes that bound her, then lifted her into his arms, wanting naught but to hold her, to stop the tears that welled in her eyes. "That's it, *ma belle,* hold me tight." With Aelia's arms looped 'round his neck, Mathieu carried her the length of the ship, then down the gangplank. "Raoul has Osric." He felt her sobbing breaths against his chest. "Your brother is safe."

He carried her to his horse and lifted her up, quickly mounting behind her.

"I see you found your lady, Mathieu," said Robert de Mortain. "And is she well?"

"Aye," Mathieu said, holding her close, feeling her shuddering against him as she squeezed his hand in affirmation.

"Then 'tis the king's wish that you join us in an hour's time."

"Agreed."

Mathieu had received the king's sanction for his marriage to Aelia, and he wanted all the Normans—particularly his father and brothers—to witness their vows. In one hour, he would return to the king's hall with Aelia.

He rode away from the wharf, stopping in a secluded lane. Turning Aelia in his arms, he kissed her softly. "Forgive me for letting them take you," he said, touching his lips to her forehead. "I was a fool to let you go."

Her chin quivered and tears fell, but she said naught, wrapping her arms 'round his waist as if she would never release him.

Naught had ever felt so good to Aelia…Mathieu's hard chest against her face, his arms 'round her back. He'd said Osric was safe, so all she had to do was relish this moment. But she only had him for one hour. Then he was to attend the king.

They held on to each other for several minutes until someone nearby spoke. "Mathieu…"

'Twas Sir Raoul.

Mathieu did not release her when Raoul continued

speaking. "Mayhap we should go to the inn. Lady Aelia can see her brother there, and I am sure the women will be able to find some decent clothes for her."

Aelia knew how she must look. She was as filthy as her ragged kirtle, but at least Mathieu did not seem to mind. In truth, he also looked the worse for wear. He had not shaved his face in days, so his beard grew thick and his clothes were as untidy as her own.

Mathieu agreed to go to the inn, and Raoul said he would ride ahead and see that all was made ready for them.

Mathieu held Aelia close as they rode through the narrow streets of London town, and before they reached their destination, she heard a child's shouts in the distance, calling her name.

"'Tis Osric!"

He ran the length of the street, shouting as he ran. Aelia let go of Mathieu and slid down to the ground, catching Osric as he ran into her arms. She heard Mathieu dismount behind her as she embraced her brother, weeping tears of relief, of joy.

"Aelia! I never thought you'd get away from those bastard Da—"

Aelia laughed and pulled him close, kissing his unkempt head.

"You're squeezing me too tight!"

She laughed again and released him as Mathieu put his arm 'round her and guided them down the street, leading his horse behind them.

"So, did you kill them? The Danes?" Osric asked Mathieu.

"No, it wasn't necessary," he replied.

"But you stole my sister away from them?"

"Aye, but 'tis a tale to be told later."

"No! Tell me now!"

Aelia's heart warmed at Osric's demand, so typical of her intrepid brother, and Mathieu's patience with the boy. She did not know what the future held for her and Osric, but for now, she would treasure these moments together.

They entered the common room of an inn and were greeted by Raoul and two Saxon women. "Lady Aelia," said one of them. "Everything is ready for you...or nearly ready."

They started to lead her away, but Mathieu kept hold of her. "Not without me," he said.

Feeling close to tears again, Aelia clung to his hand. Raoul took charge of Osric as she climbed the stairs with Mathieu and entered the bedchamber indicated by the Saxon woman.

"'Tis not much, my lady," she said, "but I hope it will do for now."

Mathieu thanked her and ushered her from the room, closing the door when she was gone. A second later, Aelia was in his arms. His mouth came down upon hers as though they'd been separated for days, rather than hours.

"How long must you stay with the king?" she asked, breathless as he unfastened her gown and slid it from her body. He kissed her injured shoulder and spanned her waist with his hands.

"A good bit of the night," he replied.

"Will he be angry if you are late?" Aelia asked, tipping her head back to give him better access to the sensitive skin of her neck.

"I cannot be late...for my own wedding."

Emotion, raw and painful, welled in Aelia's chest. She had not anticipated the kind of devastation she would feel when he went through his nuptials. "You must go then."

"What's this? Tears?"

She slipped out of his arms and turned away. "Please do not ask me to wish you well, Mathieu," she whispered.

"What's happened to my fearless Saxon lady?" he asked, taking her by the shoulders and pulling her to his chest.

"I never knew you to be cruel, but—"

"Come with me, Aelia," he said quietly, "and be my bride, before the king and all the nobles of the realm." He slid his hands 'round her waist and kissed her neck. "I'll have no other wife, Aelia."

"I don't understand…." She pulled away and faced him, feeling confused and vulnerable. "Your Norman lady…"

"Her father was persuaded to release me from our agreement."

Aelia's heart pounded so hard she was certain Mathieu must be able to hear it. "'Tis really true?" she whispered, barely able to believe what he was saying. "You want a Saxon wife?"

"Aye, *ma belle*. But only you."

She threw herself into Mathieu's arms and wept.

"I hope these are tears of joy," he said, holding her close.

She nodded against his chest.

"You are everything to me, Aelia." He fitted her head underneath his chin. "Come back with me to Ingelwald. Stand by my side as my lady. Bear my children, rebuild all that was lost in battle."

The bed creaked as Mathieu sat up and came to Aelia where she sat near the fire in their bridal chamber. She still felt dizzy from the night's events, her body humming with the aftermath of their fierce lovemaking in their room here at the inn.

Mathieu settled himself at her back and pulled her into his embrace, nuzzling her ear.

"You promised to honor and obey me, wife," he said quietly.

"Aye." She felt him take a lock of her hair and curl it 'round his finger.

"My men honor and obey me."

Aelia smiled. "Of course they do…as do I."

He swallowed, and his voice was thick with emotion. "I would have more from a wife than her obedience."

Aelia turned and looked into his eyes, which were dark with need.

She took his hands and pressed a kiss into each palm. "I love you, Mathieu. You conquered more than my lands when you came to Ingelwald. You are the lord of my heart, my body and my soul."

He closed his eyes and leaned forward, touching his forehead to hers. "And you, Aelia…I love you with all that I am, all that I ever hope to be."

He stood and took her hand, pulling her up beside him. When he cupped her face in his hands and tipped his head down to kiss her, Aelia knew her mother had been right.

This Saxon lady had known her one true mate at first sight.

* * * * *

Harlequin® Historical
Historical Romantic Adventure!

JARED'S RUNAWAY WOMAN
by Judith Stacy

He'd found her!

Kinsey Templeton's past has finally caught up with her—in the handsome form of Jared Mason. Kinsey surprises Jared in so many ways and, despite everything, he wants her. So he will have to make sure she *never* runs again....

"A fine writer with both polished style and heartwarming sensitivity."
— bestselling author Pamela Morsi

On sale May 2006
Available wherever Harlequin books are sold.

Harlequin® Historical
Historical Romantic Adventure!

HIS DUTY,
HER DESTINY
by Juliet Landon

*A promise honored,
a passion rekindled*

Bound by his word,
Sir Fergus Melrose would honor
his betrothal. His task wouldn't be
easy. Lady Nicola Coldyngham
was no longer the young lass who
had worshipped his every move.
But her defiance became his
challenge—a challenge he
was unable to resist.

On sale May 2006
*Available wherever
Harlequin books are sold.*

HARLEQUIN *Presents*

Royal Brides

**The Scorsolini Princes:
proud rulers and passionate lovers
who need convenient wives!**

Welcome to this brand-new miniseries,
set in glamorous and exotic places—it's
a world filled with passion, romance and royals!

Don't miss this new trilogy by

Lucy Monroe

THE PRINCE'S VIRGIN WIFE
May 2006

HIS ROYAL LOVE-CHILD
June 2006

THE SCORSOLINI MARRIAGE BARGAIN
July 2006

www.eHarlequin.com   HPRB0506